IN SEARCH OF A KILLER

"That's enough, Jennet," Lady Appleton said sharply. "I will not have you frightening yourself. Enough, I say. I'll have no more complaining and no more talk of danger from beyond the grave. Seeing that apparition only deepened my suspicion that something was odd about John Bexwith's death. If you can keep your wits about you, Jennet, you may prove very helpful in finding the truth."

"I will do all I can to help you, madam. Only tell me what you require."

"I mean to investigate the circumstances of John Bexwith's death. I do not for a moment believe it was caused by a visitor from beyond the grave." She gave Jennet a sharp look. "He may have died from fright, but this foolishness of believing Appleton Manor haunted must stop."

"Yes, madam."

"If it was not a natural death, and if it was not brought on by the shock of seeing what he perceived to be a ghost, then poison remains a possibility. And if murder has been done, it must be punished."

"But, madam, if it was murder, how can you ever hope to prove it? John Bexwith is long since buried. There is no evidence left of what he ate that night."

"There are people to talk to. What ingredients went into his marrow-bone pie? Who had opportunity to add more?" She looked thoughtful. "Any guilt has a way of making a person nervous, Jennet. And sometimes careless, too. I think we may still hope to discover who killed Bexwith . . ."

Books by Kathy Lynn Emerson

FACE DOWN IN THE MARROW-BONE PIE
FACE DOWN UPON AN HERBAL*
FACE DOWN AMONG THE WINCHESTER GEESE*

Published by Kensington Publishing Corp.

*coming soon

Face Down in the Marrow-Bone Pie

Kathy Lynn Emerson

Kensington Books
Kensington Publishing Corp.
http://www.kensingtonbooks.com

KENSINGTON BOOKS are published by

Kensington Publishing Corp.
850 Third Avenue
New York, NY 10022

First Kensington Paperback Printing: April, 2000
10 9 8 7 6 5 4 3 2 1

Printed in the United States of America

*For W. Merritt Emerson,
who says he wants to play
Bexwith's role "in the movie version."
Go for it, Dad!*

CHAPTER 1

Lancashire
Late August, 1559

Steam rose from the marrow-bone pie until the old man's sharp beak of a nose wrinkled in delight. John Bexwith sat at the lord's place at the elegant refectory table, one the late Sir George had looted from a monastery at the time of the Dissolution. Sir George had taken two long oaken benches as well and now all three pieces adorned the dais at one end of the great hall at Appleton Manor.

Bexwith was convinced that Sir Robert, Appleton's present master, would neither know nor care what liberties his steward took. Sir Robert hadn't seen fit to visit his ancestral estates since his father's death two years past. In the interim Bexwith had usurped first one, then another of the rights and privileges of ownership. This was his boldest act to date. This day he dined in elevated splendor, with the entirety of the empty hall spread out before him.

He'd ordered a fire built in the open hearth at the center of the cavernous room, but that had been more for show than heat. Nothing warmed Appleton. Thick stone walls defeated even the most sizzling summer day. The chill from the previous winter, and all the winters before that, still permeated the place.

Accustomed to the discomfort, Bexwith did not notice that the peat burned fitfully or that very little of its smoke reached the outlet high in the heavy-timbered roof above. Neither did he see a flash of white at the opposite end of the hall, just where the stairs turned back on themselves to reach the solar above. He was too intent on savoring, eyes closed, the wonderful aroma given off by alternate layers of artichokes, currants, succulent dates, and eryngo.

That smell fair made his mouth water, but Bexwith also relished his knowledge that the dried fruits, imported from the Levant by way of Portugal, were both rare and expensive in this part of England. So was the sugar, bought in Manchester in a great ten-pound loaf. It had cost eightpence a pound, what with being sent for all the way to London. He'd been told it came originally from the Canary Islands.

"Bring me more ale," he ordered the buxom maidservant who'd just placed his meal in front of him. She did not object when he landed a playful swat on her nicely rounded bottom. "Enough for us both," he added with a leer.

As the wench scurried off to do his bidding, Bexwith returned his attention to the dish before him. He rubbed his gnarled hands together, anticipation lighting his faded blue eyes as he thought of the pleasures to come. Henceforth he could afford to eat meals fit for a lord every day.

He dipped his pewter spoon into the pie, piercing the crust, and frowned when one of the beef bones surfaced. He pushed it aside, probing for morsels more appetizing than edible marrow. If what he'd been told was true, eryngo both restored a man's youth and acted as a potent aphrodisiac.

CHAPTER 2

Leigh Abbey, Kent
Two weeks later

Sir Robert Appleton swore under his breath. His fist clenched involuntarily, crumpling the parchment but doing little real damage to the letter he'd just read. With swift, precise movements he smoothed it out again, refolded it, and tucked it into the front of his doublet.

Seeing her husband's action, and sensing his growing agitation, Lady Appleton closed the herbal she'd been annotating and placed it on the writing table. Robert stood by the window, turned so that she could not see his face, but the bright morning sun danced on his hair, adding luster to the thick, dark curls he was so proud of. After a moment, he lifted his head, revealing eyes of a deep brown and an expression that was equally dark and brooding.

Her first inclination was to demand information. That something untoward had happened was obvious. Instead she waited, reining in a natural impatience. There was no need to prompt him. She had only to bide her time and Robert would tell her what was troubling him without being asked. That was but one advantage of his mistaken impression that servants were somehow inferior persons, incapable of carrying on intelligent conversation. When he needed to talk out weighty matters he was perforce obliged to turn to his wife.

A small, smug smile tilted Lady Appleton's lips upward as she waited for her husband to speak. Soon after they'd wed he'd been forced to admit that she was his intellectual equal. That hard-won concession had made her more resigned to the marriage, for many men would have tried to wean her of her addiction to scholarly pursuits.

It was all her father's fault, of course. Once he'd realized that she'd inherited a modicum of his intelligence, he'd given her the same education he'd have lavished on a son. Robert generally appreciated the result. At least he had, on occasion, made use of his wife's quickness of mind.

Lady Appleton readily acknowledged she had inherited three more things from her late father—his uncompromisingly square jaw, an unseemly height for a woman, and a sturdy build that did not lend itself well to the current fashion in farthingales. She sometimes wished that Robert thought her beautiful as well as clever, but all in all she was content.

The silence continued.

Frowning, Lady Appleton studied her husband's closed expression more carefully. Had he been asked to go abroad again? That seemed all too likely. In the ten months since Queen Elizabeth succeeded her half sister Mary to the throne of England, Robert's services had been much in demand.

Her effort to practice patience came to an abrupt end. "To what place do you travel this time?"

Instead of answering, Robert crossed the cozy study to the small, carpet-draped table. He filled a Venetian glass goblet with fine Rhenish from a crystal flagon, but he did not at once begin to drink. In brooding silence he stared at the huge mappa mundi which hung on the paneled wall.

France, Lady Appleton decided. The French king had recently died. Ever since, letters had been arriving at Leigh Abbey with increasing frequency. There had been missives from Nicholas Throckmorton, the English ambassador there, or rather from Walter Pendennis, a courtier Robert had known for years who was now one of Throckmorton's secretaries. There had also been a cryptic note from Queen Elizabeth herself.

As she studied her husband's profile, Lady Appleton's concern grew more intense. He looked tired. He had not had enough time to recover from the rigors of that last mission abroad. Three times in the previous six months he had made the arduous journey to the Continent, sent to Strasbourg and Geneva and Basel to treat with English exiles who'd fled their homeland during Queen Mary's reign. Some he knew from his days in the service of the late duke of Northumberland. Others accepted him as a trustworthy friend of the New Religion because of Lady Appleton. It had been through her efforts that many of them had managed to escape England and the deadly persecution of a Catholic regime.

In negotiating with the radical Protestant faction, Robert provided an invaluable service to their new monarch. Lady Appleton knew how much he looked forward to each new opportunity to prove his worth to the Crown. If he was spectacularly successful as an emissary he might hope, within a few years, to be offered a peerage as a reward for his diligent service. He'd misjudged once, assuming Queen Mary would be able to restore Catholicism to England on a permanent basis, but he'd taken pains since to study all the angles of a situation. And to listen to his wife's advice.

Apparently sensing her scrutiny, Robert turned slowly. He took a sip of the wine before he spoke. "I have no plans to leave here immediately, Susanna. In this case my presence elsewhere will serve no useful purpose."

His words confused her. "How can you refuse?" He looked startled, but before he could say more she rushed on. "I cannot imagine Queen Elizabeth will be pleased to hear you've refused a mission in her service. She expects unquestioning obedience from her subjects, now that she is in power at last. Whatever debts she may owe them are as naught compared to her sense of what is her due.''

One glance at Robert's face told Susanna her tone of voice had revealed far more of her resentment toward the queen than she'd intended. Annoyed by her own lack of control, she rose from behind her writing desk and moved away from him. She stopped before the hearth. Though she was looking directly at them, she no more saw the marble chimneypiece or the firedogs or the grate than Robert had seen the map at which he'd been gazing a few minutes earlier.

Behind her, his voice sounded faintly amused. "The queen listens to my opinions. That is bitter as gall, is it not?"

Abruptly, Susanna turned away from the fireplace, moving restlessly past a table heavy-laden with leather-bound volumes. She tried to contain her irritation, but failed miserably. When her path took her toward the oak door that led to the rest of the house, she realized that a proper wife would make some excuse to leave, forestalling conflict. After all, it was not a woman's place to question her husband. In spite of that fact, or perhaps because of it, Susanna did not open the door. Instead she made her way back across the study to the window and ensconced herself on the broad wooden bench that stood in front of it.

"Bodykins," she swore, though 'twas but a mild curse, no match for Robert's. "If I must seem a shrew, so be it." Her chin came up defiantly. Her eyes blazed.

Robert sent an indulgent smile in her direction, which annoyed her all over again. She wanted neither his pity nor his disdain.

"My poor, put-upon wife." His voice bordered on the sardonic. "It does chafe you beyond reason that the queen chose to ignore your part in the effort to keep her friends safe during her half sister's reign."

Susanna rested her forehead against the glass and stared out at fields ready to be harvested and orchards ripe with fruit. "Are my thoughts treason, do you suppose?"

"Accept the facts, my dear. It is your sex that argues against her gratitude. Queen Elizabeth considers herself perfectly fit to rule, in spite of the fact that she was born a woman, but she will never acknowledge similar abilities in any other female. If men loyal to her and her religious beliefs found help here during Mary's reign, why then of course I must have been the one who ordered it given."

Susanna did not bother to reply. It was an old bone of contention between them. These days Robert conveniently forgot how furious he had been with her when he'd first learned what she was doing. At the time, he'd been at Mary's court, struggling to appear the epitome of a loyal, Catholic subject.

It had not been such a great effort, she thought resentfully. Like so many others of his generation, he'd been raised a Catholic until King Henry broke with the church at Rome. Although the New Religion and Robert Appleton both had flourished under Henry's son Edward, the moment Mary came to the throne and restored Catholicism and it had been politically expedient to embrace one's Catholic roots and attend mass again, Robert had averred he'd been a secret papist all along.

Younger than her husband, Susanna had been unable to make such a claim and had not wanted to. In her lifetime she had known but one faith and while Queen Mary wore the crown she'd done all she could to aid the men who'd been her father's friends and co-religionists. Every night of the five long years of Mary's reign, Susanna had prayed that Elizabeth would live to succeed her half sister and restore the New Religion.

When Robert realized that she would not be baited he abandoned his verbal sparring for cajoling tones. "Come, Susanna, you know you would dislike life at court and that you have no desire to accompany me when I travel abroad. Nor do you long to be sent thither in my place. Indeed, the shortest journey over water makes you most desperately ill."

''You are unkind to remind me of my weakness.'' Susanna seized one of the cushions strewn on the window seat beside her, plucking at the red and gold crewelwork that decorated its blue velvet cover. The intricate pattern of small roses was not her own handiwork. Susanna herself was the first to admit that she had only the most rudimentary skill with a needle.

''One of us must remain in England to oversee our holdings here.''

Susanna's hands tightened until her fingers left deep impressions in the velvet. That was hardly an adequate reason to be left behind. Leigh Abbey, their principal residence, was completely self-sufficient, thanks to the efficient way she managed it. Very carefully, she set the cushion back in its accustomed place. She understood the importance of the work Robert did abroad, but she could not like his frequent, lengthy absences.

''When do you leave, if not immediately?''

''I do not know, although 'tis certain I will be dispatched soon. To France, as you must already have guessed. Matters are grave in that benighted land. There are some who think I can help right them.''

''I see.''

''Why not think of my next absence as an opportunity to pursue the scholarly endeavors you began the last time I was away.'' Robert made the suggestion in an offhand manner that offended Susanna all over again.

''While you were on that last royal errand,'' she informed him in lofty tones, ''I exhausted our entire supply of reading matter and added Spanish to the languages I already speak.''

Their eyes met.

Her lips twitched first.

Laughter followed, full-bodied and cleansing. For all their differences, they had always shared this unexpected sense of humor.

''You now mangle Spanish as badly as you do French?'' he asked, still chuckling.

The one ability Susanna had not inherited from her father was his fluency in languages. She could read Latin, Greek,

German, and French, but her attempts to communicate aloud in any tongue but her own were haphazard at best.

"Here's a thought," Robert proposed. "You might follow the example of another learned lady of our acquaintance and fill your free hours by translating Latin texts into English and thence into Greek."

Susanna sniffed contemptuously, though she knew he was only teasing her. "In my opinion, the gentlewoman in question has become quite unsettled in her mind as the result of too much study."

Closing the distance between them, Robert rested one hand on his wife's shoulder while he used the other to catch her chin and lift her face toward his own. "Today's letter was not a summons to serve the queen."

"No?"

"No."

"Then what was in it? Whence came it?"

"From Lancashire. John Bexwith, my steward at Appleton Manor, is dead."

Susanna frowned, surprised that this news should have affected him so strongly. "The man was quite elderly," she said hesitantly, "was he not?"

Robert looked surprised that she would know. He'd never taken her north with him to visit his late father's estates. Although she was the one who disbursed monies to pay for the upkeep of Appleton Manor, Susanna had never met John Bexwith. Robert had, however, mentioned the fellow once or twice, referring to him as Old John.

"Your memory is excellent," he told her, absently tucking an unruly lock of dark brown hair back up under her brocaded cap. Then, releasing her, he moved a little apart and drew the letter out of his doublet, perusing the message it contained one last time while Susanna waited, her eyes alight with curiosity. "He was found face down in a marrow-bone pie."

With that incredible statement, Robert placed the letter in his wife's outstretched hand.

Susanna blinked at him. Marrow-bone pie? She was not familiar with the dish. A natural curiosity asserted itself and was quickly repressed. A man had died. This was no time to collect recipes.

"Did his heart fail him?" she asked.

"A logical conclusion."

But other alternatives occurred to Susanna. How could they not when she was presently engaged in the writing of a cautionary herbal, a book designed to warn cooks and housewives what ingredients to avoid? She knew of at least a dozen poisonous herbs that could accidentally find their way into any dish, or be deliberately added with little fear of detection. Any odd taste could be masked by a generous use of spices.

"Do not let your imagination run away with you," Robert warned, just as though she had spoken aloud. In some few ways he knew her well.

"The news of his death troubled you for some reason," she argued. "What else am I to conclude but that you suspect he did not die of natural causes?"

"I am annoyed only. I have too many other matters to concern me to need yet another distraction. It is only your extensive knowledge of poisonous plants that leads you to jump to erroneous conclusions. Read the letter for yourself, Susanna."

She did so, then skimmed its contents again, just as he had in his reluctance to believe what was written there. "I am not the one you should be chiding for too much imagination. What nonsense this is!"

"I agree, and for that very reason I mean to let my man of law deal with the situation."

According to the letter, which had come from that very Manchester lawyer who handled Robert's legal affairs in the north, the serving wench who had found John Bexwith's body was insisting that he had been frightened to death . . . by a ghost.

"Country folk are often superstitious," Susanna mused, "but not without reason."

Robert frowned. "I'd hoped you'd dismiss the incident as too absurd to pursue. I should have known better."

As she scanned the missive a third time her interest increased with a force that was almost palpable. "Master Grimshaw writes that the apparition is female and quite young, and that she was seen again by several other servants after John Bexwith's death. Grimshaw also claims he is having difficulty finding anyone willing to replace Bexwith as your steward."

"It will take a bit of time for such rumors to fade, but we pay our servants well. Someone will eventually agree to take the post."

"Perhaps we need to show a more personal interest in your Lancashire holdings," Susanna suggested. "A visit to Appleton now would—"

"You would not care for the place."

"What has that to do with anything? It is only good business to inspect the premises of any property we own. You have not been there since just after your father's death. Two years. That's far too long to neglect your—"

"Grimshaw is perfectly capable of hiring a new steward. There is no necessity for either of us to make a long and very uncomfortable journey north."

"If you were not here at Leigh Abbey to receive your orders from the queen, you might not have to go to France after all."

"An excellent reason not to leave."

"So, you are content to wait on the whim of a—"

"She is the queen of England, Susanna."

"I will go north alone, then."

"There is no need, and if you do not have enough to occupy you here while I am gone, then pay a visit to London. Look for new tapestries. Buy books, if you wish."

She continued to argue, but Robert remained adamant. Clearly, he had no desire to return to the place of his birth, but what Susanna could not understand was why he did not want her to go there, either.

CHAPTER 3

"I am to journey out of England again, as I expected to do," Sir Robert announced. The courier who'd just left had come direct from the queen.

"Are you bound for France, then?" Susanna asked.

Once again they were in the study, as they had been a few days earlier when that last missive, from Lancashire, had arrived. Once again Susanna had a book open on the table before her. This time it was the record of grain purchases. She'd all but completed her plans for the next year's planting.

Sir Robert frowned. Dealing with the business of the estate should have been his concern. Most of the time he was well pleased to have a wife who could lift that burden from his shoulders. Every once in a while, however, he wished she were not quite so competent. It made him seem unnecessary.

"Aye, France." Susanna lifted a brow at the testiness in his voice. "I am to visit the French court first, to convey the queen of England's personal greetings to the new French queen. Another Mary."

Robert contemplated the sharp intelligence in his wife's eyes and wondered if he should say more. There were times when her insights were helpful, though of course she was only a woman, and she had never even visited a royal court.

"This one is an untried girl of sixteen," he said carefully, "and yet in that frail vessel runs the blood of the royal lines of both England and Scotland. Good Catholics, who maintain that our Elizabeth is illegitimate and a heretic as well, consider Mary of Scotland and France to be Mary of England's rightful heir."

"I do much doubt this girl-queen has any say in her own concerns. More like she is as much a puppet as poor Lady Jane Grey."

"We do not speak of the past," Robert said sharply.

He did not even like to remember what disaster had befallen them all when his own mentor, the duke of Northumberland, had tried to cut both of King Edward's half sisters out of the succession and substitute his cousin Jane, a girl who just happened to be married to Northumberland's son, Lord Guildford Dudley.

"The present is all that matters," he reminded her. "And the future."

"Where is the French court these days?" Susanna asked.

"At Blois. The new king is still said to be hunting."

Robert knew his smile had a wry twist to it. Arrangements were being made to proclaim the new king of age on his sixteenth birthday in January. In the interim, at the instigation of Queen Catherine, the king's mother, the entire court had embarked on a hunting party that was moving from one site to another as if in fear of pursuit. Perhaps they did fear it. If aught happened to Francis, his younger brother would succeed, creating the necessity for a regency that would last for several years.

"They will likely remain at Blois for some time. It seems all that recent exercise poisoned the young king's blood. His face is a mass of blotches and pimples. His physicians recommend a long stay in Touraine with frequent aromatic baths, to which end a special bathhouse is being built on the grounds of the royal château."

"Perhaps you should take the queen a salve for her husband's rash."

It was an excellent plan. Robert wished he'd thought of it first.

"And after Blois?" his wife asked.

"I am not permitted to share that information with anyone." She gave him a sharp look.

He said nothing, refusing to admit that he did not precisely know the answer to her question. He would not be told more until he reached Walter Pendennis's lodgings in Paris.

"I'll not beg to share your secrets," his wife informed him.

"It is a matter of state," he said loftily. That was nothing less than the truth. His official mission was to convey the queen's greetings and a personal gift to her royal cousin, Mary Stewart. Unofficially, he was to evaluate the political situation at the French court, then meet with a leader of the rebel faction and assess his strength. When and where that second meeting would occur was the mystery. And with whom.

When his silence continued, Susanna directed a cold stare in his direction. "God grant you a safe journey," she said stiffly.

"Will you visit London while I am gone?"

"I've the harvest to supervise first. After Michaelmas, who can say?"

Her answer annoyed him. So did her haughty manner. He considered demanding she make firm plans and seek his approval of them, but in the interest of harmony between them at their parting he held his tongue. What did it matter what she did?

"I leave tomorrow," he announced. "Have the salve ready for me." He'd depart a day ahead of schedule, giving him time to visit his mistress in Dover before he left England for France.

The thought of Alys cheered him considerably. Sir Robert smiled, looking forward to a stolen day and night with a woman who knew her proper place. Unlike Susanna, Alys behaved with becoming modesty, showing proper gratitude for his attentions. She recognized that he was master not only of the house she lived in but also of her person, providing everything from the food she ate to the clothes she wore. Alys was effusive with her thanks. And inventive.

Susanna resisted acknowledging that she was dependent upon him in any way. Indeed, she sometimes acted as if she had every right to make decisions on her own, though she knew the law as well as he did. She would admit, when pressed, that legally a wife was the property of her husband, to do with as he chose, but in practice she went her own way with a blithe disregard for his wishes. According to Susanna, they'd become partners in life when they married.

He told himself he chose to let her be useful to him. In her dull, plodding way, she did get results. She had made the estate profitable. Had she been born a man, Robert suspected they'd have been great friends. He did occasionally find her wit amusing. It was her pride that continually irritated him.

At least she did dedicate herself to looking after his interests. She'd already gone back to her ledgers. Seeing that, Sir Robert decided he had no real desire to change things. What Susanna lacked in feminine charms, Alys more than made up for. To maintain what was, after all, a comfortable balance, he could continue to pay lip service to the idea that a woman might be as capable as a man.

God knew he'd had enough practice. That was a wise opinion to hold when one was at Queen Elizabeth's court. In his heart, though, he did not believe it. Men like King Henry and Sir Thomas More and Susanna's father, who had educated their daughters beyond reading, writing, and ciphering, had done a great disservice to the others of their sex.

CHAPTER 4

Matthew Grimshaw shifted uncomfortably from one foot to the other and tried to avoid the accusing eyes charting his every twitch. He had reason to know that the messenger who delivered bad news suffered undeserved abuse. Grimshaw braced himself and spoke. "Sir Robert sends word that I am to see to the business of hiring a new steward. He says he'll not come here to Lancashire himself, not for such a trifling matter."

Ineffectual was the least of the derisive terms Grimshaw's accuser employed to describe the lawyer's shortcomings, berating him without mercy for fully a quarter of an hour. Throughout the tirade Grimshaw could hear the wind rising outside in eerie counterpoint to the hectoring voice. By the time he was at last permitted to speak in his own defense, a cold rain had begun. Great drops struck the mullioned windows, sounding like cannon shots in the sudden quiet within the room.

"A second letter to Sir Robert is sure to have the result you desire." Grimshaw ran one finger under his ruff. The sweat that had been flowing freely down his face had left it limp and discolored. "I will write to him at Leigh Abbey. I will pen the letter tonight and send it south by messenger on the morrow."

Grimshaw hoped that promise would encourage his visitor to leave. The point was drawing near at which he'd sooner brave the torrential rain himself than remain a moment longer in his own house in this company.

"You will write the letter now, in my presence. I do not trust you, Matthew."

Grimshaw went pale as ice, responding not to the calm voice but to the mad gleam in the eyes boring into him. "As you wish. Certainly."

He equipped himself with parchment and quill and ink and sat down at his writing table, eager to comply and even more eager to be done so that he might show his tormentor the door. His hand trembled so badly that he put too much pressure on the nub and left a pear-shaped blotch on the page.

"Incompetent fool."

Hastily, the lawyer began again, inscribing "Tuesday, 19 September, 1 Elizabeth" at the top of a fresh sheet of parchment. "Another letter will be all it will take. I am certain of that. You have only to let me tell him the truth, that Appleton Manor has been abandoned, that none dare remain on the grounds."

"Do so, then."

The scratching of the quill underscored the noise of the downpour outside the windows until the letter was complete. Grimshaw handed it over to be approved and waited in an agony of anticipation.

"Be warned, lawyer. If Sir Robert Appleton is not moved by this to look into matters in person, that ghost you told him of will make another deadly appearance."

"But there is no one at the manor now to see it."

A mirthless cackle sent chills up Grimshaw's spine. "Did you not know? Such manifestations have great powers. Why, this ghost of ours might easily roam here to Manchester."

Grimshaw began to shake in earnest, perceiving the words as a threat not only to his reputation but to his life. He was not accustomed to dealing with such irrational behavior. He could not predict the outcome if he refused to do as he'd been bidden. It was easiest to obey.

To make sure he got the point, Grimshaw's unwelcome guest hammered it home. "Someone else will have to die if Sir Robert does not come to Appleton Manor."

"You speak as if Bexwith's death was murder," Grimshaw whispered. "I thought . . . you told me that the old man was already dead."

"So I did." John Bexwith's murderer watched with satisfaction as Grimshaw struggled to convince himself that no crime had been committed. "Then again, a certain poisonous plant might have been added to that marrow-bone pie."

"It is not necessary to try to frighten me," Grimshaw said stiffly. "I will do what you want."

"Yes, you will." Thin lips curved into a satisfied smile, the killer abruptly left the room.

A few moments later Grimshaw heard the sound of his front door closing. His visitor was gone, out into the fury of the storm. With a deep sigh, Grimshaw rang for a servant. The sooner he dispatched the letter, the sooner he could be done with the entire uncomfortable situation at Appleton Manor.

It would become Sir Robert's problem.

CHAPTER 5

Sir Robert was glad to leave Calais behind. Once thought impregnable because of the ability of its English garrison to flood the countryside for four miles all around on half an hour's notice, it had been lost to the French as much through English incompetence as French cunning. The memory still made him bitter.

Bound for Paris, he rode across Picardy. That part of the journey he enjoyed, for all that he'd been in battle against the French there not so very long before. He simply avoided passing near Saint-Quentin, where they'd fought, where he'd been knighted by the late Queen Mary's husband, Philip of Spain.

Picardy was a fertile land, filled with cattle and red swine and sheep. The inns he stopped at were pleasant and well kept. He encountered no brigands, in spite of the fact that he traveled alone and made no secret of his nationality.

Four days after landing on French soil, Sir Robert reached Paris. The city had been built on flat land and was surrounded by vineyards and villages, removed from the countryside by crenelated walls flanked by round towers. He followed a muddy

road to a drawbridge guarded by soldiers, telling himself he
had no reason to fear. His papers were in order. Yet he took
note of the silent warning ahead. Over the narrow gate, impaled
on a spike, was a head. Farther along, on a hill top, a huge
gibbet displayed the bodies of hanged men left to rot.

No worse than London, he supposed.

As he rode into the city the street widened but became no
straighter. A filthy stream flowed along its center, enlarged by
countless tributaries feeding on the dung heaps at every door.
The stench rivaled that rising from the nearby River Seine.

Sir Robert guided his horse through an obstacle course of
children and animals. Ducks, chickens, and dogs seemed to
wander unrestricted through the narrow and excessively filth-
clogged streets. Taking a moment to get his bearings, he studied
the wooden houses that lined the way. Each plot of land gave
evidence of once having had a sameness to it: a house with a
garden in back, a stable, a barn, an oven for the weekly baking,
and sometimes a winepress near the cellar. But where boxwood
borders had once marked out vegetable patches, many of the
yards were now filled with lean-to sheds and hovels. The popu-
lation of Paris was expanding too rapidly, even as it was in
London. The old graciousness of life was fast fading.

Five bridges crossed the Seine, linking all parts of the city.
Robert thought longingly of a house on the Left Bank where
poets read their verses aloud to music. Women were allowed
to participate, which lent a coziness to the proceedings . . . and
provided opportunities for more intimate meetings at a later
date.

Business before pleasure, he reminded himself, and turned
instead toward Pendennis's small house on the Right Bank.

A pretty servant girl led him to the upper room where his
old friend was making short work of a pastry filled with meat.

"Sit, Robert," Pendennis invited, waving him toward a Glas-
tonbury chair and gesturing for the servant to bring more food
for his guest.

"You will burst out of those fancy embroidered breeches

if you eat like that every day," Sir Robert warned. Already Pendennis's paunch had increased, though height and broad shoulders disguised much of the damage done by months of easy living.

The room reeked of comfort. The polished tile floor had been strewn with pink marjoram flowers and woodruff leaves. Their sweet scent filled the air, almost concealing the stench from the street outside. The unused fireplace was also filled with aromatic greenery. Juniper boughs, he thought as he gave the returning servant a sharper look. A woman's touch was evident here.

"Paris is a feast," Pendennis declared. "All manner of food can be bought here already cooked and for little cost. The mutton is particularly good. Did you know that every Wednesday and Saturday two thousand horses arrive in Paris heavy-laden with fresh poultry and game? It is all sold in less than two hours, most of it to cookshops."

It was typical of Pendennis to accumulate such facts, and one reason why he held the position he did in Throckmorton's service. One never knew when insignificant knowledge might prove useful.

With hot food before him and a crystal goblet filled with wine, the conversation turned to mutual friends in England. It was not difficult to find topics of conversation. The two of them went back a long way, to the days when they'd both been young gentlemen being trained in the household of John Dudley. Dudley's five sons had befriended them both, in spite of the fact that Sir Robert had been a rough country lad from the north and Pendennis an equally unrefined Cornishman, the youngest son of a large family.

"Have you seen Robin or Ambrose of late?" Pendennis asked.

"Both are high in the queen's favor," Robert informed him, unable to quell a twinge of envy. "These days Robin Dudley is Queen Elizabeth's constant companion at court."

A great many things had changed since their days together

in the Dudley household. They'd gone their separate ways for a time, then been reunited during the brief period when John Dudley, by that time elevated in the peerage to duke of Northumberland, had been virtual ruler of England for the young King Edward.

"Rumor here in France has him her lover. Could he but rid himself of his wife, he might rise even higher."

Robert's grunt was answer enough.

"The Dudley's have the devil's own luck," Pendennis said.

"Luck?" Northumberland and his eldest son had been executed for treason by Edward's successor, Queen Mary. Robert had endured a few uncomfortable weeks of imprisonment himself before following the lead of the remaining Dudley sons and publicly accepting conversion to Catholicism. Henry Dudley had lost his life at the Battle of Saint-Quentin.

"What else can you call it?" Pendennis asked. "Robin was a prisoner in the Tower of London at the same time Elizabeth, then Queen Mary's heiress presumptive, was confined there. 'Tis said one of the guards pitied the poor young things and let them converse together to pass the time."

Converse? Was that the word they used for it?

Robert didn't doubt the story was true. Robin Dudley had always been one to seize the main chance. But luck had little to do with it. Say rather deviousness and cunning. It was a great pity Robin had been so foolish as to fall in love and marry young. But for that he might be ruling England now.

But for his own forced marriage to Susanna . . .

Robert retreated from that line of speculation. His marriage had served him well when Elizabeth took the throne. From that moment, he'd embraced the New Religion once more, as had Robin and Ambrose Dudley and Walter Pendennis. And Robert had also made sure the new queen learned just how many men's lives had been saved because they'd found shelter at Leigh Abbey on their way into exile.

He polished off the last of the fine meal Pendennis had

provided and turned to the matter at hand. "Tell me all you know of Blois."

Pendennis leaned back in his chair and began his recitation with what interested him most—the architectural features. "The château is actually a castle which sits on a cliff above the city of the same name. The first King Francis added a great open, circular staircase and a three-story loggia laced with windows that thrusts right out beyond the steep rock. A daring innovation at the time."

"This is the same Francis who tore down the tallest tower of the Louvre?"

Both Sir Robert and Pendennis had learned something of architecture, as well as music and art and astronomy, during their time in the Dudley household. To make the Louvre a more pleasant place in which to live, King Francis had dismantled a tower that had been eleven feet thick at the top and twenty-three feet thick at the bottom. There had been a great outcry against the destruction at the time.

"The very same," Pendennis said.

"And now we have a second Francis. I wonder what changes he will make to his world."

"He is a boy of fifteen. Sickly."

News that Francis II was in ill health, beyond the condition of his skin, troubled Robert only because the boy-king's death might mean the return of his widow to Scotland. She would be more trouble to England there than in France. It was in Elizabeth's best interests that Mary Stewart's husband stay healthy.

"Who controls him?" he asked Pendennis.

"Some say his wife's uncles, the duke of Guise and the cardinal of Lorraine. Some say his mother, Queen Catherine. In some respects it does not matter. All are most devout Catholics."

"And the remedy for England? Support the Protestant faction? Cause discord where we may?"

"Perhaps. That is what you are to assess."

"You sound doubtful. I had heard the number of French Calvinists was growing."

"Aye. They claim between three hundred thousand and four hundred thousand souls here in France. Some estimate as much as half of the nobility and a third of the bourgeoisie have been converted by missionaries working out of Geneva. Until the national synod of the Reformed Church was convened here in Paris in May there seemed a real possibility that Catholicism would be replaced as the state religion. Unfortunately, the synod coincided with the appearance of that most ominous portent, the star with the long tail. The New Religion has been blamed for every untoward event since."

Sir Robert refilled their goblets and stared broodingly into the dark wine. "We are at peace with France now. I wonder how wise it is to involve ourselves in their civil war."

"Any peace is fleeting. The queen would be foolish not to take an interest in France's internal affairs."

"And why send me? The queen's message made it clear you judged it imperative that I be the emissary sent." He'd debated whether to ask, but the question gnawed at him. He'd been wanting an assignment to France, but he was wary of the mission all the same. Mishandle his duties and he might well lose his chance for advancement at court. The new queen was as fickle as her predecessors. A man in favor one day might find himself hung, drawn, and quartered the next.

"How gratifying to know royalty pays heed to my advice." Pendennis drained his goblet in one long swallow and stared at the branches in the fireplace. "You were requested, my friend, by name."

"By whom?"

"Godefroy du Barri, the seigneur de La Renaudie. It is rumored his undertaking has the blessing of John Calvin himself, and as you are well known in Geneva, it follows that he trusts you."

"I do not know of this La Renaudie."

"He is something of a mystery. We do know he has been in

the countryside recruiting unemployed functionaries and former officers, anyone, in truth, who has suffered as a result of the economies practiced by the most Catholic cardinal of Lorraine. We suspect that his real intent is to try to capture both the cardinal and his brother the duke. Most likely kill them. He claims, of course, that he is only organizing a delegation of loyal subjects to approach the young king with a petition to redress their grievances.''

"He wants access to the court.''

"Aye. Once in, with careful planning and the support of certain noblemen already there, who knows what he might accomplish?''

"He might accomplish his own capture, torture, and execution. The risks are enormous.''

"Less, perhaps, if certain parties know that he has English support.''

"So,'' Robert mused aloud. "My real assignment is to discover just what chance this La Renaudie has to overthrow one of the powerful factions behind France's throne.'' He drank deeply and frowned. On his evaluation might rest the lives of many good men. "Where am I to meet the fellow?''

"He will send word, after your visit to Blois.''

Robert grimaced, filled with a deep sense of foreboding. He did not like to be in situations where he had so little control.

CHAPTER 6

Jennet Barton, Lady Appleton's tiring maid, stood in the middle of the sun-drenched courtyard at Leigh Abbey, arms crossed over her chest, and carefully assessed the three male servants her mistress had selected to accompany them to Lancashire. First there was Mark, the head groom who also had charge of the buttery. He was a well-proportioned fellow a year or so Jennet's senior, with mole brown hair and a plain face. Next to Mark stood Fulke, one of Leigh Abbey's two grooms of the stable. He was a strapping youth, red-cheeked and rough-skinned. Half hidden by Fulke's bulk was young Lionel, the gardener's boy, who had seen only thirteen summers but already towered over Jennet, who was of but middling height for a woman.

An adequate escort, Jennet concluded, but not a very lively one. The trip ahead promised to be fraught with difficulty and deathly dull. Unless, of course, it was true that there was a ghost.

"Since you are to go with me," Lady Appleton told them, "you deserve to know what awaits you in the north."

That they might then ask to stay behind at Leigh Abbey was a risk, but Jennet did not believe it was a very great one. The members of Lady Appleton's household were loyal, and well accustomed to her eccentric behavior. Jennet already knew the story and scarcely listened as her mistress explained about John Bexwith's death and subsequent rumors concerning its cause. Jennet had a natural talent for being in the right place at the right time to overhear the juiciest bits of news and she'd been just outside the study on the day Master Grimshaw's first letter came. Now there had been another.

"The second letter," Lady Appleton said, "was written by that same lawyer to inform Sir Robert that he's found no one willing to stay at Appleton Manor. Thus, it becomes necessary for me to go north in person. If I do not take charge and oversee the installation of new staff, the house will sit empty, abandoned, and decaying. Thieves and vagabonds will not be frightened off by this foolishness about a ghost, and I do not intend to let it deter me, either. I will not sit idly by and allow my husband's boyhood home to be robbed and vandalized."

All that sounded reasonable enough, and was delivered in Lady Appleton's most stirring manner, but Jennet wondered if there was more to this decision to travel than simple duty. Ever since Michaelmas, when the year's accounts had been settled, Jennet had noted her mistress's growing restlessness. Lady Appleton had been heard to mutter that there were no challenges left at Leigh Abbey.

Jennet herself was curious about the haunted house, though now that she thought about it she was not entirely sure she wanted to go and live in it. "What if there really is a ghost?" she asked some time later, when the two women were alone in Lady Appleton's chamber, engaged in packing clothing for the forthcoming trip.

"Why, we'll invite it to dine with us." Lady Appleton chuckled as she folded a shift made of finest lawn and tucked it into a small canvas traveling bag. "On marrow-bone pie."

Jennet failed to see any humor in the jest.

"If you are afraid, Jennet, you need not accompany me."

"I'll not desert you, madam," Jennet said staunchly. Her pride was stung by the suggestion that she might be less brave than her mistress.

Lady Appleton smiled. "Tell me, Jennet. Does it please you that Mark is going with us?"

Blushing furiously, Jennet bent to retrieve a sturdy wool cloak from the bottom of a chest. Her muffled words were barely audible. "He's nothing to me."

"And you are everything to him. It is plain he loves you, Jennet, and you could do far worse."

"Mark's a good man," Jennet grudgingly conceded, "and devoted to you, mistress. He'll protect us with his life on this journey."

"He'd make you a good husband."

Jennet spoke before she thought. "He'd turn me into a brood-mare."

Belatedly, she realized her words might offend. The Appletons had been married long enough to have had four or five children by now and yet they had none. Lady Appleton handed Jennet a pair of yellow velvet sleeves and a matching bodice and bade her fold them. If she was troubled by her failure to produce an heir, or by Jennet's careless comment, she gave no sign of it.

Was she barren? Jennet wondered. She'd never seen Lady Appleton indulge in any of the well-known treatments, yet surely she knew them. Lady Appleton had great skill with all manner of herbal remedies. She must be familiar with the garlic test.

Folding and packing occupied only a small part of Jennet's inquisitive mind. Could it be that her mistress had overheated her womb with all those baths? On the other hand, bathing was sometimes ordered to cure a too-cold womb. Then again, the problem might lie with Sir Robert.

Jennet stood still, a ruff clutched in both hands, struck by that startling possibility. A man's assets were well displayed in hose and codpiece and Sir Robert did not appear to her to be lacking in that—

"Jennet? Stop woolgathering, my girl. We've much to do to prepare for the journey."

Once again Jennet felt color seep into her cheeks as she hurried to do as she'd been bidden. She was glad Lady Appleton could not possibly guess the direction of her thoughts, and hastily diverted the conversation, changing it back to the subject she knew most interested her mistress at the moment.

"Do you think there *is* a ghost?" she asked.

"No. I do not believe anything supernatural is going on at Appleton. You will see when we get there, Jennet. John Bexwith likely died of old age, and if he did not, then his death will turn out to be a simple matter of accidental poisoning. There is a slight chance he was murdered, but even if that proves so, his killer was no ghost. Of that I am certain."

"Murder?" Jennet was no longer blushing. Indeed, she suspected that her face had abruptly lost all its color. Unaware that she was doing so, she began to worry her lower lip.

A few hours later, Jennet and Mark met by arrangement in the ornamental gardens on the south side of Leigh Abbey.

"Lady Appleton actually looked pleased by the prospect of unraveling a mystery," she told him. "And she said I need not go, that I could remain here, where it is safe."

Mark, intent on nibbling her ear, did not respond for a moment. Then, as her words took root, he abruptly released her. "You do not wish to come with me? But, Jennet, this is a great opportunity, for both of us."

"Opportunity?"

"The chance of a lifetime." Growing more confident again, Mark took both her hands in his. "Appleton Manor needs a new steward. I mean to convince Lady Appleton that I am the best man to fill that post."

"Mark Jaffrey, are you daft? There may have been one steward murdered there already. Do you mean to be the next victim?"

"Why, Jennet, do you care so much?"

Chagrined, she punched him in the arm. He laughed and pulled her closer, whispering of how good her life could be if she became a steward's wife. Then he started to kiss her again and Jennet stopped trying to talk him out of it.

But she was still uneasy about going to Appleton Manor. Deep in her heart, Jennet was certain that some terrible danger awaited them there.

CHAPTER 7

Her husband's holding lay before her, at this distance an imposing stone structure located in the southeast portion of a two-acre lot enclosed by a square moat. At a short distance from the great hall and its domestic buildings Lady Appleton could just make out a small chapel, also built of stone.

She hesitated only a moment before urging her mount across the double-arched stone bridge, noting that there seemed to be no sign of life ahead. The only movement anywhere was the stirring of leaves, brilliantly hued in this season, on the branches of a few ancient trees.

"A fine place for a ghost," Jennet muttered.

Spurred on by the comment, even though she secretly agreed with her maidservant's assessment, Susanna Appleton continued leading her small band of travelers down the slope and over the bridge. They had endured a long and exhausting journey and she was anxious for it to end. In a few more hours it would be dark and she wished to be comfortably settled in well before nightfall.

In a bolstering tone, she addressed her retinue. "If the house proves as deserted as it appears, it will still provide shelter. We have provisions with us, and firewood, too. Neither cold nor hunger will trouble us tonight.''

Two packhorses carried all they would need for the present, and Susanna began to make plans to visit the nearest village on the morrow. They'd need more supplies soon, but more importantly she wanted answers.

Within ten minutes, they reached the courtyard. An air of neglect hung about the place, more than could be accounted for by a month and a half without a steward to oversee matters. Dismounting, Susanna handed Mark her reins and strode briskly up a flight of stone steps to the porch. A heavy oaken door banded with iron was the main entrance to the house. She did not know whether to be angry or relieved when she discovered that it had been left unlocked. It swung open with an agonized creak of rusty hinges to reveal the lofty room at ground level that was Appleton's great hall.

Keep-style, the kitchen, hall, and chamber had been cobbled together end to end, but this was no castle. Susanna's knowledge of the place and its environs was limited, but she was quite certain that Appleton had never been used for the defense of the lands surrounding it. She picked her way through the soiled rushes that covered the floor, wrinkling her nose as unpleasant odors rose with each step. Rustling noises preceded her. Mice . . . she hoped.

The most cursory of surveys of the great hall revealed that the concept of a fireplace with a chimney for this principal room had not yet reached Appleton. A single opening, high above a central hearth, was deemed adequate to draw smoke from the hall.

''Inefficient,'' Susanna murmured, but she was alert to possibilities now and saw no reason why the hall could not he modernized. Her own grandfather had rebuilt Leigh Abbey. She resolved to do the same with Appleton.

Lifting her skirts carefully to keep them above the layers of accumulated filth, Susanna continued her explorations, at length mounting a dais which was lit by pale sunbeams filtering through a dirt-streaked oriel window. The illumination was sufficient, when she opened the door behind the dais, to show her the cellar beyond. She did not go in, for it appeared to be quite empty.

Opposite the window she located the narrow, tortuous stairway to the chamber above the storage room. Susanna hesitated, then squared her shoulders. She turned back only long enough to issue a few succinct orders to Jennet, Lionel, and Fulke and to tell Mark to bring a torch. He obeyed instantly, but in his other hand he carried a cudgel.

Upstairs the windows were all fitted with shutters, but one hung broken and open and let in light. An enterprising spider had spun its web across the space, but neither ghost nor vagabond inhabited the sparsely furnished great chamber at Appleton. It contained a sagging bed and a livery cupboard with a carpet and, seeming oddly out of place, a pair of virginals. It lacked a dressing box. There was no looking glass, either, and no fireplace.

Disappointed, but far from discouraged, Susanna led the way back down to the great hall. Clouds of dust billowed up with every step. ''In the old days,'' she remarked, ''it was the custom for family and retainers alike to sleep all together on pallets in the great hall.''

There were worse things, she supposed, but she had no great desire to endure rough living conditions. The sooner she installed comfortable furnishings, the better. With a delicate shudder at the thought of what she might find next, she ventured past the buttery and pantry and went into the kitchen. Like the rest of the place, the service rooms were filthy.

''Not fit for a gentleman's house,'' Mark muttered.

''It will be,'' Susanna said.

She stood with her hands on her hips and looked around her. The workrooms were a disgrace, which might well be at least a part of the reason why Robert had always discouraged her from visiting his ancestral estate. He'd not wanted her to see how general the state of neglect and disrepair was at Appleton.

"All this can be remedied, Mark."

"It will cost a fortune."

"I have a fortune," she reminded him.

Even as tired as she was after the long journey, Susanna was ready to face the challenge of turning Appleton into a second home. She discovered oil lamps and candlesticks, though neither oil nor candles were in evidence. A few mildewed and stained linens had been left behind, and some pewter. She hoped whatever gold and silver plate there had been had been stored elsewhere rather than stolen. That was something else she'd have to ask Lawyer Grimshaw about.

By the time she returned to the great hall for the second time, she'd all but given up hope that any part of the house would be comfortable to live in for the present. Even the privy had turned out to be inconvenient, having been constructed according to the old rule that dictated setting the cesspit a bowshot away from the house.

There was one area left to inspect. Bracing herself for more evidence of neglect, Appleton's new lady climbed the high, curving staircase at the lower end of the hall. She was pleasantly surprised to find herself in a solar with a fireplace. There was a washbasin set into an outer wall, too. It was getting too dark outside to see for certain through the glazed and leaded windows, but she suspected that the water drained out through the mouth of a gargoyle carved into the stone.

"I will sleep here," she told Mark, who still followed her closely with both light and cudgel at the ready. "As soon as we have eaten, instruct Fulke and Lionel to help you move all the furnishings now in the great chamber to this room."

She was almost cheerful as she went back downstairs and her optimism increased further when she saw that there was now a cheerful fire going in the open hearth. Jennet had seen to both the removal of the rushes and the unpacking of those essentials necessary for the night.

"Most excellent progress, Jennet," she called out as she approached her maidservant from behind.

Jennet jumped and let out a shriek. One hand went to her breast, as if to contain the wildly beating heart beneath the bodice of her plain blue kirtle. "Your pardon, madam," she apologized.

Susanna chose to ignore the obvious fear in Jennet's eyes, and to attribute her nervousness to the vast emptiness of the hall around them.

"We will all eat together here, as they did in days gone by." She sketched a circle around the fire with her hands. There was no reason for formality in these circumstances. They had sat together at table in every inn along the road north. Finding herself a stool, Susanna dragged it close to the welcome warmth, sat, and reached for a heel of the bread they'd brought with them.

She wondered what Robert was doing.

He'd know what she was up to by now. She'd written to him before their departure from Leigh Abbey. In a brief note she'd detailed her plans. It was as well he was in Paris, she decided. The distance between them ensured he'd had no time to reply, no chance to order her to stay at home.

She knew he'd be angry. He'd been adamant in his opinion that no one needed to visit Lancashire in person. Still, he'd not been at home to see the second letter from Matthew Grimshaw. She was not so foolish as to think that it would have changed his mind, but it was the excuse she would give when they saw each other again. By then his irritation would have faded, and she would have restored Appleton Manor to its former glory. How could he possibly object to that?

"What news?" she asked Mark as he concluded a brief consultation with Fulke and Lionel.

"No one's about." He pulled a bench up to the fire for himself and Jennet. "No beasts are stabled here. No livestock whatsoever, unless you count the trout in the brook." He whispered something Susanna could not hear in Jennet's ear and the young woman smiled.

She'd make him a good match, Susanna thought. Pretty

enough to be proud of but not so beautiful as to cause him concern. And practical. Jennet had a keen eye to the main chance. They'd make a formidable pair once they settled matters between them.

Susanna continued to watch them as they ate. Jennet cast wary glances over her shoulder every few minutes, obviously expecting to see some supernatural manifestation. Susanna could understand her uneasiness. She had to guard against becoming fanciful herself, for the atmosphere in this abandoned house was undeniably eerie.

"There is nothing here to fear, Jennet," she said to reassure her maid. Then, having noticed the speculative look on Mark's face, she informed Jennet that she would share the chamber above while they were at Appleton. Both the warmth and the company would be welcome in the bed left behind by Robert's father, but in truth Susanna's real motivation was the sense of responsibility she felt toward her servants. Left alone, Jennet's fears would doubtless drive her to seek the illusory protection of Mark's arms. No conscientious chatelaine could knowingly permit such goings-on. If Jennet wanted to marry Mark, Susanna would wish them well with all her heart, but she would not condone the sort of careless coupling that led to unwanted children and loveless marriages.

"This is a perilous cold place," Jennet said, rubbing her hands together as she held them closer to the fire. "I vow there is less draft out-of-doors than in."

"Nothing so unusual in that." Susanna studied the thick stones surrounding them. "These walls were meant to keep the inhabitants cool in the heat of summer."

"I do not believe summer comes to these parts," Jennet declared. "And I do much wonder that any survive the winter."

"And yet they must. Do not forget, Jennet, that Sir Robert lived here as a boy. The climate had no ill effect on him."

A sudden sound from the dais end of the hall undid in a moment all that reasonable words had achieved. Every face turned in that direction, wide-eyed with anticipation. The noise was not repeated, but in the breathless silence that followed, they all saw the same thing. The filthy cloth that covered the refectory table fluttered once, twice, three times, and then was still.

Jennet screamed. An answering wail, long and loud and mournful, issued from beneath the table.

"The ghost!" Jennet cried.

Susanna's heart was beating as fast as her maid's but she had to stifle a smile as she rose from her stool. She moved cautiously toward the table, not because she was afraid of what she would find but because she did not want to startle the only living creature, aside from a few mice and that one spider, who'd chosen to remain at Appleton when the servants fled.

"Good evening, Master Cat," she said as she lifted one corner of the grimy linen tablecloth and peered beneath.

Unblinking topaz eyes stared back at her.

"Will you join us?" she asked the cat.

With regal dignity, a large, ginger-colored feline emerged. Susanna hastily amended her words of greeting.

"Your pardon, for it is surely Mistress Cat, or perhaps even Dame Cat."

The creature was obviously female, so heavily pregnant that her belly was nearly dragging on the floor. And yet, with all the dignity of a queen on progress, she made her way to the hearth, circled it once to assure herself that she'd selected exactly the right spot, and then curled into a ball just as close to the warmth as she could get without having her tail catch on fire.

CHAPTER 8

Jennet squinted at the morning sun and shifted restlessly, trying to get comfortable on the leather cushion. "I do not like this Lancashire at all," she grumbled.

Neither did she like riding apillion, even behind a man as courteous as Mark. The cushion did little to pad the hard wooden frame beneath, not when it was strapped to the back of a horse that took perverse pleasure in bouncing and jouncing over every uneven roadway in the kingdom. Jennet's backside had been taking a beating all the way north from Leigh Abbey. Already bruised and sore, she was not happy to have to travel yet another bad road, even if it had been built by the Romans and ran nearly straight from Stockport to Manchester. Given a choice, Jennet would have preferred to walk all the way to the nearest village.

In front of her, using a saddle that appeared to be no more comfortable than her own perch, Mark was turning his head from side to side, alert for danger. He did not reply, but Jennet knew he'd heard her complaint. He was aware of her in other ways, too. Although her feet rested modestly on a footboard hung from the offside, she was obliged to cling to Mark's waist to keep from tumbling off the horse. She'd been gently torturing him for nigh onto one hundred and eighty miles.

"Not much farther now," Lady Appleton called back to them. "I can see a few houses from here."

She was the one who had insisted they ride to Gorebury, the nearest hamlet. Jennet wondered if her mistress was trying to impress the villagers, or if she'd simply been uncertain of the distance they would have to travel. Either way, Lady Appleton's arrival would start tongues wagging. That much was certain. She sat sideways on her horse, just as Jennet did, but Lady Appleton rode alone, resting both feet on a velvet sling and supporting one knee in a hollow cut in the pommeled saddle.

Jennet frowned. The fact that Lady Appleton had dressed for her own comfort argued against any calculated effort to impress the yeomen and husbandmen of Gorebury. She'd brought better gowns with her, but this morning she'd instructed Jennet to help her put on her old russet-colored riding dress, the one with the wool worn thin from frequent laundering. Both the little round face ruff that fastened with aglets and the ruffled cuffs had long since yellowed, and Lady Appleton had not even bothered with a safeguard to protect her skirts. So, Jennet decided, she was not interested in impressing anyone. She simply preferred to ride rather than walk.

The houses, close up, were as disappointing as Appleton had been. A poorer collection of dwellings Jennet had rarely encountered. She and Mark dismounted at the communal village well and looked around. Much alike, all the buildings were timber-framed, their roofs thatched with straw. Through doors customarily left open in the daytime, Jennet could see that the floors were beaten earth covered with rushes. Peat fires burned on raised stone hearths, creating a permanent haze, for like the hearth at Appleton, they were vented only through holes in the roof.

In one cottage a pot of porridge simmered on a trivet. In another Jennet caught a glimpse of stools drawn up to a trestle table. Every house seemed to have herbs, storage bags, and baskets hanging from the rafters, and in one place she spied a ham, but nowhere was there any hint of great prosperity.

The entire village consisted of fewer than two dozen buildings, including the mill. At least three stood empty, with holes in the wattle-and-daub infill and rot in the roof straw. Such places were likely to harbor rats, as well as hornets and wasps, and Jennet kept her distance from them.

At least there were people here, and their livestock. Pens and fences contained chickens, pigs, and cows. From somewhere out of sight, Jennet heard the bleating of sheep and when she inhaled she caught the noisome scent peculiar to puering hides in preparation for tanning.

Two women had looked up from their laundry as the riders passed them, but they'd not ceased their labor. Now they removed clothing that had been soaking in lye to beat and scrub the pieces, then hang them over nearby hedges to dry.

A middle-aged man in what appeared to be the uniform of the place, a short, belted tunic worn with long, loose hose and leather shoes with heavy wooden soles, was the first to acknowledge the presence of newcomers. He finished knocking acorns off an oak tree for his pigs, then sauntered toward the well. He did not doff his cloth cap. Neither did he speak a word of greeting, but soon others came, men and women, drawn by curiosity. Gradually, a small crowd gathered.

Still mounted, looking every inch the gentlewoman she was, Jennet's mistress studied the villagers, ignoring their rude stares and waiting for the right moment to address them.

There was no danger. Even Jennet was certain of that. She was equally sure that these people were not going to help them. As Lady Appleton began to speak, introducing herself to her new neighbors and explaining that she wished to hire servants and purchase foodstuffs, Jennet sensed invisible barriers going up, dense as any stone wall and just as impervious to sweet reason.

''We've our own work, and no need for more to do,'' said

one of the women who'd been washing clothes. She and her companion were as simply dressed as their menfolk, in long, loose, dirt brown gowns belted at the waist. The speaker had covered her head and neck with an old-fashioned wimple, but her feet were bare and her face was brown and wrinkled from exposure to the sun. Jennet tried to guess her age and could not. She might be anywhere from twenty to sixty.

The excuse she'd given struck Jennet as an odd one. October was a busy month in the south, even though the harvest season was officially over by Michaelmas. Here in the north the crops would have been in earlier. Only the slack winter season lay ahead. These people should have been glad of the prospect of employment.

"I will pay well," Lady Appleton said. "And there will be more work in the spring, honest work for any able-bodied man who can lift a stone or raise a roofbeam."

The suspicious expressions that had enlivened a few of the stolid country faces were now replaced by looks of dismay, but no one voiced any objection. The village folk remained taciturn and unhelpful, saying more by their silence than they could have with words.

"This Gorebury is a strange place," Lady Appleton told them when she'd tried again to sway them and had once more failed. "It is plain you grow barely enough to live upon, yet you show no interest in a generous offer of gainful employment."

"All the young folk are gone to Manchester," a man muttered, as though that explained his own unwillingness to work. Begrudging every word, he added, "In Manchester there be good jobs in the cloth industry."

"I will offer better working conditions and higher pay."

No one volunteered to send for a son or daughter.

"Have you a curate here?" Lady Appleton asked abruptly.

For a moment it seemed as if no one would answer. Then a new voice sounded. "Be no curate. Naught but a lay reader for the likes of us."

"And who might you be?" she asked.

"I be the new reeve what took office at Michaelmas." He puffed out his chest. "I be ale taster, too."

Jennet poked Mark in the ribs. "That great lout does not look any different from his fellows. Surely he's not clever enough to be a reeve."

"A reeve need not be lettered," Mark whispered back. "It is possible to keep accounts with a tally stick."

Solemn and pompous, the reeve explained that Gorebury's tenants paid their rents to the lord of Manchester and thus had no obligation to anyone at Appleton.

Jennet felt herself grow warm on her mistress's behalf, but if Lady Appleton was taken aback by this rudeness she gave no sign. Instead her voice went all soft and cajoling. "And you, sirrah?" she asked him. "I can see you are a fellow who seeks to better himself. What would you say if I offered you John Bexwith's old place?"

Mark's fingers tightened on Jennet's arm. She understood his reaction, but she knew, too, that he had no need to worry. She was certain Lady Appleton had no real intention of hiring this reeve to be her steward. She did but test the waters.

The big man was appalled by the suggestion. His jaw literally dropped and his face turned the color of whey.

"He is afraid," Jennet whispered. She scanned the other faces in the crowd. "They are all afraid of Appleton's ghost."

"You are quick to condemn them for that," Mark muttered, "when you are passing terrified of the thing yourself."

Jennet jerked her arm free, insulted. Mark knew perfectly well that she felt much more confident now that their first night at Appleton had passed without incident.

They left the village a short time later. Lady Appleton had inquired about provisions and had been told that no surplus food was available for sale. Jennet had expected they might have to haggle over prices. She'd never thought they'd be turned away empty-handed.

"I vow they mean to starve us into leaving," she grumbled against Mark's back. Any lingering concern about the ghost had been replaced by worries of a much more practical nature. Jennet wanted soft cushions to sit upon, and good food in her belly, and the prospect of finding either suddenly seemed remote.

"What I find curious," Mark said after a moment, "is that no one in that village made mention of the rumors that Appleton is haunted. Why not speak of the ghost? It is obvious they've all heard the tale."

"They barely spoke at all," Jennet reminded him.

"And that, too, is curious. We are strangers. Think, Jennet. At home a newcomer is made welcome. Travelers bring word from other places, and in return the locals share whatever gossip most interests them. These people did not want to hear why we'd come, nor talk to us at all. No one tried to speak with you or I. Why not? Were you in their place, would you not seize any opportunity to catch one of us away from Lady Appleton and plague him with questions?"

Jennet knew she would. She never missed a chance to find out what was going on around her, whether it was any of her business or not. The steward at Leigh Abbey was always complaining that Jennet lurked in the corners, listening to her betters when she should be concentrating on her chores.

They rode on, Lady Appleton once more in the lead. Thick, ancient hedges lined the road, but trees were sparse. A few oak and one ash were all Jennet had seen on the eastward journey. To the north, at some distance, she could just make out a flattened range of mountains, broken by deep clefts and valleys. To the south was the fertile Cheshire plain, but farms seemed both poor and far-flung in this part of Lancashire.

"Do you think this setback will discourage Lady Appleton?" Jennet asked. "Will we be leaving for home again on the morrow?"

Leigh Abbey had never seemed more luxurious, even if Jennet's own place in it was no more than an attic dormitory shared with the other maidservants. If she married Mark, she thought, they'd likely have their own cottage. The prospect brought a slow smile to Jennet's lips. Lady Appleton would not expect her to share Mark's room above the stables if they wed.

Lost in a bout of homesickness, combined though it was with passing pleasant daydreams, Jennet did not for a moment comprehend that Mark had answered her.

"Not likely," he'd said.

"What is not?"

"Leaving. If Lady Appleton cannot find workers closer at hand, she has only to journey into Manchester and open her purse. She will find someone there willing to take a few risks and live at a haunted manor."

"Then why has that lawyer, Grimshaw, not already found servants? He lives there in Manchester."

Mark chuckled. He'd plainly realized that he was in no danger of losing the plum of the steward's post. "No mere lawyer has Lady Appleton's determination. Have you ever known her to give up on a project once she'd embarked upon it?"

Jennet sighed, resigned to staying on at Appleton indefinitely. She did know how stubborn their mistress was. "How far is it to Manchester?"

"Some ten miles, I believe. Why?"

"And from Gorebury back to Appleton?"

"At my best guess, a little more than two miles."

"Faith, it felt more like a dozen!" Jennet rubbed her tender backside. She did not think she could endure the remainder of the return journey, let alone a trip to Manchester. "Help me down, Mark. I mean to walk the rest of the way back."

Before he could comply with Jennet's wishes, Lady Appleton abruptly reined in her horse. A gawky young woman was waiting at the crossroads, a maidservant by her dress. In low tones and with a hesitant manner, as if she suffered from overwhelming shyness, she spoke to Lady Appleton.

Jennet studied the girl with critical eyes. She was a sickly looking creature with an unhealthy pallor and skin that hung in folds, as if she had recently lost weight. She was also missing a front tooth, and her speech, what Jennet could hear of it, was faltering and heavy with the accent of the north country. She scurried out of the way, eyes fixed on the ground, when Lady Appleton turned her horse and, smiling broadly, spoke to Mark and Jennet.

"We are invited to stop at Denholm Hall before we return to Appleton," she announced. "The Denholms, it seems, are our nearest neighbors, and wish to make us welcome here."

Jennet reluctantly remained on the pillion, but her temper improved considerably when she got her first good look at Denholm Hall. It seemed a prosperous place, a place where they were likely to find ample provisioning. They might even be invited to stay there, in lieu of returning to that ruin at Appleton Manor.

Outbuildings abounded, almost as impressive as the house itself. There was a wooden, slate-roofed chapel. The kitchen and bakehouse were separate buildings. There was even a communal privy near at hand. A granary had been built up against the house, and several nearby barns were roofed with thatch and timber-framed. The stable was built of stone, and next to it stood a thatched wooden sheepfold. At a greater distance Jennet spotted a kiln and two large dovecotes. Chickens, geese, peacocks, and swans were also much in evidence.

"We will eat well tonight," Jennet murmured as they entered the courtyard.

Mark dismounted first, gazing about him with admiration. "I will turn Appleton Manor into a place every bit as prosperous as this one," he bragged. "Give me but a year."

Jennet stared down at him in mute amazement. She heard no doubt in his voice. When had Mark become so bold?

"Unlike you, Jennet," he said as his strong hands closed around her waist to lift her off the pillion, "I like this Lancashire very well."

CHAPTER 9

Susanna Appleton's first impression of Denholm Hall was also entirely favorable, but she had a deeper aesthetic appreciation of the architecture and design. The whole was enclosed by a wall, as Appleton Manor was, and here, too, there were traces of a moat near the stream, but the manor house was newly built.

It was situated at the center of a four-plot design. The forecourt led to the entrance, there was a kitchen garden on the service end of the house, and on the third visible side were orchards. At the back, unless the Denholms had completely and inexplicably broken with the popular new pattern, Susanna was certain she would find an elaborate ornamental garden.

Everything was carefully laid out and ordered, surprisingly modern for a place so far north of London. A kindred spirit dwelt here, Susanna deduced, someone who might well share her own avid interest in herbs and other growing things. Mistress Denholm, the woman who had sent her maidservant to fetch them thither, seemed the most likely candidate. With a keen sense of anticipation, Susanna dismounted and ascended the steps of a slate-roofed porch.

They led to an imposing front door. The woman waiting on the other side was no less massive. She dominated the parlor in which she received them and lost no time taking charge of the situation.

"Go you and see to their provisioning, Grizel," she ordered the maid who'd brought them.

With a peremptory gesture, Mistress Denholm signaled that both Jennet and Mark were to follow the girl. Neither of them even thought to disobey.

A forceful woman, Susanna decided as she studied her new neighbor. There had been a second person in the room when they'd first been shown in, a pale wraith of a girl who'd since vanished. Susanna wondered where she'd gone, and why. By the richness of her dress, she was a Denholm herself, rather than merely one of the servants. Susanna was about to inquire as to her identity when Mistress Denholm took charge once more, this time sweeping her guest out of the room before her on the pretext that she wanted to show off Denholm's grounds.

Mistress Denholm was nearly as tall as Susanna, a stout matron made to seem even more immense by the addition of all the most ostentatious trappings of mourning. Her farthingale was as wide, and the sleeves that had been added to the bodice as padded, as fashion and common sense would allow. Beneath prodigious double chins, Mistress Denholm had added a white, pleated barbe to the front of her stiff black silk hood. Susanna had the uneasy sense that she wore it to cover a neck of mammoth proportions. The hood itself had been constructed so that it dipped at the center front edge, forming a widow's peak. Mistress Denholm was wearing mourning jewelry, too, including a finger ring fashioned as a coffin and a brooch that had been designed to contain a lock of the hair of a departed loved one.

Mindful of her own extraordinary height and sturdy frame, Susanna took note of the depredations time, lack of exercise, and an excess of rich food had wrought in her hostess. In twenty years, she realized, if she were not careful, she might well attain a comparable girth herself. That thought alone was enough to produce an involuntary shudder.

Mistress Denholm's size was matched by her effusiveness. Such hearty expressions of warmth and friendliness would have overpowered a weak-willed person, and even her smile failed to lessen the effect. Unlike the rest of her, Mistress Denholm's lips were very thin, making the effort at friendliness seem both garish and startling. Susanna smiled back, berating herself for intolerance. The other woman's bossiness might be a trial, but she could not help the way she looked.

"You must tell me all the news of London and the court." Mistress Denholm's words sounded more like a command than a request, but beneath the brusque exterior Susanna sensed a desperate need for contact with the outside world. There could not be much in the way of companionship in this remote place. Gossip with the servants would only partially dispel a gentle-woman's loneliness.

"I have little firsthand knowledge of the doings there myself," she replied. "I spend most of my time in parts of Kent that are every bit as rural, and as far removed from the bustle of great cities, as you are here."

"They say your husband is much in demand at court," Mistress Denholm said bluntly. "Is that why he has not come with you?"

"He is much in demand by the court," Susanna corrected her. Mistress Denholm seemed unaware that her words might have given offense. "He is constantly being sent on one diplomatic mission or another, and all to foreign parts."

"Did he send you in his place, then?"

"Indeed, he did not. It is likely he will be most irritated with me when he hears what I am about." Fortunately, Robert's temper cooled rapidly. By the time Susanna saw him again she was sure he'd have long since forgiven her for ignoring his wishes.

Apparently pondering the strangeness of Susanna's words, Mistress Denholm slowed her pace still further. They were just passing a stone dairy when she spoke again, gesturing toward the building with one large hand. "The best equipped in Lancashire," she said proudly, "with cheese presses, churns, settling pans, strainers, and earthenware jars."

"You must sell your butter and cheese, then."

"Aye, and at a good profit, too. The only other income we have here to equal it comes from our dovecotes. We produce an average of a thousand young doves a year."

Mistress Denholm directed her guest toward a broad path that ended at the orchard. A variety of fruit trees grew inside a low hedge composed of cornelian cherry trees and rose and gooseberry bushes. A few of the roses were still in bloom. Damson, bullace, and tall plum formed the outer circle of the orchard, growing around low plum, cherry, and apple trees. Randomly mixed in were filberts, more cornelian cherries, and medlars.

"You are still picking bullaces and medlars," Susanna observed, "but I see no sign of apricots or peaches or quinces."

"It is too cold here to grow them successfully. We do better with pears."

"I am accustomed to thinking of Worcestershire for those."

"And Kent is the county famous for cherries," Mistress Denholm agreed, intending a compliment. "We cannot rival either, but neither must we import those fruits."

They smiled at each other, considerably more at ease than they had been. Mistress Denholm indicated a conveniently located bench. "Will you sit?"

"It would be pleasant to rest here awhile." Susanna settled herself at one end of the sturdy stone seat, smoothing her skirts as she did so.

With a sigh of relief, Mistress Denholm sank down beside her. Her face was ruddy from just the moderate exertion of that short stroll.

"We must dispense with formality," she said when she had

caught her breath. "I think you will find you need a friend here. My given name is Euphemia, but you may call me Effie as the members of my immediate family do."

"I am Susanna."

"Well, then, Susanna, will you accept a friend's advice?"

"That, Effie, depends not upon the friend but upon the advice."

"Have you heard . . . rumors?"

"My husband's lawyer writes that Appleton Manor is haunted, if that is what you mean." Susanna did not trouble to add that she did not believe in ghosts, for she saw no point in cutting off a potential source of information.

"That is one rumor. Tell me what Grimshaw said of the way the steward died."

"He was found face down in a marrow-bone pie. An ignominious end, I agree, but not necessarily one brought on by any supernatural cause. He was an old man, and old men die every day."

Effie Denholm's head was bowed. Her hands clenched and unclenched around the fabric across her lap. "He was sitting on the dais. He imagined himself, I suppose, in his old master's place. Overweening pride killed him." Abruptly, she looked up, eyes glittering. "Pride," she repeated. "It is said pride goeth before a fall."

Susanna was as puzzled by the other woman's intensity as she was by her apparent knowledge of what was on John Bexwith's mind on the last night of his life. "Why is where he sat at table so significant?"

"He usurped Sir George's place!"

Robert's, rather, Susanna thought, but she kept her comment to herself. If she had to, she'd demand details, but she was hoping the story would come out without prompting. She'd found that approach worked with almost everyone except her husband. He knew her too well.

Effie was no exception. After a moment she started speaking again. "Sir George Appleton was a legend in these parts,

Susanna. He left broken hearts in every hamlet between here and Manchester."

"If my husband resembles his father in appearance, then I can believe it," Susanna conceded. "Sir Robert is a most handsome man."

"Pray his morals are better than his father's!"

Startled, Susanna bit back the impulse to defend both men. In truth, Robert had never told her much about his father. He'd evaded her questions by stating that they'd not gotten along. She did know that Robert had left Lancashire when he was nineteen and joined the retinue of the future duke of Northumberland. That was nothing unusual. Most sons of the gentry received training in noble households at an even earlier age.

"I know little about Sir George and even less about my husband's mother," Susanna said carefully.

"He was a wicked, wicked man."

Curiosity warred with family loyalty. "Since he has been dead for some time, it seems pointless to revile him."

"Speak no ill of the dead, you mean? But, my dear Susanna, there is so much pleasure in it." Effie chuckled to herself, then slanted an inquisitive look in Susanna's direction. "What do you think of what he left behind? Sir George was an indifferent caretaker. Appleton Manor had deteriorated badly even before his shameful end."

Shameful end? And did that have something to do with Bexwith's death? Susanna's instincts told her there was more to this situation than met the eye, but before she could ask Effie what she meant, the older woman rose to her feet. "There is a charming fishpond this way," she said, striking out in that direction and giving Susanna no choice but to follow.

The pond was well stocked and dotted with lily pads. A willow tree dipped lissome branches near the surface at one end. "I find Appleton Manor a challenge," Susanna said as they came to a stop at bankside. She was reluctant to appear too eager for information. "The building is sound. With good workmen who know their business, I believe restoration will be complete within a year.''

''An expensive project. Three thousand pounds at the least.''

At a guess, more than that had been spent at Denholm Hall in recent years. Susanna complimented Effie on her taste, but she was more interested in returning to the subject of Sir George and his shameful end.

Susanna was reluctant to betray her own abysmal ignorance of events, but she did not see that she had much choice in the matter. ''I will tell you true, Effie,'' she confided. ''My husband has said perilous little about his early years and he has almost never mentioned his father. Will you tell me about Sir George?''

''Gladly. You should know the terrible truth.''

''Terrible?'' Susanna echoed. First it was shameful. Now it was terrible. Surely the woman exaggerated.

''He had five wives,'' Effie said bluntly, ''all of whom died before him. There were mistresses, too. Many, many mistresses.'' Her face contorted briefly, but her voice did not change. ''By the time his last wife went to her reward, Sir George was getting on in years and he was not so charming or so goodly to look at anymore. Still, he was wealthy, rich enough, he thought, to buy any woman he wanted. He could not conceive of encountering one who was unwilling. The night he died it is said he tried to seduce a serving wench, a girl new to the household at Appleton Manor. She fled his unwelcome attentions in a panic, running down the flight of stairs from the solar. He pursued her, cup-shotten and furious at the insult to his manhood.''

''He died in a fall.'' Robert had told her that much.

''Aye. Broke his neck, the randy old goat.''

Susanna considered the layout of the hall at Appleton Manor. From the dais, John Bexwith would have had an unobstructed view of the stairs to the solar.

''And the girl?'' she asked, her suspicions already forming. ''What happened to her?''

''Never seen again.

"How . . . odd."

Effie did not seem to think so. "Sir George had sent all the servants away that day. Off to the fair in Manchester. He said he was not feeling well and wished to be alone, but Bexwith afterward claimed his master had ordered the girl to stay behind."

"And no one knows what happened to her? Besides being ravished, I mean?"

"Nearly ravished, I do think." Effie's eyes glittered, as if she relished the details she was providing. "Sir George was found at the foot of the stairs, his neck broken and his codpiece askew."

"And since the girl was never seen again," Susanna murmured, "I suppose she is our ghost."

Effie looked pleased by her deduction. "Does it not seem likely she'd seek revenge? Aye. It makes a certain kind of sense. Doubtless Bexwith was involved in it all and her ghost returned for him."

After two years? And this tale did not explain the alleged sightings since, but for the moment Susanna let those aspects of the situation be.

"Tell me about her, Effie. What was her name? Had she family hereabout?"

"I do not recall. She was only a serving wench."

"Think, Effie. You must remember. 'Twas only two years ago and her name must have been on every tongue for weeks afterward."

Disconcerted by the demand, Mistress Denholm closed her eyes and thought. "Edith," she said after a moment. "I do remember now. The girl was called Edith."

"And her surname?"

"Edith. That is all I recall. No doubt 'tis all I ever knew."

"But Effie—" Susanna broke off as her companion's expression abruptly changed. She had caught sight of someone behind Susanna.

"We will talk again anon," Effie promised.

Uncertain if her new acquaintance was being deliberately evasive or merely unhelpful, Susanna turned to find that the young woman she'd caught a glimpse of inside the house was drifting toward them. She was followed at a little distance by an elderly man who leaned heavily on a walking stick.

"My daughter," Effie said. "Catherine."

On closer inspection Catherine Denholm proved to be a delicate, slender, almost childlike sprite. Susanna guessed she was no more than fifteen, but it was difficult to be certain. Her face was blank as a new canvas, unmarked by lines of thought or emotion.

"And that is Randall," Effie added dismissively. "My husband."

Susanna sent a swift, amazed glance in Effie's direction. Everything about Euphemia Denholm, especially the unrelieved black she wore, had proclaimed that she was a widow. The presence of a living husband came as a distinct shock. For whom, then, did Effie wear deepest mourning?

Catherine had little to say. Randall Denholm smiled and nodded, but when his wife informed him in a loud voice that Susanna had taken up residence at Appleton, he spat and cursed Sir George in succinct and colorful language.

"You must make allowances for Randall, Susanna," Effie said. "He's losing his hearing and other abilities, as well. I fear he's not been the man he once was for many years now."

Susanna was unsure how to take that statement. She glanced at Randall, wondering if that frail and sickly appearance was also the mark of a fellow without full grasp of his mental faculties.

The stark expression she surprised in his eyes startled her. It was gone again so quickly that Susanna thought she might have imagined it, but she could not be sure. Had it been a trick of the light, or had she seen, for one unguarded instant, the fire of a relentless hatred burning bright?

Randall took her hand in his and bowed over it in a courtly manner. "Appleton is no fit place for a lady," he said.

She spoke loudly, as Effie had. "It is my home now. I plan to rebuild."

Shaking his head, apparently at her foolishness, Randall wandered off toward the chapel.

CHAPTER 10

That evening at Appleton Manor, Susanna thought about all that Mistress Denholm had told her and all that she had not said. There had been no opportunity to ask more questions after Randall Denholm and young Catherine joined them. Immediately following Randall's departure, a servant had brought word that the supplies were loaded into a cart and ready to be transported back to Appleton Manor.

For whom did Effie wear mourning? Susanna wondered.

And whom did Randall hate?

Susanna could not help but speculate. Had that scathing look been aimed at her . . . or at his own wife? The more she thought about the incident, the more certain she became that she had not imagined anything.

She was less sure about her suspicions concerning John Bexwith's death. It was very possible she had only hoped there was something odd about his demise in order to give herself something to do. Boredom was a terrible curse. Together with her active imagination had it spawned an unknown poisonous herb or mushroom?

Certainly there was no ghost. The most likely theory was that superstitious servants had seen draperies disturbed by the passage of the cat and imagined the rest. And all too likely Bexwith had suffered a seizure and died of natural causes, or perhaps from a surfeit of rich food. She must find out what ingredients had gone into his marrow-bone pie.

A small sigh escaped her. Even if he had been poisoned, accidentally or on purpose, there seemed little chance of proving it after all this time. She comforted herself with the knowledge that her trip north had still been worthwhile. She had been wise to come and inspect the manor in person, for now that she'd seen the condition it was in, she had a new purpose. Making the place livable promised to provide her with an interesting challenge, just as she'd told Effie. By the time she left Lancashire, Appleton Manor would have not only a new steward but the beginnings of a complete renovation. The more she thought about it, the more this project appealed to her. She could scarce wait to begin.

Turning to Jennet, meaning to share some of her plans, Susanna noticed for the first time that there was a restlessness about their little band on this second night in the house. Even the cat was fidgeting. Susanna reached out a hand to stroke her, which seemed to have a calming effect. Cat, she decided, would do well enough as a name for the beast. Dame Cat, as she'd called her last night.

They were all huddled together around the smoking peat fire in the great hall. Lionel and Fulke sat directly across from their mistress. Jennet and Mark shared the bench that faced the lower end of the hall. Dame Cat's purring was the only sound in the silence. Jennet, who normally chattered cheerfully, was strangely quiet and kept sneaking furtive glances at the stairway that led to the solar.

"What are you looking at?" Susanna asked abruptly.

Jennet jumped, stuttering badly with her fear of the unknown dangers of the night. "I w-was n-not—"

"Someone at Denholm told you how Sir George died." It was not a question. It did not need to be.

After some prompting, Jennet repeated the story she'd heard from the servants at Denholm, how Sir George had sent everyone away, then died while chasing a maidservant down that staircase, a maidservant who'd vanished thereafter, never seen or heard from again. Susanna noticed that the men were listening avidly, but they said nothing.

"Is that all?" Susanna asked when Jennet stopped speaking. She had not given the object of Sir George's lust a name.

"There is one peculiar thing," Jennet said after a moment's thought. She was calmer now, just beginning to relax.

"What is that, Jennet?"

"They say there was no ghost before John Bexwith died. She appeared the very first time that night. 'Twas John Bexwith putting himself in Sir George's place at the table on the dais that raised her spirit. When the maidservant Grizel found him dead, she saw it. Plain as daylight on the stair. And all white and fluttery." Jennet lowered her voice, overdramatizing a bit because she'd realized she was the center of attention. "And then, madam, she looked at the table and saw Bexwith lying there with his eyes open wide in horror at what he'd seen."

Susanna's eyes opened a bit wider, too. "Difficult to accomplish when one is lying face down in a marrow-bone pie."

Jennet frowned, trying to work that out.

"Never mind, Jennet. I am sure the story has been altered in the retelling. But I am puzzled. Are you telling me that it was Mistress Denholm's maidservant, the same one who met us on the road and led us to Denholm Hall, who found the body?"

Jennet nodded. "She worked here then, new come to the household."

"Was it Grizel herself told you this tale?"

Jennet gave a derisive snort. "That one? She's not much of a talker. If you want my opinion, she'd be afraid to say boo to a goose."

"Can you blame her after such an experience?" Mark asked.

Tossing her head, Jennet ignored him and concentrated instead on impressing Susanna. A certain sly cunning came into her manner as she offered a suggestion. "I could find out more, madam, if you were to send me back to Denholm."

Susanna did not respond. Preoccupied, she was contemplating the fire. Why hadn't Effie Denholm told her that it had been her own maid who'd seen the ghost? She had to have known. Word of mouth spread tales quickly. Just as, two years after the fact, even young maidservants knew how Sir George had died, so everyone in the hundred of Salford had doubtless heard the rumors surrounding John Bexwith's sudden demise.

They had been interrupted. Susanna decided to believe, for the moment, that her new friend would have confided the truth about Grizel had she had more time.

Belatedly, Susanna turned to address Jennet's proposal, but as she glanced up at the two on the bench her words died in her throat. Not just Mark and Jennet, but Lionel and Fulke, as well, were staring, transfixed, at the stairs to the solar. Only Dame Cat seemed unaffected by the sudden tension in the hall. She'd curled up next to the fire and gone to sleep.

A muted thud sounded from the top of the stairwell. Jennet seized hold of Mark's arm and clung to him so tightly that he winced. Slowly, Susanna turned to see for herself what was frightening her retainers.

The light from the hearth was not bright enough to penetrate the shadows on the distant stairs, but just at the turning something was visible. An eerie shape fluttered there, glowing from what seemed to be some inner source of illumination. As they watched, the light increased enough to reveal a human form, a figure draped in thin, white fabric. Lawn, Susanna thought. The creature's pale face, its features obscured by a gauzy, fluttering veil, appeared to float above a loose-bodied gown.

"The ghost," Jennet whispered. "It is the ghost of the servant girl old Sir George was chasing!"

Susanna rose quickly to her feet and sprinted toward the

stairs, intent on proving that this was no ghost. She'd covered only half the distance to the stairway when strong hands caught her around the waist and hauled her to a stop. Struggling against the restraint, arms flailing, she landed several sharp blows, but even though Mark grunted in pain he would not let go.

"Dangerous," he gasped. "Thing's killed ere now."

"Release me at once!" Susanna was not entirely surprised when her command was ignored.

"Madam, please. You must not go up there." Eyes fearful, Jennet trailed after them, tugging at her mistress's sleeve. She dared one terrified look toward the head of the stairs. The relief that washed over her features gave all the proof Susanna needed to know that the fearsome apparition had already vanished.

Torn between frustration and a grudging appreciation of her retainers' concern for her safety, Susanna stopped trying to break free. Mark loosed her at once, mumbling apologies. One hand went to his nose and she saw that she'd struck him sharply enough there to bring tears to his eyes. In any other circumstances, she'd have apologized, but too many precious seconds had already been lost. She rushed toward the staircase.

By the time Susanna reached the top, no sign remained of either human connivance or supernatural manifestation. She had not expected there to be anything obvious, but she'd hoped to find some small indication that their ghost had been someone's cleverly arranged hoax.

"Bring me an oil lamp, Mark," she ordered.

It burned with a high, steady flame, less fitful than torches or candles would have been, but even that soft, glowing light cast shadows that appeared ominous in the aftermath of their brush with the supernatural. With painstaking care, Susanna surveyed the landing, searching for any trace of the unknown person who must have been there. She found nothing, not even their own footprints in the dust. Thanks to Jennet, the stone steps had recently been thoroughly scrubbed and swept.

"Torches," she called down to her maidservant, who had

come no closer than the foot of the staircase. "Light every corner."

When that was done, Susanna could see the length of the hall from her vantage point. She also had a bird's-eye view of an alcove hidden behind the curving staircase. The door inset there led to the buttery, pantry, and kitchen and had doubtless provided their eerie visitor with an avenue of escape. Frowning, Susanna considered the distance between the landing and the door. Without the pale illumination they had seen, in the concealment offered by darkness and shadows, it would have been the work of a moment to descend the staircase. Susanna had been delayed by Mark long enough for their ghost to escape.

"What we saw was a trick of the light," she said aloud. "A light cleverly arranged by a human hand." Unfortunately, she had found nothing to indicate just how that had been done.

"But, madam," Jennet began to protest.

Susanna cut her off with an impatient gesture. It was far too easy to entertain second thoughts, to wonder if there might have been a real ghost on these stairs. She was succumbing to the temptation herself when her sensitive nose came to the rescue, reassuring her and at the same time dispelling all possibility of the supernatural. A faint smell still lingered in the air at the top of the stairs, the distinctive scent given off by wax tapers. They had found no such luxury at Appleton Manor, and had acquired none, which meant that the woman pretending to be a ghost had brought candles with her ... and taken them away.

"Inhale, Mark," she ordered. "Tell me what you smell."

He indicated his bruised and battered nose. "I can scarce breathe, madam. Imitating a bloodhound is quite beyond me."

The torches in the hall below had already begun to destroy the evidence, overpowering the more delicate aroma of candlewax with that of burning pitch. Her expression rueful, Susanna accepted that she could rely only upon her own senses. No matter. She considered that sufficient proof. They had been gulled. It remained for her to discover by whom.

Resolute, Susanna descended the stair to explore the rooms beyond the door. As she'd expected, neither a white veil nor a filmy gown had been conveniently left behind for her to find. The door that led to the disused herb garden was firmly closed, though not latched. When Susanna peered out into a particularly dark night, she could make out almost nothing. In addition, the garden offered many places of concealment.

"Search the grounds," she told Mark. "Take Lionel and Fulke and as many torches as you can hold and look in every outbuilding. Leave no stone unturned, no door unopened."

They were afraid, but they obeyed. Likely they thought it safer to be outside the house than to remain within. Certainly Jennet was of that opinion. She busied herself building up the fire in the hearth, but her hands shook every time she added more fuel.

"What we saw was not a ghost. You have no need to fear some supernatural horror."

Jennet was not reassured. She glanced fearfully toward the staircase. "Something was up there."

"Aye, something was. Someone wants us to think Appleton Manor is haunted."

Susanna did not know yet how the trick had been done, let alone the reason behind it. Did someone want to drive them away because he or she feared Susanna would discover there was something peculiar about Bexwith's death? This seemed an odd way to go about it, raising more questions than ever. Susanna was certain of only one thing. She would not give up now until she had all the answers.

"That was no ghost," she said again when the menservants returned empty-handed.

They did not argue.

Neither did they believe her.

CHAPTER 11

Jennet stumbled along after her mistress, grumbling under her breath. She'd not slept a wink the night before, and no wonder! Who knew when that creature would appear again, or what wickedness it intended. When a spirit walked, trouble followed. Everyone knew that. Everyone, it seemed, except Lady Appleton.

Look for poisonous plants, indeed! What good was that against the supernatural?

"I fear I can be of little help to you, madam," she said aloud. "All I see is green. I cannot tell one leaf from another." Jennet exaggerated, but not a great deal.

"There were once ornamental hedges here." Lady Appleton pointed off to their left. "See there where wild rosemary grows among the wortleberries?"

Green growing things, Jennet thought. She inhaled. At this time of the year, they did not even give off much of a scent.

"This is a passable kitchen garden, but sadly neglected." Lady Appleton peered more closely at a plant. "Here are wormwood and sorrel. Every English housewife knows to gather those two herbs to keep her family healthy through the year.''

"The old man had little need for more than leeks and a few pot herbs," Jennet said.

"He had a cook," Lady Appleton reminded her, "who required more. Sage. Marjoram. Bugloss and borage. And fennel. And yet, if the cook was a poor one, someone who knew naught but boiling and roasting, then mayhap she could not tell the difference between plain parsley and dog parsley."

Belatedly, Jennet caught her meaning. "You think the cook accidentally poisoned John Bexwith?"

Jennet could not quite bring herself to suggest that the act had been deliberate, even though Lady Appleton had already mentioned the possibility of murder, back before they'd left the safety and security of Leigh Abbey. Jennet preferred to think her mistress's extraordinary interest in poisons was only the result of her great project.

Lady Appleton had begun work some time ago on a definitive herbal of hazardous plants. Its purpose was to warn the unwary housewife of the dangers present in her own herb garden and growing in the wild. She had reason to know how hazardous innocent-looking berries could be. Her only sibling, a sister, had died at the age of six from eating the poisonous fruit of the banewort plant.

"Food poisoning is one explanation, though I do not believe Bexwith ingested that particular plant." Lady Appleton was speaking in what Jennet privately called her lecturing tone. She described the symptoms a person would suffer after eating dog parsley, all most unpleasant, then concluded that since the reaction time varied from several hours to several days it was unlikely to have been the cause of death in John Bexwith's case.

Listening only as much as she thought necessary, so that she would be able to make some sensible reply if her mistress suddenly shot a question in her direction, Jennet let her mind wander to other matters. The mention of dog parsley made her think of real dogs and reminded her that the night just past had been full of terrors. She'd started at every sound, imagining a few of them, but she was quite certain she had heard dogs howling.

Everyone knew that meant disaster ahead. It was an omen of impending death, but who was it that would die? This question troubled Jennet mightily. She feared for herself but, almost against her will, she feared for Mark, too.

"No answer here," Lady Appleton concluded. She dusted her hands and placed them on her hips. "I think we must look farther afield for the answer."

"For the ghost?"

Lady Appleton frowned. "For a reason why there should be one. For a reason anyone would think seeing a ghost *could* kill him. Did he live such an evil life? Did someone want him dead? It would be very easy to poison him."

"With some plant in this garden?" Jennet kept her arms close to her sides, careful to touch nothing.

"I do not believe so. A further difficulty is that while some poisonous plants are cultivated for their medicinal value, many also grow wild."

"But the ghost—"

"There is no ghost."

"We saw it with our own eyes, madam, and so did you, a fearsome, glowing—"

"That's enough, Jennet," Lady Appleton said sharply. "I will not have you frightening yourself just for the thrill of it."

"I do not—"

"You do. Enough, I say. Next you'll be swooning to get attention. I'll have no more complaining, and no more talk of danger from beyond the grave. Seeing that apparition only deepened my suspicion that something was odd about John Bexwith's death. If you can keep your wits about you, Jennet, you may prove very helpful in finding the truth."

Still affronted by the charge that she liked being afraid, Jennet was too cross to realize at once that her mistress was paying her a compliment. Lady Appleton had snapped at her! Then the rest of what she'd said sank in and Jennet's attitude underwent a swift adjustment. She responded to the implied flattery with a sly smile.

"I will do all I can to help you, madam. Only tell me what you require."

"I mean to investigate the circumstances of John Bexwith's death. I do not for a moment believe it was caused by a visitor from beyond the grave." She gave Jennet a sharp look. "He may have died from fright, but this foolishness of believing Appleton Manor is haunted must stop."

"Yes, madam."

"If it was not a natural death, and if it was not brought on by the shock of seeing what he perceived to be a ghost, then poison remains a possibility. And if murder has been done, it must be punished."

"But, madam, if it was murder, how can you ever hope to prove it? John Bexwith is long since buried. There is no evidence left of what he ate that night."

"There are people to talk to. What ingredients went into his meal? Who had opportunity to add more?" She looked thoughtful. "Any guilt has a way of making a person nervous, Jennet. And sometimes careless, too. I think we may still hope to discover who killed Bexwith, if he *was* murdered. Now, Jennet, you are in a better position than I to question the servants at Denholm. They will talk more freely with you than with me, as indeed they already have. The next time you visit you will go armed with certain questions. Insert them cleverly enough into your conversation, and you will be able to uncover much that may be important."

"Oh, they will talk to me," Jennet bragged.

"Will the maid, Grizel?"

Less certain on that score, Jennet pretended a consuming interest in a hairy, many-branched clump of some unidentifiable plant. The distinctly unpleasant aroma that rose from it nearly gagged her and she had to beat a hasty retreat.

"Tetterwort," Lady Appleton said, glancing at it. "The juice is good for sharpening the sight. I want you to befriend this Grizel. Find out all she knows."

"But, madam, why would anyone want to kill that old man?" Jennet asked.

"An excellent question, and one of those to which we needs must discover the answer."

"But how?"

"First we must learn the identities of all the servants who were here that night, especially the cook. Then we must locate them and question them. Grizel may know where the others have gone. If she does not, Master Grimshaw certainly should. I must question him most closely about this whole affair." She glanced at the sun, which was creeping toward its zenith. "Can you bear to ride with me as far as Manchester today?"

Jennet was unsurprised that Lady Appleton had been aware all along of the discomforts Jennet had suffered from riding apillion. Her mistress missed little. Her consideration, however, placed Jennet in a quandary. "If we left now," she said carefully, "we would be obliged to spend the night in Manchester."

"Most likely," Lady Appleton agreed.

So, Jennet thought, it was going to be up to her to choose. Would they stay another night in this house which, in spite of all Lady Appleton had said, might well be home to a fearsome manifestation from beyond the grave? Or would she agree to endure the physical agony of more hours jouncing along an ill-kept road?

The solution that came to Jennet seemed to her to be truly brilliant. "You should go into Manchester at once, but there is no need for me to accompany you, since you mean to hire more maids once you arrive there. I can walk to Denholm on some pretext or other. Perhaps I might even tell them that I am afeared to stay the night alone here in this house. They will invite me to stay, and then I may begin at once to worm Grizel's secrets out of her."

Lady Appleton's face gave nothing away, but after a moment

she nodded, agreeing to her maidservant's proposal. "Very well, then. Here is the information you must seek." She ticked the items off on her fingers. "What does Grizel recall? All of it. How the dead man looked. The color of his skin. The smell of him. Next, details of the manifestation on the stairs. Third, what other servants were here that night? Fourth, which were in service at Appleton two years ago, when Sir George died?"

"Yes, madam."

Lady Appleton held up one more finger. "Who else claims to have seen our ghost and when and what, precisely, did they observe?" She hesitated a moment, then added, "And for whom does Mistress Denholm wear deepest mourning?"

Jennet waited, sensing her mistress was not yet done. She wasn't certain she could remember all those questions, but she had no intention of letting any lack of confidence show.

"Be careful, Jennet," Lady Appleton warned. "My suspicions may prove incorrect, but if there has been murder done in this house, then you must not let anyone guess that you are searching for evidence to catch a killer. To do so might put your own life in danger."

"I am clever enough to hide my purpose," Jennet bragged, determined to retain her mistress's approval, "and I am certain I can find out everything you want to know."

Even if I have to make it up, she added to herself.

CHAPTER 12

It was late that afternoon before Susanna Appleton, accompanied only by Mark Jaffrey, set out through Manchester's narrow streets for Matthew Grimshaw's house. She'd stopped first to bespeak a room at an inn which claimed to have been in business since the time of King Edward III. Susanna was more impressed by the promise of a featherbed and clean linen and the freshly washed and respectable appearance of the servants.

"Grimshaw's is a two-story house with two gables," the innkeeper had told her. "Half-timbered on a low stone base. The upper level projects over the lower."

There was nothing on the surface of that description to distinguish the place from the buildings on any other burgage, which confirmed Susanna's belief that she already had the measure of Grimshaw himself. She expected him to fit the common mold of legal practitioners outside of London. He'd have been trained in law by apprenticeship and never have seen the Inns of Court. He'd provide the community with basic legal services, such as advising litigants and handling land transfers. He might be an important figure in the local courts, even a justice of the peace, but Susanna was certain she'd find that she was herself far better educated, even in the law, than he.

Susanna's first glimpse of the interior of Grimshaw's house warned her she might have underestimated the man who lived there. She'd been prepared for the home of a rustic lawyer, high-flown with his own importance. What she found in the upper room to which she was shown went beyond that and also gave evidence of recent prosperity. There was glass in every window and the ceiling was all of molded plaster, newly done. An elaborate frieze wrapped around three walls.

The south wall was decorated with the royal arms, supported by a lion and a dragon. Two female figures flanked it, immediately recognizable as Queen Elizabeth and her predecessor, Queen Mary. The pair made a nice statement on Grimshaw's ambivalence, worthy of a rascal of a lawyer, enabling him to claim loyalty to either faction, depending upon the politics or the religion of an individual client.

On the wall opposite the two queens, a stag hunt was depicted. The tree at the center of the scene bore a crest showing an eagle and a child. Since she had long had an interest in such matters, Susanna recognized them as emblems of the Stanley family and knew the Stanleys were the most influential landholders in these parts. She supposed Grimshaw sought to flatter the local nobility, for it seemed unlikely a mere lawyer would have the right to quarter such exalted arms himself.

On the wall between these two tributes to those in power was another crest, a shield she did not recognize. "Gules three bendlets enhanced or, a chief argent therein, on waves of the sea, a ship under sail proper," Susanna murmured, enumerating aloud the elements of the heraldic device.

"The arms of the borough of Manchester," said a voice from the doorway behind her.

Susanna turned slowly. "Master Grimshaw?" By his dress alone, this was the lawyer.

"I am he." A tall, gaunt, balding man of indeterminate years, his long, lugubrious face clean-shaven, he toyed with the strings that tied his ruff and regarded her with wary eyes. "I was not expecting you, Lady Appleton. Am I to conclude you accompanied your husband on a visit to his estates?"

"Sir Robert is occupied with the queen's business. I am here in his stead, with full authority to restore Appleton Manor to its former glory."

Her declaration seemed to startle him. "You plan to stay, madam? At Appleton Manor?"

"Indeed, I do. I've come to Manchester to hire servants and buy livestock and seed. We can still plant winter wheat before the first frost. Then there is the matter of renovations. The foundation of the house is sound. Repairs will be necessary before one would wish to winter there, but they can be done easily enough by willing hands."

Grimshaw cleared his throat. "A difficult task, to find men willing, that is. The rumors—"

"Are only rumors, Master Grimshaw. There is no ghost at Appleton Manor. I believe that if we can convince the original servants to return, others will follow. Young Grizel has found new employment with my neighbor, Mistress Denholm, but what of the others?"

"Others?"

"There was a cook," Susanna had to struggle to quell her impatience. Grimshaw's manner annoyed her. She wanted to shout at him, if only to jar him out of what appeared to be a complacent stupidity. "There must have been other servants, though perilous little was done to keep up the grounds or repair the house."

"A scullion," Grimshaw reluctantly admitted, "and an odd-job man."

"They will have to do, then. Where did the scullion go?"

"I do not know, Lady Appleton. He was a lad of no importance."

"Do you know his name?"

"I do not recall it."

"The odd-job man?"

Grimshaw made a little sound of distress. "I fear I do not remember him, either. No doubt a cottar too poor to own his own plow."

Susanna knew such fellows were commonly hired to do handwork with spade and fork, or to help with sheep shearing, wattle weaving, bean planting, ditch digging, thatching, or brewing. On occasion they even found work guarding prisoners held for trial. It was possible she'd already met the odd-job man, among the sullen villagers in Gorebury.

"You are uncommonly ill informed," she accused him.

"I had little to do with the day-to-day running of the estate, madam. John Bexwith saw to that."

"Not very well." Her irritation grew with every word Grimshaw spoke, and yet she knew he was right. It had not been his responsibility to oversee Appleton Manor. It had been Robert's, and thus her own.

Defensive, Grimshaw sputtered, then volunteered the information that he had gone to Appleton Manor in person on the occasion of Bexwith's death. "There was no holding the servants there," he insisted. "The best that could be done was to store the plate and some perishable goods here in Manchester, and to sell off the livestock."

He'd had no authority to do either, but Susanna did not admonish him. She wanted answers, which required his continued goodwill. Once she had ascertained the location of Appleton Manor's portable furnishings and arranged to reclaim them, she returned to the matter of servants.

"Do you remember the name of the cook?"

"Mabel Hussey."

Grimshaw's prompt reply surprised her, and so did the content of his answer. "A woman? Is that common in these parts? In London and its environs, most cooks are men."

"Common enough. She was adequate for Appleton's needs."

"The house or the man?"

"I do not—"

"Did she cook for Sir George before she provided that service for his steward?"

"I believe so, but as I have said already, Lady Appleton, such domestic matters were not my concern. When Sir George was alive, I visited Appleton Manor only once, when Sir George decided that he required my services to make his will."

There was nothing unusual in that, Susanna supposed, and she could hardly criticize Grimshaw when she'd been neglecting the place so shamefully herself. When men owned properties spread out over the length and breadth of England, absentee landlords were more common than not. Even stewards sometimes delegated their authority, leaving bailiffs to handle the day-to-day business. But that situation was not one she endorsed, for it was almost always detrimental to the land itself.

Seating herself in one of two heavily carved chairs, Susanna regarded Grimshaw in thoughtful silence. A steward might be responsible for widely scattered estates, but John Bexwith had not been. He'd had but one demesne to oversee, and he'd neglected it sadly.

Grimshaw had done nothing to improve matters, save write nagging letters to Kent. Why? Susanna wondered about his motive more than ever, for he did not seem particularly pleased to have gotten her presence in response to them.

In his turn, Grimshaw seemed to be studying her. At last he sank into the other chair and folded his hands over a slightly concave abdomen. "How else may I be of assistance to you, Lady Appleton?" he asked.

"I wish to hire back any former servants who will come. I must find new ones, as well. Cook. Dairymaid. A plowman and a carter, a cowherd, a swineherd, and a shepherd. I will pay ten shillings per annum, and thirty for an experienced chief plowman, plus livery and an allowance of grain, flour, and salt. And a pair of gloves."

Grimshaw's small, dark eyes widened a fraction. "Most generous, madam. Hereabout you might buy a horse for thirty shillings."

"As high as twenty shillings for a woman to brew, bake, and malt," she continued, "and eighteen to a woman who will work indoors. Then I will need masons and carpenters and common laborers. I will pay the latter a penny a day, which is more than they would earn from anyone else in these parts." Briefly, she outlined her plans for rebuilding the house Robert's father had left him. "Now, about Mabel Hussey." She gathered her skirts in preparation to rise. "Where is she currently employed?"

"You do not want her back," Grimshaw said hastily.

Susanna settled back into the chair again. "Why not?"

"Well, um, I, er, that is—"

"I see. You think she might pose a threat to me because she was the one who made that marrow-bone pie."

Grimshaw looked horrified. "Oh, no, Lady Appleton. There was never any suspicion that her cooking was responsible for Bexwith's death." He sprang to his feet and came a few steps toward her before he faltered to a stop, uncertain about approaching her so closely.

No suspicion at all? Susanna found that in itself peculiar. "Perhaps you can tell me, Master Grimshaw, what is in such a dish, aside from the marrow bones?"

Taken aback by the question, he only gaped at her.

"Come, come, Master Grimshaw. Have you never eaten a marrow-bone pie? I had assumed it was a local favorite."

"Only for those of ample means." At once he looked as if he wished back that remark, but she seized on his words with the alacrity of a buckhound scenting its prey.

"A delicacy, then? And why is that?"

"Lady Appleton, I assure you the pie did not cause Bexwith's death."

"Then 'twill do no harm for me to learn how to make one for myself."

"I am a lawyer, not a cook."

"What ingredients must I purchase?"

With ill grace, he gave in. "Different cooks use different

combinations, but most include artichokes and currants and dates. And sugar. And marrow bones. Nothing harmful.''

Artichokes grew in many a kitchen garden and marrow bones, too, were easy to come by, but the other ingredients were less common. Bexwith ate well for a mere steward. ''Sugar, currants, and dates? A rich dish for a man of his . . . years.''

''Too rich, indeed,'' Grimshaw agreed, giving her remark a double meaning, ''but it did not cost him his life.''

''How can you be so sure?''

''There was another, more obvious, cause.''

''Ah. This ghost you wrote of.'' She fixed him with a steely glare. ''I do not believe in such things.''

Grimshaw backed away, his eyes shifting nervously, never quite meeting Susanna's steady gaze. ''You may not believe Bexwith was frightened to death by a spirit, Lady Appleton, but I can tell you that the servants who were there most assuredly do.''

''I would like to speak to them myself.'' She toyed with her wedding band, which was somewhat loose of late, deliberately giving Grimshaw time to recover himself. As rattled as he appeared to be, it seemed likely he believed in the supernatural, too. ''Perhaps I can convince them they are being passing foolish.''

''I will tell you all I know of them, Lady Appleton,'' Grimshaw promised, ''but I fear it is precious little. Mabel Hussey meant to seek employment in Manchester and was living in Long Millgate soon after Bexwith's death.''

''And the odd-job man?'' Susanna watched Grimshaw's face closely, thinking he was a surprisingly spineless specimen for a successful man of law. Was he always this pathetically easy to manipulate? Or simply clever enough to appear to capitulate when he realized further resistance might create greater suspicion on her part?

''I know neither his name nor his plans.''

''The scullion?''

''Richard Poulter. He had family in Preston. He may have

gone back there. It was a terrifying time for them all. They will not want to return. If you must have servants, my advice is to find individuals who have never heard of Appleton Manor.''

''I will consider what you say,'' Susanna agreed. ''Now, what can you tell me of John Bexwith? Was he from these parts?''

''Bexwith was a local man,'' the lawyer conceded, ''but he has no family left, having outlived them all.''

''What qualified him to be steward?''

''An odd question, madam. Sir George thought him adequate and your husband kept him on. I know no more than that.''

''Who would remember how he came to hold such an important post at Appleton Manor?'' she asked.

''No one I know.'' Grimshaw's wariness was almost palpable again.

Susanna favored him with a rather grim smile. ''One last matter, Master Grimshaw,'' she said as she donned her soft leather gloves in preparation to leave. ''I have told you already that I do not believe in ghosts, but since many hereabout seem to, I would like to find out all I can about this spirit who is alleged to haunt my house. I am told she is the ghost of a girl named Edith.''

Grimshaw's start of surprise checked Susanna's departure. She studied him carefully for a long moment.

''Have I come to an erroneous conclusion?'' she asked, knowing full well that Effie Denholm had confirmed her guess as to the identity of the ghost. ''When I heard the way my late father-by-marriage died, it did seem that the most likely person to be haunting the stairs to the solar would be that poor girl he'd been chasing when he fell.''

Grimshaw cleared his throat. ''Edith, you say?''

''I was informed that was the poor wench's name, but I pray you, Master Grimshaw, tell me who is it that you thought had come back to haunt Appleton Manor.''

He ran trembling fingers through his thinning hair and said, more to himself than to her, "Jane. I was sure it was Jane who had returned from the dead."

"Jane?" That was a common enough name, but not one that Susanna could remember hearing before in connection with Appleton Manor.

Grimshaw nodded, still avoiding her eyes. "Sir George's fifth wife."

"And why did you think her a likely ghost?"

Grimshaw didn't answer directly. He was still muttering distractedly to himself. "The servant that saw it would give no identity to the spirit. She did but describe its terrifying presence, how it seemed to float on the stairs, all garbed in white, billowy stuff."

With luck, Jennet was even now quizzing Grizel about what she'd seen. Or what she imagined she'd seen. Ghost stories all had a suspicious sameness.

"Tell me about this Jane Appleton, Master Grimshaw. How did she die?"

"Did your husband never mention Jane to you?"

"Why should he speak of her? She must have married his father long after Robert had left Lancashire."

Grimshaw's agitation increased. He rubbed his chin, then doubled his hand into a fist. "She'd been meant for him."

"Speak plainly, Master Grimshaw." All this wavering made her impatient. "I do not understand you."

"Jane was to have married Robert," the lawyer blurted.

This was news to Susanna, but she managed to hide her surprise. "Go on."

"After his son went south, Sir George declared he'd wed the lass himself. She was a pretty young thing and had a goodly dowry and he was always eager to acquire more wealth."

"So, he married Robert's intended bride." It did not particularly surprise Susanna that Robert had never mentioned the girl to her. Given the way marriages were arranged, their own included, handled by the families or guardians of those concerned, it was possible Robert had never met Jane. It was even possible he'd never been informed that she was under consideration as his future bride.

"How did Jane die?" Susanna asked. "And when?"

"During the epidemic eight years past." Grimshaw's eyes betrayed a deep sadness that made Susanna think he had lost loved ones at the same time. Indeed, the mysterious illness called the sweat had left few families unscathed.

"Her little daughter died with her," Grimshaw added, "a babe of less than a year."

That, too, was news to Susanna. Robert had, briefly, had a sister. With an effort, she concentrated on the present, filing away these new revelations to consider at a later time. Robert was not here for her to question about Jane, but there might be more she could learn from Grimshaw.

"If she died of the sweating sickness," Susanna said slowly, "then why would anyone think she'd return to haunt the house, and years after her husband's death, at that?"

Grimshaw ran one finger under the edge of his ruff, as if it suddenly felt far too tight. His voice sounded choked. "*Did* she wait? I do wonder, for when I first heard what had happened to Bexwith, I could not help but think that it might be the second time she'd come back from the dead to cause a man's death. Sir George fell from those very stairs, fell and broke his neck. Some might ask why."

"They did not at the time."

"No. All agreed he was cup-shotten." Grimshaw seemed lost in his own dark speculations.

"He was trying to catch a serving wench called Edith," Susanna said calmly. "A girl fleet of foot and reluctant to share his bed. Because she was his intended victim, it seems likely to me that Edith is the one doing the haunting. Why should I accept your theory in place of my own? What argues for this spirit to be a manifestation of Jane? Why not Edith?"

"Because Jane cursed Sir George as she lay dying," Grimshaw confessed in a hoarse whisper.

"Were you there?"

''No, but . . . well, I heard it from one who was.''

''Hearsay, then. Gossip. Rumor.'' She discounted all three with a wave of her hand. ''Edith still seems a more likely candidate to me.''

''But Lady Appleton, Edith cannot possibly be the ghost that haunts your house. Edith is alive and well and living right here in Manchester.''

CHAPTER 13

To reach the burgage of Oliver Ince, Edith's husband, a plain, four-room house, required a brisk walk to the shops near Salford Bridge, which spanned the river Irwell. As Grimshaw was a man of some prominence in Manchester, he was recognized at once, though not entirely with pleasure. Because she was in his company, Lady Appleton was grudgingly made welcome, too, but the announcement of her surname brought a deepening of what was already a distinct chill in the atmosphere of the house-room.

Oliver Ince was a butcher and fishmonger, a bluff, florid, barrel-chested fellow who put Susanna in mind of the queen's father, old Henry VIII, whose likeness she'd seen in portraits. "Appleton?" A sound that was very nearly a growl underscored his repetition of her name. "We want naught to do with any Appleton."

Susanna moved closer to the chimney corner. Made of both brick and stone, the fireplace was a mark of prosperity. At the back was a wide-open hearth for cooking. A baby young enough to still be completely immobilized in swaddling clothes slept in a cradle near the hearth while a toddler clung to his mother's skirts. Edith Ince paid no attention to the child, her attention fixed on the visitors. Her lips trembled slightly and her hands twisted in the folds of her apron.

Susanna wondered why, for whatever else she might have done with her life since leaving Appleton Manor, Edith was not the one who'd gone back there to play at being a ghost. This was no frail wraith, but rather an apple of a woman, red-cheeked and almost as round as she was tall.

"What do you want with us?" Ince draped one protective arm over his much shorter wife's stiff shoulders.

"I have come to ask your help," Susanna told them.

Suspicion rolled back at her in waves. Distrust of the gentry, rightfully earned in this case, prevented these good people from taking her at her word.

Grimshaw, blustering a bit in the face of opposition, placed himself at Susanna's side. "You'd be well advised to assist Lady Appleton in any way you can," he warned Ince. "I am not without power in this place, nor am I ignorant of its laws. Casting carrion into the rivers is forbidden, and muckheaps are most strictly regulated here in Manchester. Moreover, there is talk of a new law, to require all the fish dealers in Smithy Door to fix their boards over the channel."

Ince made a low noise in his throat.

With a sigh, Susanna placed a restraining hand on the lawyer's velvet sleeve. Nothing would be gained by threats. She approached Edith Ince cautiously, a serious but not unfriendly expression on her face. "I have come to advise you, Mistress Ince, that your good name is at risk. It is being bandied about in the countryside that you are a spirit, a ghost that has come back to haunt Appleton Manor and cause the death of one that dwelt there."

Ince exploded forward. Putting his wife firmly behind him, he came at Grimshaw, his meaty hands extended as if he meant to grasp the lawyer by the throat and throttle him. Susanna had barely time enough to get out of his way. Startled, she called out Mark's name. He'd been told to wait in the street and was within the house an instant later, skidding a bit as his leather shoes came in contact with the broken-flagged floor.

The abrupt arrival of reinforcements stayed Ince's attack. He dropped his arms to his sides and darted suspicious glances from Mark to Grimshaw and back again. Even together, they'd have been hard-pressed to subdue the bigger man, but with a formidable glower, Ince retreated, his fists still clenched but his temper under control. He threw his head back as he moved away, staring up at the raftered ceiling as if to seek divine assistance in that effort.

After a moment, he visibly relaxed. All the anger seemed to drain out of him. "God will dispose," he said. "What is it you want of us, Lady Appleton?"

"Answers." She seated herself on the sturdy cushioned chair he offered her and considered which question to ask first. Grimshaw had become an annoyance. She had the distinct impression that she could get far more cooperation from the Inces if he were gone.

"I wish to interview Mabel Hussey tonight," she said, turning her head until she could fix Grimshaw with a commanding stare. "Go you, good Master Grimshaw, and fetch her to the inn in Withy Grove."

Grimshaw hesitated. Susanna suspected that he was regretting that he'd ever revealed Mabel's presence in Manchester. Before he could make any excuse, Susanna caught Mark's eye.

"See him out, Mark." She gave a peremptory wave of one hand, wryly aware that the gesture was reminiscent of Effie Denholm. Then she turned her back on them both, assuming she would be obeyed.

Ince growled, his gaze flicking past Susanna to the departing men. She knew the minute that Grimshaw looked back. "I warn you, Ince. You will be assessed a heavy fine if you do not clean up that dungheap in the street." His parting shot delivered, Grimshaw left. Susanna heard the street door close behind him with a gentle thump.

Cautiously, Edith Ince and her husband relaxed, though neither was willing to sit down in the presence of a gentlewoman. Susanna had time to study the house-room more closely and found further marks of prosperity there. The Inces had two throne chairs, three chests, five brass candlesticks and one of pewter, and a great deal more pewter displayed upon a standing cupboard. Since it was close to the supper hour, dark brown bread, meat, and onions had already been set out on a round table.

"What would you know?" Ince asked.

Susanna addressed her question to his wife. "Will you tell me about the night Sir George died? I know the memories must be painful for you, but it is important that I hear the story in your own words."

Edith Ince looked at her husband. Only after Oliver nodded his permission did she finally pull up a stool to sit upon and proceed to tell a tale that was much like the one Susanna had already heard from Effie Denholm. She did not once meet Susanna's eyes.

"So, you alone of all the servants remained at Appleton Manor and Sir George made unwanted advances and you ran away?"

Edith nodded.

"Did you see him fall?"

"Nay."

"Hear a crash?"

"Nay."

"Then you have no certain knowledge of when he fell or why?"

"I were too afeared he'd catch me if I stopped running. I came all the way here to Manchester that night, I did."

"And it wasn't until the next day that you heard he was dead?"

Edith nodded.

"Did anyone question you about how it had happened?"

"Nay."

"I was told that John Bexwith knew you stayed behind at the manor. Did he never trouble you about it?"

"Nay."

"And you never came forward to tell the authorities what you knew?"

"I knew naught." For the first time, Edith looked directly at Susanna, alarm in her eyes.

Had there been a coroner's inquest? Susanna wondered. If Sir George's death was clearly an accident, she thought not.

"To speak out was to risk being blamed." Ince spoke quietly, and his point was all the more forceful for that. "Sir George tripped over his own feet and tumbled down the stair, and I'll be bound 'twas no great loss."

Oliver Ince still radiated anger. Suppressing it had colored his cheeks to a fiery red, and his hands were so tightly clenched that his knuckles showed dead white.

"Why did you attack Master Grimshaw just now?" Susanna asked him.

"Grimshaw found my Edith that post. I blame him for what happened after."

Susanna lifted one brow. The lawyer had not informed her of that little detail. "And John Bexwith? How did you feel about him?"

"He lied to Edith about what her duties would be. I do much blame him for putting her in danger." Ince scowled fiercely. "John Bexwith was a lecherous fellow, near as bad as old Sir George."

"Nay, husband. He never laid a hand on me."

Ince glowered at her.

"So, Bexwith was never . . . overfamiliar with you, Edith? Not by word, either?"

"He would have been," Ince answered for her. "If Sir George had not died when he did, he'd have had her first, as the master, then given her to his man."

Ince's blunt statement shocked Susanna, in spite of all she'd already heard about her late father-in-law. "You know this for a fact?"

"I know."

"But how? You have a prosperous business here, one of long standing. You would have been here, not at Appleton Manor, when Sir George died."

" 'Tis true. Grave matters pressed me then. I'd failed to comply with an order to sell all my tallow to the common chandler at a fixed price, and for that great sin I'd had my shop door and windows closed. I was not allowed to follow my occupation as a butcher for more than a year, though I still had my spot in the fish shambles. Still, I did hear things after, and I knew my Edith. I loved her before she ever went to Appleton. If she'd married me, she'd never have gone there."

Edith placed a warning hand on his arm and he looked down at her with a deep and abiding love in his eyes.

Ince seemed forthcoming, and yet his very honesty kept him among Susanna's suspects as a new thought crossed her mind. What if Sir George's fall had not been the accident everyone supposed? Here was Ince, unable to work as a butcher, which presumedly meant he'd had more liberty to visit his intended bride. Had he gone to Appleton Manor and found more than he'd bargained for? Could Oliver Ince have discovered his betrothed in the very act of being ravished?

On the other hand, Edith herself might have acted to preserve her virtue. Had she lied about running away before Sir George fell?

Susanna wanted to ask those questions, but she sensed that directness would avail her nothing. Neither Oliver nor Edith was stupid. It would be too obvious that her continued interest in Sir George's death was leading to an accusation. They'd only lie if they were guilty. Attempting to be more subtle, she pursued another angle.

"Why did you take the post at Appleton Manor, Edith?" She wondered, suddenly, if Ince had always been prone to these sudden violent moments. Were they the reason Edith had hesitated to marry him?

"She went to Appleton Manor because she wanted to bring a dowry to our marriage." Once more Ince answered for his wife, but she was nodding her agreement to his words. "Sir George offered better pay than anyone here in Manchester. None of us thought to ask why until it were too late."

It would have been easier to suspect Ince had some part in Appleton's haunting if he'd been a candlemaker or sold lawn or other fine linen, Susanna thought. She wanted to exonerate Ince, could almost argue herself into it, except that his moods shifted too rapidly from calm to violent to allow her to rule him out entirely.

And then another possibility struck her. If John Bexwith had known that Sir George was pushed, or even guessed it, and that Ince had done it, then Ince might have decided to kill him also. What if Bexwith had been extorting money from the Inces? Might not Ince have grown tired of making payments?

She looked at the two of them, at their comfortable little house. Surely she was being fanciful. Even if any or all of those things had happened, they still did not explain this business of a ghost, nor did they tell her who had played the part for her benefit. In truth, calling attention to those stairs should have been the last thing a murderer would want. And yet, in all honesty, Susanna knew she could not afford to eliminate any suspect.

She left the Ince house in a troubled mind, collecting Mark from the street and announcing that she intended to return at once to the inn, there to meet Matthew Grimshaw and Appleton's erstwhile cook.

"Have a care for the swine," he warned, just in time to save her from being trampled by a herd of pigs, three of which were being left off in the yard behind Oliver Ince's house. "He is a farmer as well as butcher and fishmonger," Mark added, "and owns a mare. All the swine in Manchester are collected every morning and herded to Collyhurst, a mile or so to the north, for grazing, and this is the hour at which they return. Ince's other animals are kept out of town."

"What else have you learned while waiting here, Mark? And with whom did you strike up a conversation?"

Mark's cheeks colored as he fell into step beside his mistress. "You'll not tell Jennet?"

"I swear it." She could scarce hold back a smile at his sheepish expression.

"The daughter of the house next door is a lass just turned fifteen. She spoke to me, madam," he said quickly, lest she think he'd been flirting. "It was none of my doing."

"But you did not bestir yourself to drive her away," Susanna teased him. "Very clever, Mark. It may prove to be no bad thing for us to have a friend in the house next to Edith Ince's."

Mark blinked at her, then slowly smiled, too.

"What else have you learned?"

"That tomorrow is the weekly market day. Traders come from as far as Rochdale and Warrington. We should be able to purchase everything you require to restock Appleton Manor."

"Everything? It is a considerable list. Plow animals—"

"Six oxen and two horses?" Mark interrupted as they passed the vintner's.

"Yes. That is the best combination." She was pleased by his earnest efforts to help. "Did you notice, Mark? Have we both collars and yokes at the manor?"

"Aye. Only the animals are missing. I warrant that with trained teams and a good plowman, the fields can be plowed and harrowed in less than a week. Once the last clods are crumbled with a mattock, grain seed can be sown. You have already a goodly supply of straw baskets to sow from, and I reckon a rate of two bushels to the acre, but it is oats they plant here in the north, madam, not winter wheat."

"You have given this some considerable thought, Mark."

"Aye, madam. I did talk with Leigh Abbey's steward before we came north. He was most helpful with his suggestions. And

I've asked questions here in Lancashire. 'Twas the girl told me about the oats. Temperance Strelley, her name is, madam.''

Susanna was still pondering her servant's diligence. For the first time she realized that Mark saw this trip to Lancashire as an opportunity for advancement. She wondered what Jennet's opinion was of his obvious ambition to replace John Bexwith as Appleton Manor's steward. For herself, Susanna was not displeased by the idea. Mark was untried, it was true, but he'd always been quick to learn and he was, unquestionably, loyal to her. In fact, she thought she might just send him alone to the shops along Smithy Door on the morrow. Who knew what other interesting bits of gossip he might hear?

''What further livestock do you suggest?'' she asked as they continued their journey toward the inn. They were just passing the elaborate ornamental conduit that distinguished Manchester's Marketstead Lane. Water tapped at the conduit head traveled through a pipeline from a nearby spring, she supposed, and one whiff of the stench from the rivers that met at Manchester told her why that contrivance was necessary.

In the market square itself the tollbooth, a town hall where the quarterly assizes met, dominated the other buildings. Prominently located nearby were all the trappings of the law, including stocks that were currently occupied by a scurvy fellow much befouled by the offerings of those who'd passed by during the day. Susanna and Mark gave him a wide berth and avoided, too, the scattering of peddlers with smallwares who were trying to trade on the eve of market day and thus beat out their competition.

''A few geese as well as chickens,'' Mark suggested when he had given her question due consideration. ''One or two milch cows, but the rest to breed oxen. They can feed on grass, mistletoe, and ivy. Pigs are slaughtered hereabout in November, after they've been fattened up on acorns, so I'd advise waiting to purchase a sow. Sheep, I think, would do well, but we'd be buying them less for the fleece than for their meat, milk, manure, and skin.''

"The skins? Ah, yes, for writing material. You do seem to have thought of everything, Mark." She made a mental note to see what was to be found in the local mercers' shops. Along with lace and buttons there were some who carried both paper and books. And medicines, she realized. She must also look into the availability of such items as arsenic and aqua fortis while she was trying to learn who had sold the dates, currants, and sugar to Appleton Manor.

Mark's thoughts had wandered onto a different track. "You will require a dairy maid, madam, as well as someone to be responsible for the poultry. And perhaps a maid to look after the fire in the manor house."

"Three pretty girls?" He blushed at her teasing and she took pity on him and changed the subject. "And what shall we burn, Mark? I am heartily sick of the smell of peat."

"There is firewood, for a price, and coal, and they do burn gorse hereabout, and bundles of brushwood, too. They call faggots kidds and peat is turves."

"This neighbor girl—Temperance Strelley, did you say?— must have been a veritable fountain of information."

Mark's face colored once again but he said nothing.

"You might do well to mention to Jennet just how helpful Temperance was," Susanna suggested, "and if she was also an attractive girl, why say so."

"You think Jennet would be jealous?" The hope in his voice was almost painful to hear.

"I think you deserve a good wife. If not Jennet, then some other."

They walked the rest of the distance back to the inn in thoughtful silence.

CHAPTER 14

"I have seen three queens," Jennet bragged to her new friends. That she was lying troubled her not at all.

The other maidservants drew a little closer in the maids' attic dormitory, avid interest lighting their faces. Jennet was almost as exotic a creature to them as her mistress. She was a stranger . . . from the south . . . a lucky wench who'd been to London to look at the queen.

"Three? Oh, wonderful," one of the younger maids marveled. She sidled closer, eager to hear the tale, and all her companions but one followed suit.

"Join us, Grizel," Jennet invited.

The plainest of the plain-faced maids, she seemed afraid of her own scrawny shadow. Jennet had to watch her closely to see any reaction, any indication that Grizel was as interested in hearing the tale as the others were.

Jennet patted the sweet-smelling bedtick she was perched upon, her legs tucked under her. "Come and sit down and I'll tell you everything," she promised.

The bait was too tempting to resist. Cautiously, Grizel crept closer, finally settling herself on a footstool right in front of Jennet. Her pinched cheeks were bright with excitement or embarrassment. Jennet could not tell which. Another maid giggled and was quickly shushed.

"The first queen was poor, young Jane," Jennet said, "and just my age she was when she sailed down the Thames through London on her way to the Tower. Thought she was going to be crowned, she did, but they chopped off her head instead."

A shiver of appreciation shuddered through her audience as Jennet elaborated, using details she'd had from Lady Appleton, who'd been in London at the time. She saw no reason to admit to these simple north country girls that she had herself never been away from Leigh Abbey in Kent until this very journey into Lancashire.

A hidden cache of sweet, hard sugar candies came out and was passed from hand to hand. Jennet got a lemon-flavored one and wondered who had dared invade the mistress's larder. Surely this treat was too good for mere servants.

"The second queen was Mary," she continued, sliding the sweet to the inside of one cheek so she could speak. For this story she repeated all of the oft-told tale of how Sir Robert had first seen that queen. Mary had been rallying the populace of London to defend her against some rebels. It had been a stirring scene and Jennet recounted it well enough to bring tears to Grizel's eyes.

"Then there is Elizabeth, her that folks do call Good Queen Bess. A rare beauty, she is." Jennet had a store of tales to tell about the present monarch, since Sir Robert had spent a great deal of time at her court. Lady Appleton had yet to make her personal acquaintance, but Jennet was never one to let honesty stand in the way of a good story. "The queen's maids of honor include several of Lady Appleton's dear friends," she added for good measure. That much was even true. "And the queen herself does owe a debt of gratitude to my mistress for helping her supporters get out of England, back when men were forced into exile for their faith."

At first Jennet failed to notice the little silence that fell at those words, but before long she realized that, somehow, she had made the others suspicious. A moment's consideration gave her a reason. They were still papists in these parts, for all that the old faith had once more been banished from the land.

A bit huffily, Jennet drew herself up. "Lady Appleton's husband was knighted for his services to Queen Mary," she reminded them.

"But if she helped heretics escape," one of the girls whispered, "then she were a traitor."

"My mistress has never been anything but loyal to the Crown, but she was raised in the New Religion, for that was the law of the land when she was young. And when you were, as well. She worshiped as her father did, and her husband after him. She did but obey them, each in turn, as God does command."

Jennet knew she was being less than truthful once more, but she discounted that as unimportant. If her listeners got the impression that Lady Appleton had been a loyal Catholic during Queen Mary's reign, save for helping a few poor souls escape execution, then Jennet let them think it. She smiled a little, though, at the thought. Unlike Sir Robert, Jennet's mistress had never pretended to embrace Rome, nor ever would have even if Queen Mary had lived to be a hundred.

As the night wore on, Jennet steered the conversation toward local gossip. The more she told tales of the Leighs, for whom her family had worked for generations, the more she learned about the Denholms. She was well pleased with the results of this ploy by the time she finally closed her eyes and slept. There would be no need to make up lies to tell Lady Appleton after all.

The following day passed slowly, and another evening was almost upon Jennet before Mark returned with Lady Appleton to her husband's manor. Jennet's betraying heart beat a little faster at her first glimpse of his familiar mole brown hair. 'Twas just that she'd been getting nervous of spending a night here alone, she told herself. She had no particular need for Mark's company.

Jennet's eyes narrowed as she watched the arrival of several packhorses and other animals. In the train were two new menservants and a puny female who'd lost what looks she might have had to the swine pox. Jennet's face fell as she inspected the newcomers. She'd hoped several women would be joining the household, including at least one wench strong enough to do the heavy work. Then Jennet's hands would be freed for other, more amenable chores. After all, she was supposed to be Lady Appleton's tiring maid, even if her tasks did usually extend well beyond dressing her mistress and arranging her hair.

"Where did you find that thin stick?" she hissed at Mark as soon as he dismounted. Her disdainful gaze raked over the maidservant and her nose wrinkled. The newcomer looked clean enough but the faint odor of garlic clung to her.

"Her name is Bess," Mark said, "and Lawyer Grimshaw brought her. He was waiting with her when we returned to the inn last evening."

Jennet snorted derisively. "Are any of these pitiful creatures the cook we were promised?"

"Grimshaw claimed he knew where the cook was, the one who was here before. Mabel, she's called. But then he said he could not find her, that she's no longer in Manchester. I think he brought Bess as a peace offering for Lady Appleton." Mark allowed himself a brief smile. "He is much in awe of our lady mistress."

"And these others?" The dregs of humanity, in Jennet's opinion, and they looked scared of their own shadows, too.

"Not a promising lot, and well I know it, but the best we could manage. We've brought ample provisions, though. And more coming."

Jennet waited. There was something in Mark's manner, in the way he toyed with his cap and fiddled with the reins, that promised further revelations, but not the welcome kind.

"You might want to continue to do the cooking yourself," he suggested.

Jennet sighed, hating the knowledge that the only way they'd eat well was if she prepared all the food. She did not care to work that hard, sweating over the hearth, turning spits, trying to guess what herbs to add to the sauce. Then she brightened. Bess would earn her keep, after all, and the new menservants, too. No reason they could not behave as underlings should. There were many tasks even an ignorant northern clod could perform . . . under Jennet's diligent supervision.

It was a miracle, Jennet decided several hours later, that the fool girl hadn't burned the house down right along with the roast capons. Still and all, the meal had been served, all had been fed, and Lady Appleton had seemed pleased with the result.

Jennet and her mistress retired together to the solar they had turned into a bedchamber. As a result of the trip to Manchester, Jennet now had a trundle bed of her own. She pulled it out and prepared it for the night while she waited for the questions she knew were coming.

Lady Appleton would be pleased when she'd heard Jennet's report. It was one Jennet could take pride in. Following up the night's success, she'd pursued Grizel in the morning. Before leaving Denholm to return to Appleton, she'd made promises of friendship, hinted at confidences, and offered the ultimate lure, the hope of escape from servitude in this dull and barren place, this Lancashire. The poor silly creature had been powerless to resist temptation.

"What have you learned?" Lady Appleton asked as Jennet started to help her with her laces.

For the journey to Manchester she'd worn her most elaborate bodice and kirtle and gown, not quite court dress but complicated enough to require a maid's assistance. Bess must have helped her last night and this morning, Jennet decided. The knots were all in a tangle.

"Grizel," Jennet said as she struggled to undo the laces that held a bright yellow sleeve to a darker-colored bodice, "is terrified of her mistress."

"Afraid? Why?"

Because Mistress Denholm is built like a battering ram, Jennet thought. One blow from her fist and a poor, bumbling serving wench would end up with a broken arm . . . or worse. Aloud she said only, "Her lady has a forceful way about her."

"A formidable woman," Lady Appleton agreed, "but is there any particular cause for the girl's fear? Does Mistress Denholm beat or otherwise mistreat her retainers?" The first sleeve slipped free and she turned to give Jennet access to the other.

"No more than most."

"Mind what you say, Jennet."

"Must I speak no ill of my betters, madam?" She gave an ironic twist to the word, and Lady Appleton had the grace to wince.

"You must speak the truth, Jennet, but without undue elaboration." Lady Appleton hesitated, then added, "I would much appreciate hearing your opinions, unflattering though they may be to the gentry."

"They are careful what they say there," Jennet told her. "It did seem almost as if Mistress Denholm had heard that her servants were gossiping the last time I was there, that she had ordered an end to such loose tongues. Still, a mistress cannot be in the maids' room in the middle of the night, and I contrived to share a bed with Grizel and one other girl. I told them what we saw here and they were proper terrified, they were."

"Oh, Jennet. I had hoped you'd not give credence to these tales of a ghostly presence. It is difficult enough to find servants without more stories getting started."

"For all the good that girl Bess is, you might have left her where you found her." A point broke in her hand and she muttered further condemnations under her breath.

"Never mind about Bess now. Tell me what else you learned at Denholm."

"Grizel's father is also in service there. He is the tiler hired to redo the chapel floor."

"And the Denholms themselves? Did their servants speak of the family?"

"Not as much as I thought they would. They're . . . protective of that girl. Catherine." Odd, that was, now that Jennet thought of it, but she could not put her finger on the reason why she felt as she did.

"Protective?"

"She's frail, or so they say. Needs looking after, for she's impulsive, too. They say she often does an injury to herself through carelessness. Climbs trees to rescue cats and the like."

"They?"

Jennet knew Lady Appleton had always disliked the attribution of gossip to that vague "they" and had to hide her smile. "Her own mother says, with some regularity, that Catherine wants watching. Ofttimes she says so to the girl herself. This Catherine has never been heard to answer back. Indeed, she speaks so little that one wonders if she is slow-witted."

"What of Master Randall Denholm? What is it that ails him?" The disrobing complete at last, Lady Appleton slipped a night robe on over her shift for warmth and gestured for Jennet to build up the fire.

"Now he's a strange one." A note of disdain came into Jennet's voice as she coaxed the dying embers to life. She wrinkled her nose as smoke drifted out at her. She was accustomed to better fireplaces at home in Kent.

"How is he strange?"

"He spends all his time in the garden, tending herbs and flowers like a goodwife. Mistress Denholm has little use for that, and less for him. He is afflicted with deafness, and swelling of the knees, no doubt from all that kneeling in the garden. And impotence."

Lady Appleton tried unsuccessfully to hide a small smile. "I thought you said the servants were reluctant to gossip about their betters."

Jennet laughed. "That last is old news. He was kicked in the privates by a horse years ago. Managed to get Catherine on his wife afterward, but the effort must have finished him." She tried to picture the frail old man making love to his massive wife but in that endeavor even Jennet's rich imagination failed her.

"She must have been a handsome woman once," Lady Appleton mused. "We all thicken with age, Jennet. Even young maidservants. Mark may have told you that we found and talked with Edith yesterday."

Jennet could not contain a little gasp. "Edith, madam?" She recollected that name well. It was Edith who was supposed to be haunting Appleton, or so Mistress Denholm had told Lady Appleton who had told Jennet.

And Mark had *not* said a word. She'd have something to say to him about that on the morrow.

"Indeed. She's very much alive and well. And she is not our ghost, not even if, as I believe, we saw some human creature pretending to be a spirit. Edith was never any part of that. Once she was a plump and pretty girl, attractive to young men and old alike. After two years and the bearing of two children, she has a girth that makes her seem to be with child even though she is not."

Jennet chewed on her lower lip, distracted. If having children turned women into mountains, that seemed an excellent reason not to marry, almost as sound as the one she'd already expressed, several times, to Mark, that too many children could turn a lissome, comely women into a lifeless, haggard stick, more worn and twisted with each successive birth. Childbearing had done that to many she knew back home in Kent.

And yet, when Mark was giving her his full attention, when he was blatantly trying to seduce her, it was hard to remember why she didn't want to let him come too close. Jennet had known him for years without ever suspecting he'd suddenly gain this power to attract her. Sometime when she wasn't looking, he'd grown into his feet.

Jennet realized that Lady Appleton had been speaking to her and that she hadn't heard a word. She mumbled an apology, then flushed guiltily when she caught sight of her mistress's knowing smile. Though she didn't truly believe she was fooling anyone, Jennet pretended she'd just been pondering Lady Appleton's announcement.

"So Edith is not dead," Jennet mused, "and she is fat, besides. Then who is it that is haunting Appleton?" Jennet realized then that she'd made one mistake. She had never asked the maids at Denholm who they thought the ghost was. She'd just assumed that her mistress already had the right of it, for it was not like Lady Appleton to make mistakes.

Instead of answering, Lady Appleton posed a question of her own. "What did Grizel see the night John Bexwith died?"

"A flash of something white on the stairs."

"No more than that?"

"She admitted she added more details later, after others saw the spirit, too."

"What others?"

"Now there is a most strange thing. When I pressed her, she grew confused and did not seem to know who else claimed to have seen her ghost. She would not explain how she knew any had."

"Is she the sort of girl capable of making up a story to gain attention?"

"She's not clever enough. But she might well think first of a ghost if she were frightened. She's the most superstitious person I've ever met. Carries a stone to bed with her to ward off nightmares, and did so even before Master Bexwith's sudden death."

"Carbuncle, no doubt. There are many people who believe it can drive away devils and overcome sorrow, and keep one safe from shipwreck and drowning, too."

Jennet sniffed disdainfully, completely forgetting that she still had moments when she believed Appleton Manor might have a resident ghost.

"So, what Grizel saw might have been the wind stirring a paper or a piece of fabric. A pity she insists it was white or we might put the blame on Dame Cat. No matter. Now we must find out what persons saw this apparition later, and what, precisely, they did see. It is possible the story grew from nothing at all. Or that others were treated to the same vision we were, designed to build on the wild claim Grizel made. The real question is, Who would want to frighten everyone away, leaving Appleton Manor abandoned and empty?"

"Outlaws?" Jennet suggested, seeing visions of Robin Hood and his band making themselves comfortable in the great hall for the winter.

"Someone more closely involved with Bexwith, I do think. Now, tell me, Jennet, what Grizel said about his last moments. Did she see him fall ill?"

"No, madam. Grizel served him his meal and went off to fetch ale from the buttery, but someone had taken away the candles, so she had to go and fetch a lamp from the kitchen and there fell into some talk with the cook, who warned her that Bexwith meant to have her warm his bed. Grizel did not believe it. They argued over it and all in all it was near to half an hour before she went back and found him dead."

"And the condition of the body?"

With a grimace, Jennet repeated all she'd learned. Grizel hadn't wanted to talk about that, either, but she had confirmed that Bexwith's eyes, when they'd lifted his head in hope of reviving him, were wide open and staring. "In horror," she added, as Grizel had.

"Making Grizel look for some cause of it. What about smells? Did she notice his breath?"

"Death smells." Jennet did not need to elaborate.

"Had he vomited?"

"Grizel did not approach close enough to tell. It was the cook who touched him."

Lady Appleton nodded, unsurprised that Grizel had been so cowardly. "She'll not have noticed the color of his skin, then, either, but mayhap Mabel Hussey did. We must locate her, and the other servants. What did Grizel tell you of the meal Bexwith ate?''

''Marrow-bone pie is marrow bones, currants, dates, artichokes, sugar, and . . .''—Jennet struggled to remember the odd name Grizel had used—''eryngo.''

''Eryngo?''

Had she got it wrong? ''That is what Grizel said, madam. Is it an herb?''

'' 'Tis the candied root of sea holly.''

''A poison, madam?''

''No. Still, this detail may be important. Master Grimshaw did not mention eryngo. You have done well, Jennet.''

Basking in the praise, Jennet dared ask again the question her mistress had evaded earlier. ''Madam, if this Edith is not Appleton's ghost, who is?''

''There is no ghost,'' Lady Appleton reminded her in stern tones.

''Yes, madam.'' Jennet sighed. ''But if there was one, who do people think she would be?''

With a rueful half smile, Lady Appleton relented. ''Lawyer Grimshaw's suggestion is that she is Sir George's fifth wife, Jane, a woman who died of the sweat some eight years past.''

Jennet frowned, once more gnawing thoughtfully on her lower lip. This time she really was concentrating on the mystery. ''That could be the answer.''

''What do you know of Jane Appleton?'' The current Lady Appleton's voice sharpened and her face took on the pinched look it sometimes got when she was expecting unpleasant tidings.

Jennet remembered several things all at once, things she'd heard about Jane during her visit to Denholm. It would not be politic to repeat all of them, she decided, at least not until she could determine just how much her mistress already knew.

''The maids at Denholm spoke of her,'' Jennet said cautiously.

"Why would those at Denholm now know anything? The woman died years ago and she was not wed all that long to Sir George. I understand that she was a great deal younger than he. I cannot imagine she would have much in common with Effie Denholm. Do you mean to say she was often there as a guest?"

"Guest?" Jennet permitted herself a small, superior smile. She did have in her possession information that Lady Appleton lacked. "No, madam, she was never a guest there. She was family. Jane was Mistress Denholm's elder daughter. It is for Jane Appleton that she still wears mourning."

CHAPTER 15

The letter from his wife arrived just after Sir Robert Appleton finished a fine breakfast of fried tripe, grilled beef, and excellent thick soup. Enclosed in it was a list of ingredients.

"She feared the pot of salve to treat King Francis's rash would be broken in transit," he said, glancing at the first part of the message, "and sends me the recipe in the event I need to procure more." The mixture was composed of Saracen's root, St. John's-wort, herb-of-the-sun, serpent's-tongue, and oil of lavender.

Blessing his wife for her thoughtful gesture, Sir Robert resumed reading the short letter. A moment later he swore fluently. He had to take a long swallow of ale before he could control his anger.

"Trouble?" Pendennis asked.

"When you marry, Pendennis," Robert advised his old friend, "make certain you have chosen a biddable woman."

She had written on the first of October. On that very day she'd left Kent. By now she'd have long since reached Appleton Manor. It was far too late to go after her and bring her back, even if he could simply abandon his mission and return to England.

Resigned, Sir Robert folded the letter together with the list of ingredients and tucked them into the front of his doublet. He'd known life with Susanna would be difficult, even before he'd married her. She'd gotten too much education. He'd agreed to the match because she also had a great deal of money, and because the duke of Northumberland was her guardian and had thought her a suitable bride.

"She has done nothing to threaten your mission, I trust." Pendennis sounded only mildly concerned.

"No. This is a personal matter. Against my wishes, she has gone north to deal with a problem at my estate in Lancashire."

"Women should not meddle in men's business," Pendennis said. "You may be sure that I will heed your advice. When I wed, I will select a bride who understands that."

Sir Robert found he had to laugh at his friend's naive certainty. It had been his experience that most men underestimated their wives. At least he'd been forewarned what to expect from his. "Susanna claims women should run things. She says men always make matters more complicated than they need to be."

"Queen Elizabeth is a woman and she's shown no great inclination toward simplicity."

Sir Robert did not answer. He had difficulty enough understanding his wife's thought processes, and he knew her well. He feared he'd never comprehend the queen's mind.

CHAPTER 16

The twenty-second day of October, the second Sunday Susanna had spent at Appleton Manor, began badly and got worse. She'd grown accustomed, in Kent, to breaking her fast with manchet bread and ale or butter and eggs. The new cook, who had arrived the previous day, sent by Master Grimshaw, provided brawn and mustard, beef, and what Jennet said was called brewis, slices of bread with fat broth poured over them.

She was further disappointed by the church services in the village. The lay reader could barely mumble his way through the service in the Book of Common Prayer. On the way home, detouring toward Denholm, she broached the subject of praying in her own chapel instead.

"But you have no chaplain," Mark pointed out.

"Then I will hire one. Many country households keep a chaplain and have him double as a clerk or schoolmaster. Sir William Cecil has one at his house in Wimbledon. Perhaps he can recommend a candidate." She frowned. "I believe I must write to the local bishop for permission."

"This is the territory of the bishop of Chester, madam, but no one at present holds that seat."

"Chester? Not Chichester?"

"No, madam."

"A pity. I am acquainted with the bishop who held Bath and Wells until Queen Mary's reign. 'Tis rumored he'll soon be installed at Chichester."

In truth she was better acquainted with his wife. Susanna smiled, remembering her last meeting with that very determined lady. Agatha Bárlow had but one goal in life. She would have each of her daughters marry a bishop, too. Susanna did not discount the possibility. There was nothing more powerful than a mother's love.

By the time they came to Denholm, Susanna was beginning to feel more cheerful again, but her good humor abruptly vanished at the discovery that Effie and her entire family had gone to Manchester during the week. The Denholms had a town house there and they meant to remain long enough to attend church services at St. Mary's before they returned to the country.

"A pity you did not know about the town house," Mark said as they turned away. "You might have stayed there instead of putting up at the inn."

"And have her servants report my every movement to their mistress? Thank you, no."

Susanna's second trip to Manchester had been brief and frustrating. Her search for someone who sold eryngo had been futile. Few had even heard of the delicacy. She could readily understand why. The sea holly grew plentifully near her own home in Kent, along the shore, but here it would be a greater rarity than the currants and dates, especially in its candied form.

The process was complex enough to make the end result expensive. The roots, which were of the bigness of a man's finger, had to be picked, washed, and then boiled until they were soft, then peeled and divested of all their pith. Then they were soaked a whole day in a syrup of sugar, white of egg, rosewater, cinnamon, and musk. Finally, they were heated over a very hot fire for one hour. Eryngo, this candied root of sea holly, had a very sweet and pleasant taste and was said to restore the aged and amend the defects of the young.

Someone he knew must have given Bexwith the ingredient. But who? And how had it been procured?

Jennet, fidgeting nervously at Susanna's side, made her aware she'd reined in her horse and had been staring back at the walls of Denholm, saying nothing, for several minutes. Annoyed, both at herself and the maidservant, Susanna snapped at her. "What ails you, girl?"

"I like not this wilderness."

"Do you expect to encounter the ghost between Denholm and Appleton?"

Jennet didn't deny it, but she made a valiant effort to appear unconcerned. "There have been no further appearances of the ghost. Perhaps it would be wise to leave well enough alone."

Not possible, Susanna thought. There were still too many unanswered questions. Repairs on the manor house kept her occupied, but not too busy to continue to contemplate the mysteries surrounding Bexwith's death . . . and that of Sir George.

And leaving Denholm, routed, meant a lost opportunity. She could scarce question Effie's houseservants while their mistress was away, but there were others here. She turned her horse. "I believe I will stop a while and view the floor in the Denholms' chapel. Did you not tell me, Jennet, that the tiler is Grizel's father?"

Jennet's long-suffering sigh answered her.

Dismounting, Susanna walked briskly to the chapel. Her first glimpse of the interior brought her to a halt, pleased and amazed by the quality of the workmanship. A multitude of tall, narrow windows shone with stained glass. And the light glancing through them illuminated a pattern of concentric circular bands of two-color, decorated floor tiles.

"Magnificent." What had been merely an excuse to poke about now became a very real desire. She wanted to meet the artisan who had produced this floor. She wanted him to come and work for her.

Jack Brown the tiler was not difficult to locate, but he turned out to be a sinewy little man with bulging biceps and a surly expression on his thin-lipped face. He heard Lady Appleton out in silence, then grunted in what she hoped was agreement to work for her.

"I have need of roofing tiles, as well."

He cackled at that. "Roof and ridge tiles require no skill."

"You are a craftsman. I understand that. But if you—"

With remarkable rudeness and lack of respect, Jack cut her off in midsentence. "I've no use for Appleton. My girl was a bonny and buxom lass before she went to work there. Fear of the place and its ghost have turned her into a shadow of her former self. No good will come of opening that accursed house again. Your husband, madam, should come and close it up. Or burn it down, mayhap. Total destruction is the only way to root out evil."

"Nonsense. There is no longer any evil present, and I do much doubt there ever was. Men may be cruel, Master Brown, but the places in which they live are innocent of all malevolence."

"I've no use for Appleton or the Appletons."

"We pay well."

"Aye. So Grizel was told."

"Your daughter had a fright, but I assure you that my husband's manor is not haunted."

"So you say."

"So I say." She stood as tall as he and stared him square in the eye.

"Appletons have much to make up for. Your husband should have kept tighter rein on that old lecher he left in charge."

"I agree. Things will change now. My next steward will be a married man." The tiler's attitude made Susanna wonder if he, too, might have thought he had reason to rid the world of

John Bexwith. She added Jack Brown to her list of suspicious characters.

Brown, meanwhile, indulged in a long, brooding silence, then rewarded her with a curt nod. "Then again, I am all but finished here. And so I will work for you. For a price."

An hour later, Susanna resumed the journey home, her skills at haggling sorely tested but her newest plan, to renovate Appleton's chapel, now well advanced. "The tiler will visit later in the week," she told Jennet and Mark. "He's agreed to design a paving similar to that at Denholm and make the segmented tiles for the circular arrangement and the decorated oblong tiles to use as borders, but he informs me that kilns are fired only in the summer months. This is the season for digging clay and carting it to yards, where it is left in heaps until Christmas. Fortunately for the leaks in Appleton's roof, Master Brown will be able to use ready-made tiles for repairs there. He's willing to do that much now, and begin to plan the design for the chapel."

"If he cannot fire the kiln, and if the work at Denholm is nearly finished, why does he linger there?"

"A good question, Jennet. Perhaps the winter's lodging was part of his fee. And he does have a daughter in service at Denholm."

Once more reminded of the reason behind her interest in Grizel, Susanna looked back over her shoulder at the distant manor house, wishing she'd thought to take time to inspect the herb garden while she was there. Another day, she decided. Now she was ready for home and her dinner.

Susanna and her servants rode on to Appleton Manor. Silence met them, a great, blissful quiet. For the first time in days, no workmen were abuilding because it was the sabbath. During the past week, when Susanna was not making a quick visit to Manchester or overseeing the planting, she'd spent most of her time supervising the beginning of repairs to the house.

"I have not seen Dame Cat lately," she remarked to Jennet as she dismounted.

Neither Jennet nor Mark had, either.

Leaving her mare in the stable, Susanna searched there first. She was not overly concerned, for she had a good idea what the cat was doing. She was, however, mildly curious to know how many kittens had been born.

Later that afternoon, her stomach full and nothing more pressing to do on this day she'd planned to spend visiting her neighbor, Susanna began a methodical sweep of the outbuildings in search of the cat. Within an hour she met with success.

The nest was hidden in the chapel, behind the altar. Susanna leaned closer, counting heads, but before she could finish enumerating Dame Cat's litter, she made a discovery that quite distracted her.

"White cloth," she whispered.

The kittens were curled up on top of a piece of fabric. Their mother might have found it anywhere, mayhap caught on a branch. Or hidden somewhere close at hand. A pity Dame Cat could not talk, for this, most assuredly, was part of the costume worn by the ghost of Appleton Manor.

CHAPTER 17

"She took Bess with her," Jennet grumbled as she and Mark walked the short distance from the house to the small private chapel at Appleton Manor.

"Do you hear me complaining?"

Although Mark smiled at her, and seemed willing to do most of the actual work she'd been assigned, Jennet was not appeased. She'd been given the responsibility for cleaning out the chapel. It was an important task, but she felt she was missing out on the adventure, for who knew what might be happening at Denholm?

"I am glad you are here and safe," Mark said.

"Here and given much to do in little time," Jennet shot back.

She surveyed the interior with a sense of vague foreboding. Everything was covered with dust, and in the dim light the thought of all the long-dead Appletons beneath their feet in the vault increased her sense of dread. When Mark touched her arm she jumped and shrieked. He barely contained a laugh as she glared at him.

"Tidy the place, she says," Jennet grumbled, trying to ignore the frisson of awareness that streaked through her when he took hold of her again, offering a soothing stroke of one thumb along the side of her face to ease away her fright. Her voice was a trifle husky as she continued her litany of complaints. "And at the same time she forbids me to disturb Dame Cat and her litter."

"Duty must always come before personal desires," Mark murmured, "but in this case my personal desires and my duty are as one." He slid his hand down to her shoulder, forcing her more deeply into an embrace. His lips were only inches from her own. "I have been wanting to talk with you alone, Jennet. You have been avoiding me."

"If you are going to ask me to marry you again, you may save your breath." She pulled away and stalked toward the altar Lady Appleton had told her concealed the cat's nest. She'd been avoiding temptation, 'twas true. Ever since they'd come to Appleton, Mark had changed, become more compelling. Where once she'd been certain of her ability to remain in control, now she doubted herself. "I have no mind to become any man's possession," she muttered as she reached her goal.

Mark took the rejection with his usual good humor, mostly because, Jennet supposed, he did not believe she meant what she said. Men! They were an arrogant species.

A closer look at the chapel confirmed that opinion. Sir George and his five wives were buried in the vault beneath, but above ground there was a brass memorial. It showed the man's likeness in such great detail that Jennet could see Sir Robert's resemblance to his father, though she did think her master was more handsome. The wives, however, were etched with a sameness that robbed them of any individual identity, as if each of them had lost her personality upon becoming Lady Appleton.

Dame Cat sent a baleful glare in Jennet's direction when the maidservant knelt down in front of the altar. The feline was lodged in comfort and did not mean to allow either herself or her litter to be disturbed.

"No respect for religion," was Mark's indulgent comment as he, too, bent to inspect the little family. He was smiling as he said the words.

Grim-faced, Jennet ignored him. She stood again, took up a rag and bucket, and started the cleaning. An hour passed. In spite of her best efforts, Jennet remained all too aware of Mark's nearby presence. The pull of passion was there, no doubt of it. The practical side of her nature urged her to encourage him, too. If Lady Appleton left him in charge at Appleton Manor when she returned to Leigh Abbey, he would doubtless become an important member of the local community.

Jennet tried, briefly, to imagine a future here together. A third aspect of her character, a deep-rooted superstitiousness, kept interfering. Lady Appleton thought she had proof the ghost was contrived, but Jennet was not convinced. A bit of cloth lying beneath a litter of kittens did not settle anything. It might be, as Lady Appleton claimed, a piece of the apparition's veil. Or it might be something else entirely.

Everyone knew there *were* ghosts. Why, old King Henry's fifth bride—or was it his sixth?—was said to run shrieking through the corridors of Hampton Court, begging them not to cut off her head.

The cleaning progressed while Jennet's imagination roamed freely. At last, careful not to disturb Dame Cat, she came to the final chore and stuck her rag beneath the altar to clean out the accumulation of dirt. To her surprise, her fingers encountered the sharp corner of a solid object. Perplexed, she drew out an oddly shaped box.

"What have you found?"

Jennet looked up, surprised to find Mark at her elbow. He had to have been watching her closely indeed to appear so quickly. The thought pleased her.

"I cannot tell," she said, "but I do think it was deliberately hidden here."

"Open it," he suggested.

Jennet needed no urging. Curious, she lifted the lid to reveal a small, mottled object nestled on a pad of velvet. With instinctive distaste, she recoiled, thrusting the box away from her. "What is this thing?"

Mark frowned, then took the case from her to examine its contents more closely. Slowly a sardonic smile crept over his features. He removed the mysterious object and offered it to her. Reluctantly, she let him place it on her palm.

"What is it?"

"It seems Sir George had papist sympathies." Mark chuckled at her confusion. "The box is a reliquary, and that appears to be a knucklebone."

Jennet hastily dropped it, wiping her hands on her apron as she made a low sound of distress.

Mark laughed outright. "What? No respect for a saint's relic? 'Tis said such things have miraculous powers."

His mockery irritated her so much that her fear vanished. "I do much doubt that," she declared. "If it were so, then papists would still rule England. 'Tis more likely this is a fraud sold at some fair." With as much dignity as she could muster, Jennet got up off her knees, dusted her skirt, and turned her back on Mark, leaving the bone where it had fallen. "This chapel is clean enough," she declared. "Add fresh rushes and we are finished with our task."

When she got no answer, she glanced over her shoulder. Mark had retrieved the relic and was placing it almost reverently back inside the box. Jennet frowned. All of a sudden she felt as chilled as she had been by the sight of the ghost. Was this discovery an ill omen? Try as she might, Jennet could not shake off the premonition that worse discoveries were yet to come.

CHAPTER 18

"Join us," Euphemia Denholm invited.

Susanna hesitated, not because she objected to the chance to talk to her near neighbor, but because she could not sit without taking up a needle to help in the embroidery of a particularly complex piece of tapestrywork.

The entire distaff side of the household at Denholm had been recruited to complete the project. Next to Mistress Denholm sat her daughter, Catherine, and then, in descending order of importance, all the maidservants, Grizel included. The invitation was meant to include Susanna's maid, as well. Susanna could only hope that young Bess had more skill with embroidery than she did, else Effie was going to have to pick out and rework a great many stitches after they left.

"I am not known for my needlework," she warned as she took the place made for her on the bench, between Effie and Catherine. Bess settled herself farther down the line, smiling shyly at Grizel, as if she already knew the other girl.

Did she? Susanna wondered, but she left that question for later. It was well she'd decided to leave Jennet at home, she thought. This was not the time for distraction, and Jennet, for all she meant well did not go unnoticed long, even when she was in the company of her betters.

Her own fault, Susanna realized. She'd encouraged the younger woman to express herself freely. Like Mark, Jennet would do anything for her, and for both of them Susanna felt an almost sisterly affection. To those who believed in a strict hierarchy, in separation of the classes and the superiority of gentle or noble birth, such behavior was nigh unto treasonous.

"This is to be a gift," Effie informed her as they sat and wrought. "For a wedding. You'll not know the bride, but the family is an ancient one in these parts. Connected to the Stanleys."

Susanna let her hostess rattle on, all the while looking for an opening. She ran idle fingers over the silken textures, hesitant to spoil such a masterpiece with her own inept additions.

She had questions to ask, but she knew the interrogation must be done subtly. She took the first stitch, uncertain whether she would mention Jane's name at all. Or Edith's. She did not want Effie to think she'd been investigating the past, not if there was even the slightest possibility that someone at Denholm was involved in murder.

With a skeptical glance at the section of tapestry beneath Susanna's hands, Effie cleared her throat and hesitantly asked, "How do you occupy your time in Kent if not in needlework?"

"With my herbs and potions, and the compiling of a cautionary herbal."

Effie looked puzzled. "Do you mean to say you are a writer of books?"

"Not yet, but my goal is to produce a complete compendium of the dangerous side effects of plants. My sister died many years ago from eating banewort berries, which she mistook for cherries. Such deaths can be prevented if every gentlewoman and goodwife's training in the preparation of herbal remedies includes detailed descriptions of harmful herbs."

"Banewort? What is that? I do not know it."

"In these parts it is called dwale. I have seen it growing by the highway, and henbane, too. There are thimbleflowers under a good many hedges, and cowbane grows in ditches and stagnant water. Another poison, tansy, grows hereabout as a roadside weed, for it thrives on peat land. Monkshood does not grow wild in England, but I fully expect to find it in some gardens, as it also has so many medicinal uses."

"I am sure Randall permits no poisons to grow in our herb garden." Effie drew herself up a little straighter and sniffed, as if she'd just been insulted.

"Ah, but that is the point, you see. Everyone does, sometimes without realizing it. Poisonous plants almost always have benign uses one would be loath to do without. My herbal will be a warning to housewives, a clear indication of how much is safe and what to avoid. And, as far as may be known, what course to follow should accidental poisoning occur."

Every ear was now cocked in Susanna's direction, but it was, surprisingly, Catherine who spoke. "Father warned us about cowbane."

Susanna's interest quickened. "What did he say?"

"That some poor fool in Red Bank had mistaken it for smallage and boiled it in a sallet for supper and was found dead the next day."

Effie looked disapproving. "Enough of this dismal talk. Let us speak not of deadly herbs but of those that heal."

Mischief sparkled in Catherine's eyes as she addressed a question to Susanna. "Then tell us, Lady Appleton, what antidotes do you recommend should one be accidentally poisoned?"

"That is difficult to answer. At home I keep many ingredients at hand. In case of accidents." Unable to resist the chance to educate a young gentlewoman, Susanna offered up her opinion on the efficacy of universal cures. "Some claim any poison can be expelled from the system by ingesting wormwood. Others swear by a dose of unicorn's horn. Or they recommend swallowing a toadstone. I believe it is necessary to know what poison has been consumed before selecting a likely cure. And any such remedy must needs be administered quickly if it is to have any chance of success. Cures are effective only a fraction of the time and some poisons simply work too fast. In those cases nothing can be done.''

''So, you account yourself a skilled herbalist,'' Effie mused. ''Mayhap you'd be willing to make a suggestion or two to help my dear husband's condition.''

At her side, Susanna felt Catherine tense, but she kept her attention on the girl's mother. ''I will be delighted to try. Deafness, if caused by accident, apoplexy, or a fall, can sometimes be restored in part by a mixture of gall of hare and grease of fox. Warm it to the temperature of blood and dip black wool in it and put that in the ear. Another remedy, though I cannot vouch for its effectiveness, advises using the black wool to apply juice of wormwood tempered with the gall of a bull.''

''Randall's deafness does not concern me as much as another ailment.''

Stiff knees, Susanna recalled. She searched her memory for cures. ''Have you tried a poultice of rue and borage mixed with honey? That does well to reduce swelling.''

''It is greater swelling I desire.'' Effie had bent over her work, making it difficult for Susanna to hear her next mumbled words. ''It availed me nothing to apply an unguent compounded of castor oil, spikehead seeds, earthworms, and fermented goat's milk.''

For a moment Susanna thought she had misunderstood. Was the problem gout? For that there were several possibilities. ''Populeon ointment,'' she mused aloud, ''made of poplar buds. Or stag's marrow, or one can also lay on the affected part a paste compounded of styrax, bitumen, sandarac, myrrh, and camphor. Or, an alternative might be cantharides paste, made from the dried, crushed bodies of beetles, but that can also be a poison and must be used with care.''

''Cantharides?''

Something in Effie's tone made Susanna aware that she had

erred. Jennet's report had included deafness and trouble with the knees, it was true, but she had also said Randall Denholm was impotent. She gave Effie a sharp look. Had they been talking at cross-purposes? "There are some who think that cantharides is also an aphrodisiac."

There were some who thought eryngo was as well.

"I knew I had heard of it before. 'Twas in that connection. But a poison, too? What a pity. Love potions always seem to have some negative aspect. I have heard one method certain of success is for the man to eat the genitals of a cockerel, but Randall refuses to cooperate."

The compound of earthworms and goat's milk made perfect sense now, and Susanna had difficulty holding back a chuckle. It was apparently a local cure for male . . . difficulties. To judge by Effie's reaction, it had not been a success.

"He might find the candied root of sea holly more palatable," she suggested. "Eryngo, it is called."

"I have never heard of it. Is it difficult to obtain?"

"It would seem so."

Certainly no one in Manchester would confess to selling any to John Bexwith. Could Randall Denholm have grown and candied his own in hope of a cure? He might have offered to share his success with his neighbor. Except that if Effie was to be believed, he'd not met with success. It was a puzzle Susanna could not solve. Not yet. There were too many pieces missing. And, in truth, it might have no bearing on Bexwith's death at all. She had to keep reminding herself of that. The old man might simply have died, for no reason save that his time on this earth was finished.

Slowly, Susanna became aware that her hostess was staring at her, a peculiar look on her face. It seemed prudent to drop all discussion of sea holly for the present. Susanna did not want anyone to guess that she suspected Bexwith's pie had been poisoned, especially when it was equally possible it had not been.

"I know no sure cure for impotence," she told Effie,

"although another possibility I've heard suggested is a powder made from the heel bones of a pig." She could not hold back a small smile at the lengths to which some people would go in their search for a cure. They appeared to work just often enough to keep hope alive.

"I have been told that if a man's member is curved or crooked it may be made straight again by the application of compresses containing an ointment of fresh butter, linseed oil, and sweet almonds," an elderly maidservant said.

Conversation became general then, since nearly every woman received some instruction in the use of herbs during girlhood. For all Effie's disinterest, Susanna was certain she'd been properly trained in the distilling and decocting of medicines. 'Twas likely she simply had as little aptitude for that as Susanna did for needlework.

Another maid offered up her grandmother's recipe to cure chilblains.

"A tasty list of ingredients," Susanna remarked, her voice so low only Catherine heard and responded with a muffled giggle. "Did it fail to remedy the chilblains, 'twould also make a fine sauce for a roast."

CHAPTER 19

An hour later, Susanna excused herself from the needlework to visit the privy. She could not bring herself to go back. Of their own volition her feet took her toward the herb garden, a much more natural environment than the confines of the house.

Did Effie know anything about Bexwith's death? Susanna asked herself that question as she wandered among the rows of plants, recognizing many of them from her own garden even though at this time of year, nearly the end of October, most had gone by. Only bare stalks remained.

Effie had misled her about Edith, but that could be no more than a mother's desire to deflect attention away from her own daughter, Jane. Or that she really believed Edith had disappeared and was thus a likely prospect to haunt the manor.

It was odd she still wore mourning for her eldest child after all these years, but mayhap their relationship had been especially close.

What else? At their first meeting, Effie had neglected to mention that Grizel had found Bexwith's body, that she'd been in service at Appleton Manor before coming to Denholm Hall. But Susanna had not asked.

"Good day to you, Lady Appleton," said a whispery voice. Randall Denholm rose unsteadily from behind the hedge that bordered the garden. "Fumes," he said.

Approaching him with caution, Susanna peered at the small plot of open ground where he'd been working. Randall Denholm had been laying out roots to dry in the sun. "Monkshood?" she asked, speaking more loudly than usual.

"Aye. In three or four days I will grind these to powder."

'Twas clear his hearing loss was only partial. "For what purpose?" she asked.

"To kill rats . . . and other vermin." He chuckled and looked sly.

"You have a fine garden." Susanna edged away a few steps. "How came you to have so great a knowledge of herbs?"

A faraway look came into his faded eyes. "Once long ago I was a novice in a monastery. I had no great calling for the religious life and gladly left it when my elder brother died and I became my father's heir, but during the time I was cloistered, I was put to work in the herb garden and discovered I had a rare talent for making things grow."

Surprised by his candor, Susanna gave him a hard look. Perhaps he was as addlepated as he sometimes appeared. Surely no sensible man would speak so openly of papist roots.

"A garden soothes a man's soul," he said.

With that Susanna had to agree and for a few minutes they chatted amiably enough of herbs and their uses. All the while, she continued to catalog the contents of his garden. She found but one other deadly poison—mandrake. A quick glance from the plant to the man caught a crafty look in his eyes before he made his expression carefully blank again.

"Work to do," he told her and shuffled off toward a patch of rosemary that needed covering before the first frost.

Mandrake. Susanna closed her eyes, trying to remember all she knew of the herb. Like the root of the sea holly, the mandrake's root was also said to cure impotence. Had the root of one been substituted for the other? A frown wrinkled her brow as she tried to make that theory work. Mandrake was a poison, it was true, but its effects would not be consistent with what she knew about the way Bexwith had died. For one thing a man poisoned by mandrake should have taken much longer to expire. As much as a whole day. And he'd have had to eat a great deal of the plant.

Frowning, Susanna considered Randall's explanation for growing monkshood. No doubt he had reasons for mandrake, too. But when she looked around, thinking to ask a seemingly innocent question about the use of mandrake oil to remove warts, Randall Denholm was gone. She finally caught sight of him halfway across the orchard, hobbling away from her as fast as his walking stick would let him.

Robert would say she was making much of nothing because she was looking for real-life examples to use in her herbal, that she thought this must be a case of poisoning because that interpretation would be more useful to her than the death of an old man from natural causes. Perhaps Robert would be right, but Susanna could not shake the sense that everyone she'd met since coming to Lancashire was hiding something from her.

Even Robert was holding information back, she realized. In truth, his behavior had been suspicious from the start. He had not wanted her to make this journey.

One explanation for her husband's reticence came readily to mind. He doubtless had once kept a mistress here in Lancashire. He did not want them to meet.

Foolish man, to think he must hide such a thing from her. Someday, Susanna decided, she must find a subtle way to tell him she already knew all about Alys of Dover.

CHAPTER 20

Navigation along the Loire River was well organized and swift, and boatmen bragged that they could journey all the way from Orléans to Nantes in but six days. There were a number of royal châteaux in the Loire Valley, among them Blois.

Woods stretched to a depth of several miles along the river in the vicinity of the village beneath the castle, forests filled with oak and beech, poplar and chestnut. Sir Robert Appleton came by way of Saint-Dié and approached from a direction that gave him a spectacular view of the royal château where it perched on the cliff: The place had a hybrid appearance, a facade of white stone in one wing, one in the Gothic style in another.

As he came closer, Sir Robert was amazed at how absurdly easy it was to approach. He went unchallenged until the very last moment, when royal guards in striped uniforms of blue, red, and white stepped forward holding halberds. Even then, their manner made the weapons appear more ceremonial than warlike.

The papers Sir Robert carried led to an invitation to stay the night and sup with the court. He was shown to lodgings across the courtyard from the white stone wing. On closer inspection, he noted a profusion of tiny, diamond-paned windows and narrow doorways there. The doors were small where he was, too. He had to duck to avoid striking his head as he passed through them.

Contriving to lose his way en route to supper, Sir Robert managed to explore a number of little galleries. From the many windows and balconies he got a sense of the plan of the place, but he also found himself taking simple enjoyment from his glimpses of wide terraces and formal Italian gardens.

The meal, when at last he reached his place at table, was elegant and very refined, with napkins changed after each course, service dishes of silver, and forks as well as meat knives at every place.

Sir Robert's attention was drawn at once to King Francis's wife, the young woman who was queen of Scots in her own right. She was sixteen and enchanting, a tall, slender creature with delicate bone structure, a swanlike neck, and long hands. Her air of fragility enhanced her beauty.

The poets who sung her praises had failed utterly to capture the essence of Mary Stewart. Sir Robert studied her closely as she put aside the black velvet mask lined with white satin that every lady at court seemed to wear. Her small mouth was perfection.

Noting that she ate sparingly, he watched her sample cheese from Milan and apricots imported from Armenia. Soon she put aside those foods in favor of candied cucumbers and two patés, one made of larks and the other from artichokes.

Some might say she was too pale, but that pallor was offset by a perfect complexion in a perfect face, oval in shape and small in proportion to her height. Almond-shaped, amber-colored eyes were topped by delicately arched brows the same color as her hair, which was a bright, golden red. The color, a shade just lighter than auburn, was not unlike that of her English cousin Elizabeth.

When he realized he was beginning to fall under Mary's spell, Sir Robert exerted himself to seek flaws. It was a difficult task, but in the end he managed to find three. Her ears were too large. Her nose was a little too long and slightly aquiline. And then there was the canopy over her head. Queen Mary and King Francis each had one. His was made of purple damask and had the arms of France emblazoned on it. Hers was crimson and she had quartered the arms of England with those of France and Scotland. She'd had the same usurped arms engraved on the silver plate being used at table.

Sir Robert caught himself speculating. Would there be any profit in presenting himself not as an Englishman loyal to the present queen, but as one anxious to recruit French and Scots assistance in overthrowing the heretic Elizabeth and replacing her with another Catholic Mary?

It would not be a difficult role to play in one respect. His father *had* been a papist all his life. Many of the people of Lancashire still were, in spite of decrees issued in faraway London. And Sir Robert himself had once been a devout Catholic. He had fallen easily back into papist ways when the other Mary reigned in England. Had she lived, he'd be a model Catholic courtier still. Oh, it would be easy enough to once more adopt the appearance of that faith, but the necessity of acting as if he wanted a second Mary, born of a Scots father and a French mother, to mount the throne of England in Elizabeth's place would soon have him grinding his teeth.

In truth, he'd prefer almost any man of any faith to any queen regnant. Unfortunately, there were no male heirs left. If not Mary of Scotland, descended from King Henry's elder sister, then the choice was between Mary's father's half sister, Margaret Douglas, countess of Lennox, and Frances Brandon, duchess of Suffolk, the daughter of King Henry's younger sister. The best solution, flawed though it was, remained forcing Queen Elizabeth to marry, turn the reins of government over to her consort, and bear him sons.

On his second day in Blois, Sir Robert was allowed to present

Queen Elizabeth's present and his own to the queen of France. She thanked him prettily and dismissed him. That night, when he'd climbed the stairs from the inner courtyard to the southwest wing, he tried to take reassurance that this mission had not been a waste of time from the sheer splendor of his lodgings. The walls were so heavily carved they looked like brocade and the bed hangings were brilliant with gold and fine embroidery. He had tiled floors, coffers for his belongings, of which he'd brought but few, a comfortably padded chair, and a prie-dieu.

Sir Robert smiled at his own conceit. This meant nothing. The French were not making any special effort to impress him. This was simply their way. Overdone. Ostentatious. He'd heard it said that here a courtier was expected to have at least thirty changes of raiment.

His own appearance had not compared well to the standard he saw at every meal. In spite of the fact that the court was still officially in mourning for the late King Henri, most garments were colorful and elaborate. Sir Robert's doublet, the best he had brought with him, was very plain by comparison, mere velvet, decorated with only a starched collaret and a bit of lace. His hose were not silk. And he had no beard.

Then again, neither did the young king. Francis II was a poor specimen of manhood, but what came after? An even younger boy, another of Queen Catherine's sons.

A knock sounded and, as if he'd conjured her, the queen mother of France swept into his chamber. She was masked, but he had no trouble recognizing her. The royal chins were unmistakable. Queen Catherine was a great, gross figure of a woman. He'd noticed at table that she ate with a glutton's fervor.

"Madam," he said, and sketched a bow. "I am honored."

Her voice was disguised by the fact that she had to hold the mask in place by a little knob caught between her teeth, but what she said was perfectly comprehensible. "Were you sent here to poison my son?" she asked in French. She held the small pot of salve he'd given Queen Mary.

Sir Robert took heart from the fact that the queen mother had come in person and alone. Unless she had left guardsmen waiting in the passageway, it seemed unlikely she meant to have him thrown into prison. His reply was in French as fluent as her own, and without her betraying Italian accent.

"It is a recipe of my wife's and I assure you, madam, that she is most careful to avoid poisons. It is her great mission in life to compile a book on dangerous herbs."

"And this salve contains what ingredients?"

"All harmless, I do assure you." He enumerated them, grateful that Susanna had thought to send him the recipe.

When he had done, the queen mother extended the small pottery jar toward him. "Rub some on the back of your own hand, over the veins."

With a silent prayer that this was indeed the same salve he had sent to the young king and not some deadly substitution, Sir Robert removed his glove and did as she commanded. Queen Catherine would be a powerful ally. Even as the often ignored wife of King Henri II, she had changed life in her adopted country. With her from Italy had come an improved sidesaddle, an interest in astrology, a sweet called iced cream, the art of fencing, and the concept of the hired bravo. She'd make a good friend, but a very dangerous enemy.

"If your queen be content not to meddle in the affairs of France," she said quietly, as she waited to see if there would be any reaction, "there will be no difficulties from my daughter-by-marriage. France does not desire to annex so troublesome a place as England."

Sir Robert said nothing.

"As to your mission here," she continued, "we are well aware you mean to meet with our enemies. Advise your queen well, Sir Robert. She has nothing to gain by involving herself in the affairs of France."

As he maintained his silence, unable to think of anything he might say that would not condemn him, he wondered who had betrayed his mission to the queen mother. Did she have her own spies everywhere? Or was someone he trusted, Pendennis perhaps, a traitor to England? That he'd briefly toyed with changing his own allegiance enabled him to believe the same temptations could entice any man.

"Your wife interests me," Queen Catherine said after a short time had passed. "Tell me more about this herbal of hers."

Robert obliged, explaining briefly how the death of Susanna's sister, Joanna, had made her realize that many leaves, berries, and roots were quite deadly, thus inspiring her to begin a book full of warnings for both cook and goodwife. "As yet, she has not progressed very far," he remarked, saying to this audience the same thing he'd said many times before to friends and acquaintances, making light of Susanna's project. "As you may imagine, it is both dangerous and difficult to experiment freely with poison."

The moment the words were out, he wished them back. Had the queen mother cast some sort of spell on him? How else could he explain that he'd completely forgotten that her family, the Medicis, were as notorious in her native Italy as the Borgias. Their enemies had an unfortunate tendency to die of poison.

The queen mother let his words pass without comment. Apparently satisfied the salve would have no ill effects, she retrieved the pot and started to leave. At the heavy door she looked back at him.

"I believe I would enjoy meeting Lady Appleton," she said. "A pity that will never happen. I do much doubt I will ever visit England and you, Sir Robert, would be well advised not to return to France."

CHAPTER 21

At Appleton on St. Crispin's Day a cart entered the courtyard and a stoop-shouldered woman descended. She was fair-haired, a rather fleshy creature with wide hips and an ample bosom. In her youth she'd have been considered buxom. Now she was just fat.

"I be Mabel Hussey," she announced, "come back to me post."

Susanna received her in the hall, surprised and pleased to have found Sir George's cook at last. Since her first trip to Manchester, she had made some progress on the house, but precious little in solving the mysteries of Appleton Manor.

She studied Mabel's face intently, searching for some clue to her character. Its most prominent feature was a sharp nose, but there were other distinctions. Deep bags under the eyes gave her the aspect of a sorrowful hound and she had a wide, thin-lipped mouth. It was a face that had no claim to charm or beauty and yet in the eyes there was an astuteness that looked promising. Susanna's overall impression was that she and Mabel would deal very well together.

" 'Tis well spoke of ye be, madam," Mabel said with cheerful bluntness, "but ye'll have need of me, I warrant. I say it that shouldn't, but here be the best cook in Salford Hundred." She thumped her chest with one meaty hand.

"Indeed." Susanna doubted the claim. The herb garden she'd found gave little evidence of an interest in seasonings. On the other hand, she could understand why Mabel would exaggerate her abilities. She wanted her position back.

"Ye would have known that," Mabel continued, "had ye stayed at the inn on Shude Hill instead of the one in Withy Grove."

"A mistake, I do assure you, for I was most anxious to find you and retain your services. How is it that Master Grimshaw did not know where you were?"

"Grimshaw? What has he to do with anything? Meddling old fart! 'Twere he what sent me away. I did mean to stay on here, ghost or no ghost, until he did close up the house."

"He never contacted you afterward, in Manchester?"

"Nay. Did he say he had, then?"

"He said you had left by the time he tried to find you."

Mabel laughed aloud, showing a mouth full of large, yellowed teeth. "I do wonder . . . what is it ye could learn from me that he does not want ye to know?"

"My question exactly." Susanna motioned for her newly acquired cook to sit in the best chair in the hall and filled pewter tankards with perry for them both. "Do you know what happened to the others who once worked here?"

"The girl, Grizel, went to Denholm Hall. Her father insisted. Furious, he were, when he heard she'd been near seduced by the old man. The scullion, a lad called Dickon, found work as a butcher's boy."

"What butcher?"

"Oliver Ince."

"Well," said Susanna. "Well."

"Even so. The odd-job man, a cottar by the name of Adam Bone, from the other side of Manchester, he's not gone far, either. Since he lost his holding he'll do any work to put a roof over his head. The town took him on as a swineherd to take the pigs to Collyhurst every morning and bring them back at night."

It seemed, Susanna thought, that she'd be making yet another visit to Manchester soon. She leaned toward Mabel and lowered her voice. "There is another matter you might help me with. It is this marrow-bone pie. Can you tell me what ingredients were in it?"

"A lot of fancy nonsense is what," Mabel grumbled, but she rattled off the same list Grizel had.

"And where did you get the recipe?"

"From John Bexwith himself."

"And where did you get the eryngo?"

"From Bexwith, too. He bought all the ingredients, even the artichokes, in Manchester."

But Susanna knew he hadn't gotten the eryngo there.

"Waste of money," Mabel muttered.

"Expensive for a mere steward," Susanna agreed. "How do you suppose he came by the wherewithal to buy such things?"

"I fancied he learned some poor fool's secrets."

"You think he extorted money from someone?"

"Stands to reason he did not earn so much by honest means. And he did tell me he planned to eat well from that night on. Him, not the rest of us."

"Who?"

"I know not. Nor care to, either. Let his secret die with Bexwith."

There was food for thought. Had she not already considered this very possibility when she'd seen the relative luxury of Oliver Ince's house? "Is it possible this unknown person might have preferred to end Bexwith's life rather than continue to pay for silence?"

"Murder? The man died of a surfeit of rich food. Old fool."

"Did he? Or was a deadly poison contained in the marrow-bone pie?"

Surprised and insulted by this suggestion, Mabel drew herself up straighter and slammed the empty pewter tankard down on the refectory table. Susanna refilled it.

"His death was passing strange," she reminded the affronted cook. "Did you know by sight each item you put into the pie?"

Susanna could see the possibility she had accidentally caused Bexwith's death begin to prey on Mabel's mind. The woman had no skill at hiding her reactions, which was reassuring. That inability and the cook's voluntary return to Appleton Manor strongly suggested she was innocent of any intention to harm Bexwith.

"Should have stuck to plain pottage," Mabel muttered under her breath.

"You added no spices, no herbs beyond what Bexwith provided?"

"Nay, madam. Not a one. And I took his word for it that what he gave me were eryngo and artichokes and the rest."

"What about the kitchen? Could anyone have come in while the pie was there, before or after it was baked, to add something to it?"

"It did sit to cool a bit while no one was about. Any might have entered." Relief flooded her features but was quickly followed by a considering frown. "But how could anyone have come and not been seen at dinnertime? All of us were about the house."

"Unless the poisoner was one of the servants," Susanna pointed out. "But it does also occur to me now that if someone gave Bexwith a poisonous root and told him it was eryngo, he would not know the difference." Nor would Mabel. Substituting monkshood or mandrake or some other root for eryngo in that manner would be far easier than sneaking in and sprinkling the powdered leaves of some poisonous plant into the finished pie.

"Would not cooking kill the poison?" Mabel asked.

"Some, like dog's mercury, are rendered harmless by heat, but not all." Briefly, Susanna told Mabel about her herbal and her interest in poisonings, accidental and deliberate. Then she asked about the condition of the body. "This can tell us much," she explained. "Skin color, for example."

"He were covered in pie."

With a grimace, Susanna soldiered on. "Smells?"

Mabel gave her a look.

"I know the dead give up their bodily fluids, but had he been sick before he breathed his last?"

"Aye. When I did lift his head I could see froth and vomit along with bits of the pie."

"Grizel says his eyes were wide and staring."

"Aye. The pupils were big, too."

"And she spent a half an hour's time with you between serving the dish and finding him dead?"

"Aye."

"No more?"

"Nay."

Sipping perry and watching Mabel, Susanna sensed that the cook was a woman both outspoken and forthright. That she was telling the truth as she knew it seemed certain.

"How do you feel about Lawyer Grimshaw?" she asked.

"I've no ax to grind with him now I'm back."

Which did not explain his failure to let her know Appleton was inhabited again. "He said you were afraid to return."

"Never held with a ghost," she declared. "Never saw one with me own eyes."

"And if you had seen something that night?"

Mabel chuckled. " 'Twould be doubting it I'd be, even then, I warrant."

"So, no one saw it, aside from Grizel?"

"Nay."

That was odd. Susanna was certain Grimshaw had said in his first letter that the other servants had seen it, before Appleton Manor was closed up and they went their separate ways.

"There seems to be some question as to *who* is haunting Appleton." Susanna told her. "And I wish I knew who would want to. In any event, the appearances are as contrived as a player's spectacle.'' She described what she'd been told and what she had seen herself, adding, ''What I saw lacked only trapdoors and flashes of light.''

Mabel nodded and sipped and sipped again. ''Just so. Well, there's many a lass might have liked to see Sir George meet his maker, but none, I do think, who'd try to hurry him along. And as for John Bexwith, what harm did he ever do?''

''That is my exact question,'' Susanna told her, ''though there are those who say the master and his man were both threats to womankind.''

Mabel's hearty laugh boomed forth. ''Aye, but is that such a bad thing? I knew them both well, if ye do take my meaning, and I came to no harm from it.''

''There's a difference between willing and unwilling,'' Susanna commented dryly. ''Tell me about Edith Ince.''

The story was the same one Susanna had already heard. Mabel and the other servants had gone to the fair. Bexwith had found the body on his return. Since everyone knew what Sir George was like, it was immediately clear that his death was an accident. Besides, no one had wanted to make a fuss.

''No one questioned Edith?''

''No need. If it had not been Edith, 'twould have been some other young wench. And by the look of it, she suffered enough.'' Mabel winked. ''Had his codpiece unlaced, he did, when he fell.'' Then she chortled. ''Died as he lived, and that be the Lord's own truth.''

''You've little pity for the girl.''

Mabel sobered instantly. ''Aye, and I do see that a young lass might think Sir George a ripe old horror. But in his youth, ah, there were a man. Is his son like him?''

''In appearance, or so I surmise. In his profligate ways, I do hope not. Can you tell me how John Bexwith came to be steward here?''

''He and Sir George did know each other as lads. They shared a wildhead youth and managed to take it well into their middle years with them. Why, I remember me once, and it must have been after Sir George had taken him his third wife, he and Bexwith put on masks one night and entered a neighbor's house. Sir George had a quarrel with the fellow but he weren't at home so they plucked his children out of their beds and tossed up the bedding and bedstraw and told the fellow's wife that they'd come to kill him. It was all a great jest, prompted by overindulgence in fancy French wine, but the family were proper terrorized before they'd done."

"Can such antics have gone unpunished?"

"He were charged in Chancery. Not the first time, either. But Sir George never did more than pay a fine. Had the magistrates in his pocket, he did, and that's the Lord's truth, too."

Susanna shook her head, dismayed by this further proof that Robert's father had been a lawless and irresponsible sort, prone to go his own way without regard for others.

"Most times when he entered a man's house and that man were not at home, Sir George had other things on his mind. He'd tear up the bed, all right." Mabel was laughing again. "Terror of the neighborhood, he was."

"I am surprised the Denholms agreed to his marriage with their daughter."

Mabel shook her head solemnly from side to side. "A pity, that were. Sweet young thing. Brought music and laughter into this house . . . for a time."

"And her parents? What did they think of this elderly son-by-marriage?"

Mabel just shook her head, reluctant to guess. "Never once did they come here when she were Lady Appleton. And 'twas rare she went to them."

Susanna frowned. She needed to think about all Mabel had said. There would be time for more questions later. "I will send the cook Master Grimshaw provided back to Manchester this very day," she declared. She had to wonder now if he'd been sent as a spy. No doubt Robert's profession made her overly suspicious, but she would not be sorry to see the last of that particular retainer.

"I were housekeeper, too," Mabel said. "Sir George did keep but a small staff."

"Then you shall be housekeeper again. I've household staff you have not met and some few from Manchester that you may know already." She named them, but was not surprised when Mabel had heard of none of them, not even the girl Bess. Grimshaw had apparently been careful to hire only servants who had no prior connection to or knowledge of Appleton Manor.

Briefly, Susanna wondered if she should dismiss all the new staff and let Mabel find replacements, but she rejected the idea at once. Help had been hard to come by. She would simply have to be careful what she did and said in front of Bess and the others.

As she'd promised, Susanna led Mabel to the kitchen, gave the cook a generous bribe to be on his way quickly, and introduced his replacement to the rest of the staff. Jennet looked the newcomer over thoroughly, her manner suspicious, and Mabel returned the examination in kind.

It did not surprise Susanna that her tiring maid sought her out within the hour. She found her in the stillroom she had set up since coming to Lancashire, grinding basil to use in a poultice to treat workmen's blisters.

"Madam, are you certain you want that Mabel Hussey back?"

Susanna smiled to herself, unable to resist baiting the girl. "Why should I not, Jennet? She claims to be an excellent cook." Susanna pretended to concentrate on the rhythm of mortar and pestle.

"Aye. I do remember how she cooks," Jennet muttered. In a louder voice she asked, "Is she not the one who made the marrow-bone pie?"

"I am convinced we've naught to fear from Mabel Hussey's cooking."

"Did the ghost kill Master Bexwith, then?"

Exasperation made Susanna's voice sharp. She wielded the pestle with greater vigor. Would she never be rid of this superstitious nonsense? "No, Jennet! Ghosts do not kill."

Her maidservant looked puzzled for a moment, but then her expression cleared and delight underscored her words. "Oh, excellent, madam! You have reasoned out that there was no murder at all!"

Jennet's relief was so intense that Susanna did not have the heart to contradict her. And how could she admit to a girl who admired her mistress's cleverness that she was more uncertain of what was true and what was not at this moment than she'd been before Mabel's return to Appleton Manor?

CHAPTER 22

"There was a rumor," Pendennis reported, "that La Renaudie was here in Paris last week, lodging with a Calvinist lawyer, but we were unable to confirm it, or to make contact with him."

"An elusive fellow," Sir Robert remarked. He'd already given Pendennis an account of his adventures in Blois, though he'd omitted Queen Catherine's final gesture. An hour after the queen mother's departure from his rooms, a lusty Scotswoman from Queen Mary's retinue had appeared at his door.

"La Renaudie is a man I grow more and more loath to trust," Pendennis admitted.

"What have you learned?"

"That he was convicted of forgery and fled France for Geneva. There he began to recruit malcontents: students, artisans, unemployed soldiers, and mercenaries. By some mysterious means he obtained a pardon from Henri II just before that monarch's death. Thus he has been able to return to France with his new followers and reclaim his estates in Périgord."

"But he still foments rebellion?"

"More than ever. He seems to target the landless younger sons of noble families."

"I mislike the sound of this," Sir Robert said.

"You have no choice but to meet with him."

"Aye. The queen commands it. Does it strike you we've too many queens these days, Pendennis? Catherine wants to be regent in France. Marie of Guise, Queen Mary's mother, is already regent in Scotland. Elizabeth controls England."

"Do not forget the regent of the Netherlands," Pendennis pointed out with a smile. "Margaret of Parma."

"That Scots clergyman, Knox, has the right of it," Sir Robert grumbled. " 'Tis a monstrous regiment of women."

"Knox does object, I think, only when they are Catholic women. Still, it is as well our Elizabeth does not ally herself with her papist sisters. Working together they would be a formidable force indeed." He grinned suddenly. "Speaking of forceful women, did you find your letter?"

Sir Robert grimaced. "Aye. Another from my wife, as I am certain you have already divined. Full of questions this time."

"About your mission here?"

"No. This enterprise is of her own making. She is still in Lancashire." She wanted his impressions of certain people she had encountered there.

"Well, 'twill keep her occupied while you are away," Pendennis said.

Sir Robert let Pendennis think so and kept his concerns to himself. He could not like Susanna's stated intention to dig into both Bexwith's death and his father's. She might uncover far more than she expected, and as long as he was stuck here in France, he had no way to stop her from making matters public.

Late that night, when he was alone, he took up pen and parchment and began his answer to her letter. He had little hope he could convince Susanna to return to Kent. He reasoned that if he told her most of what he knew, however, he might limit the number of questions she asked the neighbors.

He began with Grimshaw, an easy task since he'd had but few dealings with the fellow. He'd met the lawyer once, he wrote, when he'd gone north to settle his father's estate.

He remembered the journey well. Newly knighted, fresh from the Battle of Saint-Quentin, he'd received word that his father was dead. He'd ridden night and day to reach Appleton Manor, anxious to be done with the business of burying the old man so that he might return to court. He had not even bothered to return to Kent first and tell Susanna what had happened. He'd made do with a curt note, informing her that Sir George had died.

Sir George's death had been an accident. Randall Denholm, as nearest justice of the peace, had ruled it so. Of the involvement of the girl, Edith, no mention had been made. Not to him. By the same token, Susanna's report of the events leading up to Sir George's fall came as no surprise. He wondered what age this Edith was. The last he'd known, his father had been fond of very young women. The older he'd gotten, the younger he'd liked them.

Sir Robert had not stayed at Appleton Manor any longer than necessary. John Bexwith had been in charge for years and Robert had been content to let that arrangement continue. He'd ordered the accounts sent to Leigh Abbey for Susanna to oversee at Michaelmas. Otherwise, Bexwith had been given complete freedom to run the estate.

When he had written all that in his letter to his wife, Sir Robert added what little he knew about the other servants. He did not, in truth, remember much about any of them. He'd been nineteen when he'd left Lancashire for good. In the fifteen long years since, he'd been back only that once. He'd never met the girl Grizel, nor Edith, either. He remembered Mabel Hussey more for her gooseberry tarts than her person. Bexwith had been in the background all of his life, but Sir Robert had never known much about the person behind the steward. He had not cared to learn.

He paused as he considered what to say about the Denholm family. They had been his neighbors as a boy. He'd certainly known Jane well when she was a girl. But what did he really have to say about Randall or Effie? They'd been aloof from him when he was a child, wanting no more to do with him than they had with their own children. Catherine had not even been born yet when he'd lived in Lancashire. He remembered that there had been several other children who'd died young, and wrote that down, but there was little else he could tell Susanna. Certainly he could not write that Denholm and Appleton had shared the services of a Catholic priest well after such a thing was against the law of England.

Sir Robert was of two minds how much to say about his father and Jane Denholm. There was much he could reveal, but to what purpose? Both were long dead. It might be best to let their secrets, and his own, die with them.

Reading his wife's letter once more, Sir Robert realized that she'd unearthed a good many facts for herself in the short time she'd been at Appleton Manor. This missive had been penned right after Mabel Hussey's return, and had taken some two weeks to reach Paris. He wondered what else she had learned in the interim. Perhaps nothing. He hoped that was the case. After all, she was a stranger, a "foreigner" by local standards. With luck, she'd already found out all she was going to.

Sir Robert added a paragraph strongly suggesting that she return to Kent and was about to seal the letter when he remembered the gift the queen mother of France had sent, along with the delightful Scotswoman to share his bed that last night at Blois. It was a single, thrice-folded piece of parchment. Written on the outside, in French, was an inscription: "For inclusion in Lady Appleton's cautionary herbal."

Sir Robert thought a moment longer, then added a single line beneath Queen Catherine's words. He enclosed the sheet inside his own thrice-folded letter to Susanna. He was smiling to himself as he sent for a servant to take the packet and start it on its way back to England. It was a good thing that he trusted his wife, he thought. Otherwise it might prove passing dangerous to thwart a woman who knew as much as she did about poisons.

CHAPTER 23

Susanna Appleton took her letter from the messenger and glanced at the seal. As she'd expected, it was an apple pierced through with an arrow, her husband's crest. She lost no time breaking the wax and unfolding the missive. A quick glance told her that the speed at which a message could be carried from Paris to Lancashire was improving. He'd written on St. Martin's Day, the eleventh of November, and this was only the twentieth, the Feast of St. Andrew.

She smiled slightly, struck by a thought. How slow people were to change. The law had reduced the number of saint's days in England from ninety-five feasts and thirty saint's eves to twenty-seven, but the old dates still lingered in memory and the discarded names were difficult to abandon entirely. Even the courts still divided their terms by the old calendar.

Her smile faded as she began to read. Torn between pleasure and frustration, she skimmed the rest of the missive from her husband. He wanted her to go home, back to Leigh Abbey, but he gave no reason that made sense to her. He spoke vaguely of the dangers of lawless Lancashire, but she well knew that he was the one in the Appleton family who took risks daily. Every time he went abroad there was a possibility that he would not return.

Shrugging her concern for his safety aside, Susanna read the letter again, more carefully this time. In spite of his obvious disapproval because she'd disobeyed him and journeyed north, he had endeavored to answer her questions. Unfortunately, what he had to say did not help. The servants now at Appleton Manor were unknown to him, except for Mabel. He had little to say about Bexwith and seemed to know Lawyer Grimshaw even less well. Neither did he have anything of value to report about his father's neighbors at Denholm.

"I shall be greatly distressed," he wrote at the end, "if I return home to find you still in the north. I desire your presence at Leigh Abbey and trust you will be there, waiting for me and tending to your duties as my wife."

"But you are not here to enforce your will," Susanna said softly, "and to my mind, I am tending to my wifely duties very well indeed."

For the last few weeks she'd been extremely busy, supervising the building and repairs she wanted done before winter. She had not had time yet to journey a third time to Manchester and pursue her inquiries, though she had spoken again to Jack the tiler. He made no secret of his dislike for Bexwith or his opinion that the steward had deserved an ignominious death. Had he taken a hand in it? He'd certainly had motive and opportunity. On the other hand, he seemed the sort more likely to bludgeon an enemy to death than resort to poison.

Turning her attention to the second page, Susanna noted that on the outside, beneath the strange handwriting that earmarked the contents for her herbal, her husband had penned an enigmatic sentence. She had to read it twice before she understood.

"From a very great lady," Sir Robert had written, "whose family knows well the properties of *aqua tofana.*"

Aqua tofana. Susanna stared at the name, searching her memory. *Aqua tofana* was also known as *aqua di Napoli*. It was a poison. Arsenic combined with cantharides, if she remembered aright. Four to six drops in water or wine were enough to kill a strong man in minutes, and that method of ridding itself of enemies was popularly believed to be a favorite of the Italian family of the queen mother of France.

With fingers that trembled just a little, Susanna opened the paper. Inside had been written, again in French, that a very simple and effective antidote for "all poisons that speed the heart" was to force the victim to vomit up the evil, then dose him with a mixture that contained a large quantity of poppy syrup. "Though it be a poison in itself," Susanna translated, "given as an antidote it does not kill."

She studied the list of other ingredients, assessing their probable effectiveness. Nettle root. Columbine. Wormwood. Those were familiar antidotes. But mixed with dried saffron? Burdock root? Dandelion root?

Leaving the letter from Sir Robert on a table, Susanna took the second page and sought the greater privacy of her stillroom. She spent the next few hours making notes in her herbal, oblivious to any distraction. She was not sure she trusted this remedy, coming as it did from the notorious Queen Catherine, but it made more sense as a cure than hanging part of a stag's heart in a silk bag around a victim's neck in order to draw poison out of the body.

If there had been poison used against John Bexwith, what poison had it been? Susanna turned her attention to the question, searching through all those toxic plants she'd marked for inclusion in her herbal, looking for any that were readily available in Lancashire and would produce wide, staring eyes and would act in half an hour or less.

Unless Bexwith's retching had sent him into the pie with such force that he lost consciousness and smothered. Susanna shuddered, but it was a possibility she should consider, even if it did increase the number of entries on her list of possible poisons.

It meant she had to reconsider mandrake and banewort, too.

What irony if banewort turned out to be the most likely cause of death. No one had mentioned dry, red skin, though, a characteristic effect. And usually, in the first half hour, the victim had only lost the power of speech, not consciousness.

A more likely suspect was the thimbleflower. Cooking did not lessen the potency of the poison. It showed effects in twenty to thirty minutes, though it generally took longer than that to kill.

Setting aside the possibility of death by asphyxiation, Susanna finally narrowed her suspects down to three: monkshood, cowbane, and henbane.

Monkshood could cause death in ten minutes. The antidote was yew. She made a note to be sure she had an ample supply on hand. She liked to be prepared for any eventuality, and with monkshood, those who were treated and survived were almost fully recovered twenty-four hours later.

Death from ingesting cowbane came as quickly as twenty minutes. The root had a sweet taste, too, making it easy to confuse with edible plants. If the queen mother's mixture worked against poisons that speeded the heart, it should be effective against that one.

Then there was henbane, for which nettle alone was a known remedy. The root could kill in a quarter of an hour, but what if it had been cooked? She could scarcely experiment on her retainers as she'd heard the Medicis did.

The pounding of a headache finally forced Susanna to stop puzzling over a mystery she despaired of solving. It did no harm to keep all manner of antidotes near at hand, but she was no closer to deciding if murder had been done, let alone by what means.

What did she know? That Bexwith had showed signs of recent prosperity, possibly from extorting money from someone about Sir George's murder. That theory held up only if Sir George had, in fact, been pushed down those stairs. The only hard evidence Susanna had that anything untoward had happened at Appleton Manor was that someone had gone to a great

deal of trouble to create a ghost to blame, even having it
"appear" to Susanna herself.

That meant something. But what?

She pushed away from her worktable and went in search of
food and drink, but she was only temporarily abandoning her
quest. Before she left Lancashire, she silently vowed, she would
have all the answers.

CHAPTER 24

At that same moment, Catherine Denholm watched with
unbridled curiosity as the girl called Bess, now a serving maid
at Appleton Manor, delivered into Matthew Grimshaw's hands
at Denholm Hall a piece of folded parchment. He read it
through, smiled to himself, and placed it on the desk in Randall
Denholm's study. A coin changed hands, and Bess departed in
great haste.

Hesitant, Catherine hovered in the doorway. She had almost
decided to retreat when Matthew looked up and saw her.

"Catherine!" His delight was evident and he opened his
arms. "My dear cousin, come and let me have a good look at
you. I vow you become more like your sister every year."

"I am nothing like Jane," Catherine murmured, but she
obediently entered the room and endured her cousin's welcom-
ing kiss.

"How old are you now, my dear?"

"Fourteen, cousin."

"A woman grown. You'll be thinking of marriage soon, I
warrant."

"I've time yet," she protested softly, but he did not seem to hear. As Matthew babbled on about Jane, Catherine stopped listening. It was a great waste of time, she felt, to pretend she was interested when she was not. Instead she let her cousin ramble on while she drifted toward the desk. When he was sufficiently distracted by the sound of his own voice, she took a closer look at the letter he'd been reading.

The last words inscribed were "From my lodgings in Paris, this eleventh of November, your devoted husband, Robert Appleton, Knight." Catherine would have recognized the Appleton crest even without the signature. She wondered what Sir Robert had written to Susanna, but resisted the temptation to read a personal message. Instead she plucked up the letter whole and secreted it in the placket in her skirt. Grimshaw never noticed.

Later she would decide if she could safely return her prize to Appleton Manor or if she would have to destroy it. Catherine did not understand why anyone would steal from their new neighbor, or think they could frighten her away with tricks, either. Her acquaintance with Susanna, brief though it was, had convinced Catherine that Sir Robert's wife was a strong-minded woman. To terrorize her would take far more than an eerie figure standing on the stairs and pretending to be a ghost.

CHAPTER 25

It was St. Catherine's Day, a full month after Mabel Hussey's return to Appleton Manor, before Susanna managed to make time for another trip into Manchester. It was not that the distance was so great. She simply had to look to the restoration of her husband's estate first.

Once again Susanna left Jennet behind and took Mark with her into town. Jennet was not pleased. She was beginning to have suspicions about Mark's sudden interest in visiting Manchester.

"Does she know that you met a young woman on your last visit?" Susanna asked as they neared the bridge across the river. She had no specific plan to further her inquiry by using Mark's acquaintance with Temperance Strelley, the girl who lived next door to the Inces, but she did not object to having him visit Temperance again, either.

"Nay, Lady Appleton. I'd not trouble Jennet with my private business."

"You must have hinted at something. She is most put out with you of late."

Mark only smiled with a smug, masculine superiority that made his mistress want to box his ears. Jennet deserved a few bad moments for the hard time she'd given Mark in the past, but he did not need to take such pleasure in taunting her. "I'll not have needless cruelty in my household," she warned before she let the matter drop.

"Shall I pay my visit to the Strelley house now or later, madam? It is market day. There's much to be bought for Appleton Manor."

"Have you a list?"

Mark tapped his forehead. "All in here, it is, madam. Safe for the nonce."

"And the cost?"

"They will send you bills, if you wish it, madam, or you might trust me to make payment."

Quickly calculating, Susanna delved into the leather pouch she wore at her waist. The purchases she knew of were many and varied, and would have to be made at a dozen different shops. Some, spices and cloth, she would purchase herself, but Mark would need sixpence apiece for the pigs. Fifty shillings for a hogshead of claret. Four shillings fourpence for a barrel of small beer. Oranges were three shillings tenpence for four hundred in Kent but might be far more dear in this remote place.

"What sell they in the shops near the spot where Oliver Ince has his butcher's stall?"

"South side of Conduit Place," Mark mused. A moment's thought and he had the answer. "On the north side they sell grain, crockery, wooden vessels, and fruit."

"Good. Inquire there about the oranges and at the same time observe the butcher's boy, one Dickon by name. Strike up an acquaintance with him if you can, but be careful that Oliver Ince does not recognize you as my man." She handed over a sum of money and instructed Mark to meet her in two hours' time at the shop of a draper.

"The fish market is near Smithy Door, which is hard by the man's house. What if Ince is there instead?"

"Why, the better to question his employees. I mean, as you know, to go and speak with his wife while you seek out the lad. If Ince is there, 'twill make no matter."

She said the words with confidence, but in her heart Susanna hoped to find Edith Ince alone. There was still a chance, however slight, that Oliver was behind the death of the steward. He'd hated the man enough to kill him and it seemed suspicious to her that he'd taken in the scullion from Appleton and not troubled to mention that fact to her on her last visit.

No one, Susanna had long since realized, was very forthcoming. They were all hiding things from her. In order to get to the truth, she could very well end up uncovering every one of their small secrets. Matters would be much simpler if people only told the truth, but she supposed that was too much to expect. She was, after all, a stranger among them.

Oliver Ince was not at home. Edith smiled a welcome, inviting Lady Appleton in with an openness that was almost enough to make her seem innocent of any crime. Her expression was equally guileless when Susanna asked after Dickon.

"Oh, aye. Oliver did take him in. A good man, my Oliver." Responding to a cry from the cradle, she lifted the younger child out and began to nurse.

" 'Tis strange no one mentioned to me that he'd once worked at Appleton Manor."

Edith blinked at her in surprise above the downy head of her small daughter. "But, Lady Appleton, you did not ask."

"Master Grimshaw knew I was looking for him," she said after a moment, silently acknowledging the rightness of Edith's point.

A disdainful sound told her what Edith Ince thought of him.

Susanna frowned. She had not asked the Inces about Dickon, but she had demanded information from the lawyer, and Grimshaw had first insisted he could not even remember the boy's name. When pressed, he'd recalled it but hinted the lad might have gone to family in Preston, which was some distance from Manchester. Had Grimshaw deliberately lied to her? Had he known Dickon was in Manchester all along, just as he'd known where to find Mabel Hussey?

"Did you know what became of the man, too? Adam Bone?"

"He were taken on as swineherd," Edith replied promptly. If she was trying to hide something, it was not that.

"I would speak with both of them," Susanna told her, "to learn all I can of what happened at Appleton Manor." Belatedly, it occurred to her that Adam Bone and the boy Dickon and Mabel, too, must have known where Edith was. How, then, did the rumor that she was Appleton's ghost get started?

The answer troubled her, for it had been Euphemia Denholm who had let her jump to that erroneous conclusion. To protect her late daughter's reputation? Perhaps. But something did not fit. The more Susanna learned about these people, the more confusing matters seemed.

"Oliver keeps the lad busy." There was the first sign of hesitation now in Edith's words. "We've naught to hide, and yet he will be angry, I fear, if young Dickon be distracted from his work. And he does not know anything. He'd have told me if he did."

"I'd still like to speak with him myself, if your husband will allow it."

Edith was silent for a long moment. The older child, awakened from a nap, wandered into the room, and for the first time Susanna looked carefully at him. It had been scarce two years since Oliver and Edith married. This was either a very big boy for his age, or she'd been breeding ere they wed. Through narrowed eyes she regarded the child more closely still, looking for any resemblance to the Appletons.

As if she followed her visitor's thoughts, Edith hastily divested herself of the baby, returning her to the cradle, and snatched up her son. "He's Ince's get, and make no mistake about that. Sir George never touched me."

"Now, Edith, it is common knowledge that Sir George had his codpiece all undone when he was found dead."

"Then he were relieving himself, or found a more willing woman after I fled."

No nervousness accompanied this statement. Her eyes did not shift away. Her hands did not tremble. She believed what she was saying and Susanna believed it, too, even if it did complicate matters.

Had there been another woman there that night?

Mark was waiting for his mistress when she came out of the draper's shop, and took the packages that contained crimson satin at three shillings a yard and yellow kersey at four shillings sevenpence an ell.

"I need also to purchase eight pair of knitted hose," she told him as they began to walk toward a shop that carried such things.

Three shillings and fourpence changed hands. Once more in the street, Susanna asked Mark for his report.

"The boy knows nothing. He saw no ghost at Appleton. Nor any strangers about. Neither did he know Sir George."

"Did he watch Mabel prepare the marrow-bone pie?"

"No, madam. He was busy with his own chores."

Susanna frowned. Did it matter? Mabel hadn't added the poison, if there had been poison. Someone else had slipped that in. Or given Bexwith a poisoned root, convincing him it was candied eryngo. Ince? His wife? Dickon himself, already promised employment? If any of those three had, the lad would never admit it, not unless she had more than guesses to go on. Grizel's father? One of the Denholms? Grimshaw? Everyone seemed to have disliked Bexwith, but where was a strong enough motive to kill?

The next stop was for spices, and Susanna vented her frustration on the shopkeeper, who dared charge ten shillings and sixpence for a pound of cinnamon. A like amount of ginger was more reasonable, at three shillings and eightpence.

Susanna left their purchases at the inn where she would spend the night. She meant to attend church at St. Mary's on the morrow, then return to Appleton Manor, but first she had another task to perform. In Mark's company, she began the long walk to Collyhurst. It was only midafternoon, giving her ample time to confront Adam Bone.

He turned out to be a surly, sly creature, who answered questions with great reluctance. It soon became plain that the swineherd could tell them no more than young Dickon had. He did, however, deny he'd seen any ghost. Only a body and a hysterical serving wench.

Discouraged, Susanna returned to Manchester with nothing for her pains but sore feet and a lingering smell of pig. She debated paying an evening visit to Matthew Grimshaw, torn between the urge to confront him with the knowledge that he'd lied to her and an equally strong desire to avoid him altogether until she knew more.

"Where was Grimshaw when Bexwith died?" she murmured aloud.

"With Mistress Denholm," Mark replied.

At her invitation he was sharing a pot of ale with her in the common room at the inn, a situation that had earned them several curious stares and one look of outrage. She was the only women in the place, and though she was clearly of gentle birth, she was just as clearly treating a servant as an equal. People did not know what to make of either circumstance.

Mark's words took a moment to sink in, and even then she wasn't sure she'd heard correctly. "What did you say?"

Mark seemed surprised that she did not already know. "He visited Denholm Hall that day. Grizel told Jennet and she told me."

Bewildered, Susanna took a long swallow of her ale. "Why do you suppose he was there?"

Mark frowned. "Jennet did not say."

"Which means she did not think to ask." Susanna sighed as she reluctantly reached that conclusion. She would question Jennet when they returned to Appleton Manor, but she did not think there would be more to learn. Not yet.

"Madam," Mark said hesitantly. He ran one finger around the rim of his cup. "What if you are wrong? What if there has been no crime committed, after all? This could be no more than an old man dropping dead and a maid's runaway imagination."

"You think Grizel invented our ghost?"

"I think she is not so sure of what she saw as it first seemed. Jennet says she is oddly hesitant to speak of it, but that she came to Appleton Manor to visit without a qualm the last time her father wanted to measure the chapel. She was not as afraid as Jennet thought she'd be. I am thinking that the shock of finding John Bexwith dead may have addled her brain."

"Then how do you explain what we saw?"

"There is that."

"Yes. There is that."

Susanna said nothing more, but she was thinking hard. Had someone seen in the girl's fanciful story a means to accomplish some other end? The result of the rumor had been to leave Appleton Manor deserted. Had that been the intent?

Or had someone simply wanted to encourage Sir Robert to come north?

The latter idea alarmed her, but the more she thought about it, the more sense it made. How had she altered matters, she wondered, by coming in his stead?

CHAPTER 26

Early in the morning on the first Sunday of December, Sir Robert Appleton presented himself at a modest country house just outside La Rochelle. The town was a stronghold of those with Calvinist leanings.

He was shown at once into the principal room, but it was not La Renaudie who waited for him there. A small, delicate female figure stood in a window alcove, shadowed by a burgundy-colored velvet curtain that had been looped back just to her right. Behind her the diamond-paned leaded windows overlooked the cobble-stone courtyard below. She had obviously been watching his arrival.

"Mademoiselle," he said with a deep bow.

He thought she smiled, but he could not see her face well enough to tell. Was she La Renaudie's mistress? She was not his wife, of that he was certain. And there was no sign of the elusive rabble-rouser himself.

"Come," the woman said, speaking a charmingly accented English. "Services are about to begin. I think you will enjoy hearing our new French versions of some of the Psalms."

As she came into the light, Sir Robert saw that she was young, and very beautiful. Her dark hair and eyes were in stark contrast to pale, flawless skin. "How shall I call you, ma belle?" he inquired.

A faint smile flickered and was gone. "Diane," she said.

Two hours later, Sir Robert was no closer to knowing her identity, but he had ascertained that she was a widow, and a wealthy one at that. Her household was run with an efficiency even Susanna would have approved, but with considerably more emphasis on luxury. The mysterious Diane was a hedonist, for all her claims to follow Calvin's teachings.

At long last, La Renaudie arrived for their meeting. He brought with him a secretary and a servant and, to Sir Robert's surprise, he did not dismiss Diane. Observing them together, Sir Robert concluded that his earlier guess had been correct. She was the man's mistress and appeared to be completely devoted to him. A great pity, Sir Robert thought. He had begun to hope the lovely Diane might be willing to provide him with a pleasant diversion during the night ahead.

Recalled to business, he listened with growing alarm as La Renaudie outlined his plans. There was an element of fanaticism in the plot that boded ill for its success. Sir Robert diplomatically declined to point out the flaws, for he had come only to listen and observe.

None of his impressions of La Renaudie were favorable. The fellow thought very highly of himself, refusing to entertain the slightest doubt that he would succeed. He based his certainty not only upon his own abilities but upon those of one he called only *le chef muet,* the silent leader. At the penultimate moment, he claimed, this powerful nobleman would reveal himself and lead them to victory.

"How can I ask my queen's help without knowing the name of this eminent person?" Sir Robert asked.

La Renaudie was adamant. "Those who know are willing to face torture, even death, rather than reveal his identity too soon."

Sir Robert could guess who the silent leader might be, but even if he was right, he had no faith in the outcome of the revolution La Renaudie seemed so sure would succeed. All the same, he demanded details. He was somewhat surprised to be given them.

"We plan armed uprisings in Normandie, Bretagne, Gascogne, Champagne, and the Limousin," La Renaudie confided. "The main force will gather at Nantes, at the mouth of the Loire, for from that point they will be in a position to attack any of the royal châteaux in Touraine. Wherever the court is, we will have access by land and water."

More and more, Sir Robert was reminded of the ill-fated rebellion Sir Thomas Wyatt had attempted in England during the reign of Queen Mary. This plan had many of the same flaws, not the least of which involved the number of people who knew details of it in advance. La Renaudie did not intend to move against the court until March. In three months a great deal could go wrong.

The delay was in large part due to a desire to solicit aid from abroad, in particular from the church leaders in Geneva and from the English queen. Sir Robert suspected that Elizabeth would be sensible enough to avoid such a dangerous entanglement. In fact, he intended to advise her to do so, but he said nothing of that to La Renaudie. This revolt was both ill planned and ill timed and he suspected that it would end by accomplishing the one thing the rebels least desired, a union between the rival Catholic factions headed by the Guise brothers on one hand and the queen mother on the other.

As the day turned to evening, Sir Robert's dislike of both the plan and the planner increased. When, on his way to bed, he came upon La Renaudie in a hallway, blatantly seducing one of the maids, Sir Robert was appalled.

It was true enough that he was not always faithful to Susanna, but he had never taken another woman in the same house where his wife was staying. His certainty that La Renaudie would be spending the remainder of the night in Diane's chambers made the Frenchman's actions seem even more reprehensible.

"You do not approve," Diane remarked the next morning as they watched La Renaudie and his men ride away.

Sir Robert considered her gravely, wondering to what, exactly, she referred. He was tempted to warn her against her lover. Both as a man and as a political force, La Renaudie was dangerous to all those foolish enough to become involved with him. In the end, however, he said only, "I am but a humble messenger, ma belle. I have no opinions of mine own."

Diane smiled at that, and reached up to touch his cheek with one soft fingertip. "I think you are much, much more than a messenger, Sir Robert Appleton. And you are most assuredly not a humble man."

He caught her hand, lifting her knuckles to his lips. Her eyes danced with a challenge, daring him to try to seduce the rebel leader's woman. He contented himself with issuing an invitation.

"If he does not succeed, Diane, and you find yourself in need of refuge, remember always that you have a friend in England."

CHAPTER 27

"She continues to ask questions."

"She will learn nothing," Grimshaw said in a placating voice. He hoped he was telling the truth. "There is nothing for her to find out."

"We accomplish nothing, either."

"Sir Robert is not even in England," Grimshaw pointed out. "The letter I saw indicates he may be abroad for some time yet."

"The letter you lost."

Grimshaw made no reply. There was nothing he could say. He hadn't a clue what had happened to the thrice-folded piece of parchment. His only real regret was that he'd not thought quickly enough and said he'd burned it after perusing its contents. If he'd been clever, he'd never have confessed to misplacing it.

That letter, wherever it was now, had indicated that Lady Appleton had asked specific questions of her husband, questions about those she'd encountered at Appleton Manor and Denholm Hall and in Manchester. Grimshaw did not like the implications, but neither could he think of anything he could do to rectify the situation. He had not spoken directly to Lady Appleton since her first visit to the market town.

A harsh sound, the clearing of a throat, broke into his thoughts. "I suppose that girl, Bess, thought better of her theft and returned the letter to Appleton Manor."

"No doubt of it, though of course I have no way of confirming my suspicion without betraying that she stole it in the first place to bring to me."

"How much does the cook know?"

"Very little, I do think, else Lady Appleton would have made some move by now. Sir Robert's wife did not speak to the coroner or to the constable or to any other justice when she was in Manchester." Neither had her man been anywhere near them. Grimshaw, himself one of Manchester's justices of the peace, took hope from that. "Perhaps she does not suspect there was anything unusual about Bexwith's death after all."

He wished he didn't.

"Then why all the questions? Why her annoying interest in poisons?"

Grimshaw swallowed hard. "Poisons?"

"She does not believe in our ghost."

In spite of his best efforts to deny the truth, Matthew Grimshaw was no longer able to ignore the oddness of John Bexwith's death. "The ghost," he began, his voice tinged with desperation, "the ghost—"

"The ghost may serve my purpose yet again, even with all the people presently living at Appleton Manor. The servants are still properly frightened of spirits and keep to their beds at night. Only Lady Appleton seems to lack fear . . . to the point of most foolhardy behavior."

Grimshaw bit back a sound of dismay. This was madness, surely. Why could not his employer leave well enough alone?

"I must have Sir Robert here in Lancashire. Did the letter hint at any affection between husband and wife? Can we use her to lure him north?"

''What difference would that make? Until he's finished with the queen's business, he'll not be allowed to come here.''

''But there might be word waiting for him upon his return to England, a message that will bring him north in all haste. Not her death. That could be too easily handled by minions. No, an accident, I think. Something crippling, so that she cannot travel south and he must perforce come to her. Yes. He must find an alarming message waiting for him at Leigh Abbey, instead of his beloved wife.''

''Lies?'' Grimshaw asked hopefully.

A contemptuous look was his only answer and he knew the truth without hearing it. Lady Appleton was going to have an accident in which she would be seriously hurt. And there was nothing Matthew Grimshaw dared do to prevent it.

CHAPTER 28

Susanna woke, pulled from a deep and dreamless sleep by a loud thump. It was not repeated and she was uncertain whence it had come.

The room was chilled, for the fire had gone out, but it was warm enough beneath the piled blankets. The hangings around her bed kept out the cold, as well, but they did not quite meet on the side she was facing.

She attempted to drift off again but it was no use. It was not just the hangings that were at fault. The old wooden shutters, which she had not yet replaced, were cracked and bowed and let in the bright beams of a moon at the full.

For some reason, this excess of light was sufficient to hold back slumber. Reluctantly, she threw aside the covers and shoved the bed hangings the rest of the way apart and felt with her bare toes for the leather shoes she'd left on the cold stone floor.

It was the business of a moment to struggle into her warm velvet night robe and open the shutters the rest of the way. A film of frozen condensation coated the newly installed glass windowpane, obscuring her view, but there was now light enough within the room to show her that the washbasin had a thin coat of ice atop the water. She considered waking Jennet, whose job it was to tend the fire, but the maid's gentle snores deterred her. Jennet worked as hard as anyone at Appleton Manor. Susanna stirred the embers back to life herself and let her servant sleep.

A faint sound caught her attention just as the flame caught, a low moaning that seemed to come from outside. Puzzled, Susanna returned to the window and wiped a patch clear with the side of her hand. Her view encompassed the rear of Appleton Hall, extending as far the apple orchard and including the small stone chapel where Dame Cat had made her home.

It was the chapel that drew her gaze. A dim light shone inside, a light that should not have been burning at this hour of the night. *So,* she thought, *our ghost has returned.*

Hoarfrost covered the ground and from this angle, by the light of the moon, Susanna could just make out a track where someone had walked. Each step had made an impression, leaving her in no doubt that a flesh-and-blood person had crossed the yard, and recently, to haunt the chapel.

Convinced the specter would flee again if she did not hurry, Susanna did not waste time waking her servants. Armed only with the fireplace poker, she hurried down the stairs and out into the night. She slowed her pace as she approached the chapel door, proceeding more cautiously.

The door creaked softly as she opened it, but there was no other sound but her own breathing and the pounding of her heart. Tightening her grip on the makeshift weapon until it bit into the soft insides of her hands, she advanced one slow step at a time.

Within, the moonlight created an eerie effect, its beams distorted by the stained glass in the windows. The single candle guttering on the altar revealed little beyond a small circle of light.

"Are you there?" Susanna whispered. Then, in a stronger voice, she issued a challenge. "Show yourself and state your case. Ghosts do not haunt without reason."

Nor did they light candles, but at this moment Susanna was unsure which she'd less like to encounter, a spirit or a fellow human being bent on mischief. Either would be unwelcome, but she could hardly shirk her duty now. This might be her best chance to find out the truth.

Pale, filmy fabric stirred, catching Susanna's attention. Her quarry was behind the altar. As she watched, an equally pale bare arm was extended. The apparition beckoned, wanting her to come closer.

She wished she'd brought a torch.

She wondered why the cat and her kittens made no sound.

She obeyed the summons anyway, approaching the mysterious spirit who had been haunting Appleton Manor. Her trepidation increased, in spite of her growing certainty that this was no supernatural being. A ghost could not have made those footprints, she repeated silently, to reassure herself. And she was dealing with a small person, one she could overcome physically if it came to that. Those thoughts gave Susanna the courage to continue.

Almost at her goal, she extended her own hand, palm up. "Talk to me," she urged. "Tell me why you have come."

What was now clearly a woman, her face hidden by a thin veil and her form draped in the loose, concealing folds of some heavier fabric, backed away. When Susanna began to follow, her quarry turned and ran.

"Stay!" Even as she called out, Susanna knew that the only way she'd persuade the other woman to talk was to catch her. Intent upon learning who had come to haunt Appleton Manor, she launched a rapid pursuit.

She never saw the opening beneath her feet. One moment she was racing across solid stone. The next she was plunging downward, straight into the vault that held the remains of all the past generations of Appletons. Susanna felt a sharp pain in her leg as she landed, but she had no time to cry out. Her head struck against the side of a coffin and that rendered her unconscious even before her bruised and battered body came to rest on the flagged floor of the crypt.

CHAPTER 29

Jennet was puzzled to wake and find the shutters open wide. Grumbling to herself, she got out of bed and went to close them again, not even noticing that Lady Appleton was gone from the room. What she did see was a ghostly figure fleeing from the chapel, its shape even more fearsome in the moonlight.

"Lady Appleton! 'Tis the ghost!" Jennet all but threw herself into the large bed, but there was no one there to offer comfort. A terrible coldness came over her as she realized what that meant.

Lady Appleton had gone ghost hunting. Jennet was sure of it. And she was certain, too, that something terrible had happened to her mistress.

Her shouts roused the household. Jennet was trembling so badly that she could scarce make herself understood. Bess paled at the very mention of the ghost. Mark's expression grew grim when he heard that Lady Appleton was missing.

"Where did you see the ghost?" he demanded, shaking Jennet a little in his agitation.

She jerked away from him, rubbing her bare, bruised shoulder and pulling the coverlet she had wrapped about herself tight once more. "It was coming out of the chapel."

"Fulke. Lionel. Bring torches and come with me."

Jennet and the other women servants followed after, terrified of what they might find and yet equally afraid to remain behind. Mark went first, cautiously, into the chapel.

"Why has the vault been opened?" Jennet heard him demand. No one had an answer for him. "Be careful where you step," he ordered next, sounding authoritative and in control, but in the next moment, just as Jennet braved the interior, he cried out in dismay.

His torch, held out over the gap in the paving stones, revealed what Jennet most dreaded. The body of her mistress lay fully six feet below the servants who'd gathered to search for her.

"The ghost has killed her," Bess wailed. Hands over her eyes she turned and ran, nearly colliding with the open door of the chapel on her way out.

Mabel moved a little closer to the opening. "Mayn't be dead." She grabbed Lionel and shoved him toward the hole. "Ye be most agile. Get ye down there and see."

Scrambling to obey and fighting tears at the same time, the lad leapt into the vault. He pushed aside a fireplace poker that had fallen with her and knelt by Lady Appleton's side, then looked as if he feared to touch her.

"Put your fingertips on her neck," Jennet called down.

She was determined that Mabel should not be the one to take charge. Lady Appleton was her responsibility, not the cook's. Indeed, it was most suspicious that the cook was taking such an interest. The other servants Lady Appleton had hired since coming north had all followed Bess's lead and fled. And Mabel was dressed, her kirtle laced up over her shift as if she'd been up already when the alarm was sounded.

"She's alive," Lionel called. "I feel the rush of her blood. But she's very cold." He struggled out of his heavy wool shirt and put it over Lady Appleton, shivering as his torso was bared to the cold December night.

"We must lift her," Mark murmured.

"May be she is injured," Mabel objected. "Ye could make matters worse."

" 'Tis certain she is injured, but 'tis just as certain that she's cold and unconscious. We can do nothing for her until we get her out of there."

Suiting action to words, he sent Fulke for a ladder, then carefully lowered himself into the vault. Working together, he and Lionel lifted Lady Appleton's limp form high above their heads, high enough that Mabel and Jennet could catch hold of her and slide her onto the floor of the chapel.

Her breathing was very shallow and she had a lump rising on the back of her head, but there was another injury, as well. Lady Appleton had a deep gash in her leg, one that ran from ankle to knee.

Jennet bandaged it as best she could with strips Mabel tore from the bottom of her shift and handed over. Jennet hoped to stanch the flow of blood, but she knew her own shortcomings. It was Lady Appleton who understood doctoring and remedies.

"Bring her inside," Jennet ordered, her voice unsteady and tears prickling at the backs of her eyes. "We must send to Manchester for a physician."

"Little good that will do." Mabel grumbled. Then she suggested calling in a cunning woman who lived not far beyond Gorebury.

Torn between her uncertainty about Mabel and her need to help her mistress, Jennet chewed her lower lip until it bled. She did not quite trust Mabel, but neither did she fear her. It had most assuredly not been Mabel she'd seen running away from the chapel in filmy white robes.

"Send for both," she decided at last. Lionel and Fulke could be dispatched each for one.

Lady Appleton moaned softly. She opened her eyes and called out for water.

Abruptly, Jennet forgot everything but seeing to her mistress's comfort.

CHAPTER 30

With the dawn, word came to Denholm Hall that a terrible accident had befallen Lady Appleton. The story had already been embellished, turning the apparition in the chapel into a fearful specter that smelled of fire and brimstone and had long talons for fingers. All the servants had reportedly left, running clear back to Manchester. It was even said that Lady Appleton was like to die from her injuries.

Believing the last to be true, Catherine Denholm fled to the sanctuary of her father's study, deeply troubled. Susanna had been lured into danger, but had the intent been merely to frighten, or to do grievous harm?

At first she was unable to understand how the stone that covered the entrance to the family vault had come to be removed. Then she realized that she knew who had been in the chapel earlier that evening. A little sob escaped her. As much as she wished she had the strength of character to tell her neighbor everything she suspected, she did not dare speak up.

Catherine roamed her father's study, idly picking things up and putting them down again, trying to think, trying to reason out not only what had happened but why. Nearly an hour passed, in which she came to no clear conclusions. Then her mother interrupted her, demanding to know what she was doing.

"Nothing," Catherine said.

"Then why did you start when I spoke? Why do you twist your hands together?"

" 'Tis nothing." Around her mother, Catherine nearly always felt ill at ease. And sometimes guilty, too, whether she'd done anything wrong or not.

" 'Tis something. Tell me now, Catherine, or it will go hard on you."

"I was only thinking."

"About what?"

"I was wondering why so many people wish the Appletons harm."

"What people?"

"Cousin Matthew. Jack the tiler. You and Father."

At first she thought her mother would not answer. Then, with a grimace, Euphemia Denholm said curtly, "You know why Randall and I disliked Sir George. That old reprobate was to blame for Jane's death."

"But—"

"Your father is ... disturbed in his mind. He has never gotten over losing Jane. But he is still head of this family ..." Her voice trailed off as she made a helpless gesture with one hand, as if to say, What can we do but accept our duty?

"I do not understand how you can defend actions that harm another. You—"

"Let it be, Catherine. Do as your father and I tell you, always, and all will be well." Without another word, Euphemia left the room.

She assumed she would be obeyed.

The confrontation only increased Catherine's anxiety. For a long while, in the quiet of the study, she stood with head hung low, her mind reviewing all the unanswered questions.

Why would no one explain?

Catherine shuddered, remembering what she'd been coerced into doing, but she was suddenly certain that if she tried to tell anyone that the ghost was a fraud she would only make matters worse. She would be blamed. The authorities would think she'd devised the scheme herself, that she was mad. She'd be locked up for the rest of her life.

She had no real choice. She had to continue to be an obedient daughter. She did not dare confess to Susanna Appleton or anyone else.

Guilt threatened to overwhelm her.

What if Lady Appleton died?

Tears flowed at that thought and Catherine bolted, fleeing in spite of the cold to seek what comfort she could in Denholm's dormant flower garden. But there was no respite there, nor inspiration. No escape from the terrible possibility that she might share the blood of a murderer.

CHAPTER 31

A week after her fall, Susanna was ill-tempered and restless. She could hobble about on her injured leg, but it pained her too much to stay up for long. She knew rest was essential for a full recovery, so most of the time she remained in her bed, one foot propped up on pillows, thinking about all the things she'd rather be doing. For a woman who usually enjoyed good health, this was an ordeal.

She did not even have Jennet for company. With the desertion of most of the servants, her companion had been recruited to help the few who were left. Mark had gone into Manchester twice, offering employment, but he'd found no one willing to take on Appleton Manor's ghost. Word had spread far and wide that the specter was out for blood. Few wished to risk life or limb by coming near.

Gossip had also reached Jennet that Mark was taking time to pay calls on Temperance Strelley, which put the maidservant in a foul mood to match that of her mistress. Susanna did not know whether to be amused or irritated by the reaction. Since she'd been the one to suggest that Mark continue to visit the

Strelley house, the better to find out what their neighbors, the Inces, were up to, she could scarce demand that he stop going there now.

When she felt better, Susanna promised herself, she would sit down and have a heart-to-heart talk with Jennet about men and marriage and compromise. She was, after all, something of an expert on the subject.

A faint rap drew her attention to the door. Catherine Denholm hesitated in the opening, her eyes darting nervously about the bedchamber as if she, too, expected to be confronted by a supernatural being.

"Ah—Catherine. Come in, my dear." If Susanna's voice sounded heartier than usual, it only reflected the fact that she was starved for conversation. Her smile was genuine. Trapped here as she was, she much preferred a visit from Catherine to one from Catherine's overwhelming mother.

"If I do not disturb your rest . . ."

"Never think it. I've rested enough to take me into the new year." Susanna patted the side of the bed. "Come and sit down and tell me how the world outside does."

"Much the same as ever, I do fear."

As Catherine launched into an amusing anecdote concerning the escape of a milch cow from the barn, Susanna's eyes narrowed. Away from Euphemia's dominance, her young daughter was a surprise. Her narrow face and high forehead would prevent her ever having the softly rounded features that presently constituted beauty, but the blossoming of color on her cheeks worked wonders and her dark eyes were marvelously expressive.

" 'Tis a dull time of year," Catherine concluded. "We have nothing better to speak of than cows . . . and your impending demise. Your fall in the chapel has sparked much speculation."

As if uncertain how Lady Appleton would take that news, Catherine shifted her gaze to the distant horizon visible through the window. She toyed with a lock of dark brown hair, waiting for some indication from her hostess that this was an acceptable topic of conversation.

"What? Am I dead and risen again?" Masking more serious thoughts, Susanna kept her tone of voice light.

A smile lifted the corners of Catherine's mouth as she met her neighbor's eyes once more. "I do not doubt it," she said with a chuckle. "You must know that gossips will invent what they cannot otherwise learn."

"I know that all too well. 'Tis true among servants in particular."

There was something about Catherine's bearing, she thought, that reminded her of another. Euphemia, no doubt. Certainly it was not Randall. Though at first Susanna had thought the girl much resembled her frail father, now she was of another mind.

"I fear the servants at Denholm do eagerly await whatever news they can glean from your retainers."

"My present staff or those who have most precipitously left?" A wry twist lifted one corner of Susanna's mouth. She had no reason to expect loyalty from those servants she'd hired since coming to Lancashire, but she had counted on their staying in her service for the year they'd agreed to.

"Oh, those who fled, to be sure. They have the far more interesting tale to tell."

Susanna wondered. Jennet had an admirable imagination and she did like to be the center of attention. And it was but a short walk overland from one house to the other.

"Have they all gone on to Manchester?" she inquired aloud. "These former employees of mine?"

"I believe so. They dared not linger near Appleton Manor and its evil spirits."

"I find I cannot blame them," Susanna admitted. "They fear what they do not understand."

Catherine hesitated, then blurted. "Why are *you* not frightened? You have suffered an injury because of this ghost. You must know it means to harm you."

"Does it? Why? 'Tis against my nature to let mysteries go unsolved, and therefore I must continue to seek answers."

"I do not understand you."

Susanna rather thought she did, for Catherine's pink cheeks had abruptly lost all their color.

"This ghost is no ghost," she said calmly, her eyes fixed on the girl's face. "Ghosts do not need candles, nor do they leave footprints."

Her visitor's already pale complexion turned deathly white. "You *know* this?"

"I know this. Someone seeks to trick us and I will discover who it is if it takes the last breath in my body."

Her words hung in the air between them, a challenge and a declaration of war. It required Dame Cat, who had been curled with her kittens in a basket on the far side of the bed, moved there to keep Susanna company after her fall, to break the tense silence that ensued. She landed with a small thump on the top of the coverlet.

Catherine gasped, her hand flying to her throat, then managed a sheepish smile as she extended one hand toward the cat. The feline sauntered toward the newcomer, sniffed, then nuzzled.

"Sweet," Catherine murmured.

"I call her Dame Cat." *Patience,* Susanna warned herself. If she put too much pressure on young Catherine, the girl would flee.

Hesitantly, as if she longed for an excuse to linger yet feared the outcome, Catherine began to stroke the now purring creature. After a moment she ventured a comment. "I have seen this pretty puss about, before you came."

Susanna introduced the kittens, who were awake now and mewing. Catherine relaxed visibly, enough to advance an opinion that one of the area's tomcats, a pure white creature who roamed the fields between Denholm and Appleton, was likely to have fathered them.

The young woman's demeanor puzzled Susanna. Catherine did not seem impulsive, as Jennet had reported, nor in need of watching. Studying her as she sat and played with the cats, reviewing their conversation, Susanna came to the conclusion that Catherine was a shy, self-contained girl, but pleasant company when she wished to be. Did that mean she might be devious, as well?

Susanna remembered the first time she'd seen Catherine, at Denholm Hall. The girl had given an impression of drifting when she walked. All in all, she possessed exactly the right physical qualifications to be Appleton Manor's ghost.

The two properties were close together, especially if one traveled on horseback and overland. It would not be difficult, even at night, to come to Appleton Manor from Denholm Hall and slip away again without anyone being the wiser.

But why would she? There had been a scheming, conniving mind behind the ghostly appearances. Unless Susanna was much mistaken, Catherine was too sweet-natured to have devised such a plot.

Looks could be deceiving, as Susanna well knew, but to do such a thing on her own, to lure Susanna toward what might have been her death? No, if Catherine was the ghost, and that was by no means certain, then she had not conceived the idea of haunting Appleton Manor on her own.

Susanna wanted the ghost to be someone else. She could think of two other girls who could have played the part of the supernatural being, at least for size. Both Bess and Grizel were slender, though neither had Catherine's gracefulness.

One of the three. That seemed sure. It only remained to discover which one. And why. And who had put her up to it.

"Does your injury pain you?" Catherine asked.

"Not so much anymore. My leg suffered most of the damage and it is healing well."

She had come back to consciousness in the chapel just in time to prevent Jennet from sending for medical help. She'd taken charge herself, giving instructions to both Jennet and Mabel.

Between them they had nursed her admirably, first applying

sicklewort to stanch the bleeding from the cut, then washing
the wound with comfrey juice to guard against deadly inflam-
mations. She'd been obliged to send Jennet out for more comfrey roots, the only part of the plant that was available fresh
at this time of year. On her return, Susanna had supervised the
reduction of the roots to pulp, making sure that Jennet strained
the pulp through linen cloth before she used it to make the
poultices that would stave off infection. Susanna acknowledged
that she had been most fortunate. Fever had troubled her only
during the first night.

"Can I give you something for pain?" Catherine sounded
genuinely concerned. "I have heard that poppy syrup is effective."

"I save my poppy syrup for more urgent needs. For the
times when my leg troubles me, I use lettuce cakes." She
plucked up a thin brown wafer from the table at the bedside.
"These are made from the white juice of wild lettuce. When
it dries to this form it becomes a mild narcotic. One of these
cakes is enough to allow me to sleep even when the pain is
troublesome. It is also an additional preventive against devel-
oping fever."

"I wish I could do something to make your recovery easier."
Catherine continued to stroke Dame Cat.

"Only finding out the truth about the ghost will do that,"
Susanna said gently. She considered asking Catherine outright
about her part in this. Would she admit to being the ghost? Or
would she flee?

Patience, she warned herself again as she saw a haunted
look come into Catherine's eyes. This confrontation must wait
until she was back on her feet. Then she could deal better with
this young woman's reaction to the accusation, hold onto her
with physical force if necessary.

In spite of her desire to find Catherine innocent, Susanna
reluctantly admitted that her neighbor was the most likely suspect. The time would come when she would have to force a

confession from her, and then deal with whatever fiend had inspired this dangerous mischief.

"Mayhap there is some errand I can run for you," Catherine suggested. "We go to Manchester tomorrow." At the thought, she abruptly brightened. "I could take messages to my cousin!"

"Your cousin?" Susanna was not aware that she knew any of Catherine's relatives, aside from her parents.

"Matthew Grimshaw. The lawyer. He is my mother's sister's son."

"How odd."

"Odd?"

"That I did not know. I'd have thought either Grimshaw himself or your mother would have mentioned the relationship ere now."

The expressions that flickered in rapid succession across Catherine's face were impossible to interpret, but at her first opportunity she bade Susanna farewell and all but fled the bedchamber.

"Odd, indeed," Susanna murmured.

CHAPTER 32

"It is about time you got back," Jennet complained.

Mark scowled at her and hung his coat on a peg by the kitchen door. "I've had a long, cold ride. If you've naught good to say to me, pray be silent."

"Is she more amenable?"

"She?"

"Do not play games with me, Mark Jaffrey. I know you visit a woman when you go to town."

"In truth, Jennet, I did not have time. I've been too busy looking for new servants to hire, and trying to talk Master Grimshaw out of writing to Sir Robert."

"What?"

"You heard me. He wants to know how to reach Sir Robert. Lost his temper with me when I told him I had no notion where my master was."

Jennet did not wait to hear more. She was already halfway to her mistress's chamber. The sound of the lid of a cookpot lifting told her Mark had not followed her. She'd deal with him later, she vowed. For the nonce she had news to report to Lady Appleton.

Disappointment darkened her expression a few minutes later. Lady Appleton did not seem to be either surprised or distressed by Jennet's revelation.

"I meant to write to him myself," she declared.

"Master Grimshaw?"

That got a laugh. "Robert. Let Grimshaw say what he pleases. I will send a letter of mine own to counter his report."

"Do you know what he will say?"

"I can guess that he urges Robert to call me home, to stop me meddling in the matter of the ghost. Well, I will not go, and indeed, my injury gives me just the excuse I need to stay."

Jennet privately thought Lady Appleton overconfident, but she said nothing aloud. 'Would you not like to go back to Leigh Abbey? If we left now, we could be there by the time Sir Robert returns from France."

"And how did you guess, I do wonder, that he had gone to France?"

Jennet looked down at her shoes. Her mistress knew full well she listened at doors. Indeed, she encouraged it at times. There was no call to make her admit it aloud.

A sound that smacked of amusement spared her making any confessions. "I cannot travel, injured as I am, and there's an end to it." Lady Appleton pulled the covers up to her nose and closed her eyes.

Though she'd expressed her fears before and been rebuked, Jennet blurted out what she was thinking. "I am afraid for us all. And Mark no longer cares. He has a new love to distract him."

"Then win him back," came muffled advice from the bed.

"You do not understand," Jennet wailed. "I do not want him back if he means to stay here." Appalled, she clapped her hands over her mouth. She'd never meant to say so much.

Lady Appleton opened one eye. "Bodykins," she muttered.

"Such a pother over nothing." Then she sighed and sat up again, pounding the cushions into shape to support her back.

Jennet hastened to her mistress's side, eager to help and even more eager to hear what Lady Appleton advised.

"I am aware that Mark wants to be steward here," Lady Appleton informed her.

"And?"

"Stop mangling your lower lip, Jennet, and think logically about your own prospects. I do mean to appoint him my steward as soon as this matter of the ghost is settled. You could live in fine style at Appleton Manor, Jennet. All you need do is marry him."

"There will be none of us living here if that ghost has its way."

Lady Appleton remained stubborn. She refused to admit that she might be courting disaster. "Give me mine herbal, Jennet. Then go and talk to Mark. Win him away from the attractions of Manchester and think about what I have said."

Jennet obeyed, at least so far as to fetch the book. She had no choice when Lady Appleton used that particular tone of voice. But her opinion did not change. The ghost would be back. She was certain of it. And she was much afraid that the next time it came to Appleton Manor they would all perish.

CHAPTER 33

Off East Anglia, fierce gales at Christmas wrecked a French fleet on its way to Scotland. Sir Robert Appleton and his friend Walter Pendennis left Calais for Dover shortly afterward. They had a safe but unpleasant crossing. For them the worse storm came after they'd arrived at the English court.

Two letters were waiting for Sir Robert, both sent on from Leigh Abbey by his steward. The first, from Matthew Grimshaw, would have him believe his wife lay at death's door. The second, from Susanna herself and written at a later date, did no more than hint at trouble at Appleton Manor. It consisted primarily of an account of various servant problems.

The truth, Sir Robert knew, would be somewhere in between. There was no question now but that he'd have to go north to see for himself what was happening there. But first he had to report to the queen and she was not yet ready to receive him. Just as he'd had to wait in France for his summons to Blois, now he cooled his heels at Greenwich. He grumbled at the delay, but no one rushed Her Majesty.

"I have called in every favor I can in an effort to arrange

an earlier audience,'' he complained to Pendennis. ''One would think that with Northumberland's surviving children now in such high favor here at court I'd have been in to see her and on my way again already.''

''Why such a hurry? And in winter, too. Are there not enough delights here to keep you busy while you wait?''

Pendennis's gaze drifted to a bevy of beauties, young women who served the queen as maids of honor and who were not at all adverse to dalliance with her courtiers. Under other circumstances, Sir Robert might have agreed with his old friend. This time, however, his irritation and resentment grew with each new delay.

''What is she thinking, to make me cool my heels after insisting that I be the one to make the journey to France in the first place?''

''She is the queen. She does not need reasons.'' Pendennis gave him a sharp look. ''What is it that really troubles you?''

''My lady wife.'' Sir Robert all but snarled the admission. Susanna was creating trouble for him in Lancashire. If he did not get there soon, who knew what might come out?

At last Lady Sidney, the late duke of Northumberland's daughter and a lady-in-waiting to the queen, succeeded in arranging an audience with Her Majesty. Surrounded by close advisers, standing, Elizabeth Tudor sat in regal splendor on a gilded chair. Sir Robert was obliged to kneel. She said nothing at all when he had finished imparting his intelligence about the French rebels. She did not signal for him to rise, either. Indeed, she seemed to have forgotten that he was even there in her presence. Her eyes were unfocused, her mind clearly far away. Robert was not at all sure she was thinking about what he had said. For all he knew, she might be dreaming of Robin Dudley, or some other lover, or of a new gown.

''Madam?'' Sir Robert dared speak only after one knee made an audible creak as he shifted his weight.

Impatiently, she motioned for him to stand. Her eyes were sharp once more, but still she put off giving him his freedom.

"We must think carefully about what you have told us," she said. "We may have more questions. Stay you here at court and await our pleasure and we promise you that we will speak with you again. Twelfth Night is almost upon us. You will take part in the festivities."

With that, he was dismissed. Anger darkened Sir Robert's countenance as he made his way back to the small, dank chamber, sparsely furnished, which had been assigned to him. With real longing, he remembered the apartment he had occupied at Blois.

Queens! He wished them all to perdition. Elizabeth might take months to decide the French question. In the meantime she expected him to dance attendance on her. Literally.

The queen and his wife had much in common and not just that they were the same age and both well educated. Each had the potential to destroy all he had worked for.

The next day, Sir Robert informed Pendennis he was leaving.

"You risk offending the queen if you go now," his old friend warned.

The risk was greater if he did not go. "My wife needs me," he lied. He produced Grimshaw's last letter. "This should be enough to convince the queen that Susanna's life is in danger. Entrust this missive to Lady Sidney and let her present it to the queen when Her Majesty seems in a good mood, along with my promise to return as soon as may be."

An hour later he stopped to look over his shoulder at the spires of Greenwich. It was not too late to turn back, but he'd made his decision and would abide by it. He went to a "dying" wife. The queen would forgive that. In this world, appearances were everything.

Robert had been telling himself for weeks now that Susanna was unlikely to unearth certain facts that were better kept quiet. Her last letter had forced him to admit the truth. His wife had a dogged sort of determination in any endeavor she undertook. Left to her own devices, searching for other answers, she would eventually find out about the foolish vow he'd made fifteen years earlier when, desperate to avoid a betrothal to Jane Denholm, he had informed both their families that he would never marry. He meant, he'd told them all, to join the priesthood.

The ploy had initially yielded positive results beyond his wildest dreams. Denholm had accepted his decision without a qualm. He'd actually been pleased about it and bored Robert with tales of his own brief sojourn in a Benedictine house. Even though training to be a priest during the reign of Henry VIII meant leaving England, Robert had briefly considered making good on his impulsive threat, drawn by the allure of gaining personal power within the church hierarchy. Then a better opportunity had presented itself, a chance to advance in the secular world of the royal court. Sir George Appleton, eager to preserve his own safe existence as a secret papist, had proposed to send his son to a noble household known to fervently embrace the New Religion. Robert had gone willingly to John Dudley, just at the start of that politician's meteoric rise to power.

During the long ride north, Robert tried to view his situation from all angles. What if Susanna had already learned his secret? What would she do? Although she'd never been a Catholic, neither was she one of those radicals who thought all papists were the devil's spawn. She might be inclined to protect him.

And if not? Or if the story got out anyway?

Bandied about by the wrong people, his hasty words could be exaggerated and twisted, used by his enemies to ruin his chances of becoming an influential diplomat. His future depended upon keeping everyone convinced that his loyalty was now and had always been to the New Religion, his only lapse the politically expedient conversion while Mary reigned. The revelation of long-ago events in Lancashire could be as much of a detriment to his career as any present failure to shine at court.

If the queen learned he'd once wanted to become a priest, she might believe he remained a devout Catholic, that he still harbored a secret allegiance to Rome. She might also think he supported Mary Stewart's claim to her throne. She might even believe he would conspire against her.

Conversely, Elizabeth might accept his word that he'd long since converted to the New Religion, that he was completely loyal to her. She was as unpredictable as her father and her half sister had been. That was the real trouble, the uncertainty. One day he might be her trusted emissary to France and other foreign points. The next he might find himself in the Tower of London, about to be executed for treason.

Best to take no chances, he decided, and urged his horse to greater speed as he traveled ever northward. With luck and cunning, his youthful indiscretion might yet remain buried in Lancashire.

CHAPTER 34

The morning after Twelfth Night, a full month after the fall in which she'd been injured, Susanna Appleton insisted upon resuming her normal routine. Her leg still pained her, and she suspected she would always carry a scar and perhaps continue to limp somewhat when the weather was damp, but since the alternative had been death, she was well enough content. She felt nearly as sturdy as she'd been before the fall.

There had been no sign of Appleton Manor's ghost since that night in the chapel. Susanna was uncertain whether to be pleased or upset about that. She wanted another chance to unmask the specter and she'd never get it if it did not pay a return visit. Had it been Catherine? Had she scared her off? If there was one thing Susanna Appleton hated, it was unanswered questions.

The continuing shortage of servants was also distressing, but the lack was not insurmountable. The workmen, fortunately, had already finished the most necessary repairs on the manor house before they'd been frightened away. The improvements gave Susanna immense satisfaction. The place was less drafty now and provided a modicum of comfort even when the cold breezes of January blew. There was nothing she could do about the central fire in the hall until spring, but even that burned with less smoke now that she had supplies of seasoned wood.

In better spirits than she'd enjoyed for some weeks, Susanna entered the kitchen. The first thing that struck her was the absence of heat. It was scarcely cold, since the cooking fires never went entirely out, but it was obvious to her that no one had yet begun to prepare the morning meal. Most peculiar, she thought. It was nigh onto eight of the clock. Had the household possessed a full complement of servants, someone would have been demanding breakfast long ere now.

Cautiously, she searched the large room, looking for any sign that Mabel had been up and about. She found nothing. With growing trepidation, she approached the room her cook and housekeeper had claimed as her own. It was a narrow little nook, just off the pantry, containing no more than a bed and a chest for storage.

There was no sign of Mabel.

Frowning now, Susanna widened her search. The premises were not so large that it took long. By the time she'd gone through all the service rooms, she was calling for Mark and Fulke and Lionel.

"I fear some harm has come to her," she explained after she told them that Mabel was missing. "Search all the outbuildings and everywhere in the house."

"No doubt she simply fled," Jennet muttered.

"In the middle of the night? Why?"

"I never trusted the woman."

"Again, why?"

But Jennet could offer no solid reason for her feelings, only the revelation that Mabel had been fully dressed the night Susanna fell. Susanna gave her tiring maid a sharp look and ordered her to join the search.

They found Mabel soon after, unconscious and very cold, in the cellar behind the dais in the great hall. This large storage room had not been empty since Susanna's first trip to Manchester, but neither was it a place Mabel often needed to go. The stores kept there were building supplies and seed for spring planting and other items not in everyday use.

"She'd no business in here," Jennet said. "This is a trick of some kind."

"She did not hit herself on the head." Feeling carefully, Susanna located the lump that had rendered the cook senseless. She did not seem to have any other injuries, but she'd been lying on the cold stones for some time. Her limp hands were icy. "Move her into the hall, near the fire. We must warm her."

"She fell and struck her head while up to no good. Perhaps she meant to rob you."

"Give up your foolishness, Jennet. Mabel is as loyal to me as you are."

Susanna half expected her maidservant to suggest that Mabel was their ghost or, alternately, that she'd been attacked by it. If Jennet's white face was any indication, she was frightened by this latest turn of events. To forestall any further speculation, Susanna issued orders for the care of the stricken woman. Jennet seemed grateful to have something to take her mind off her worries. She hastened to obey, leaving her mistress alone in the cellar with the cook.

Mabel moaned.

"Can you hear me?" Susanna whispered.

"Madam?"

Good. She had her senses. "Who struck you, Mabel? Did you see . . . anyone?"

In spite of her pain, the big woman managed a weak smile. "No ghost, madam. This were real enough. Felt like a cudgel, it did, on the back of me skull." She tried to reach up and touch the spot, but Susanna caught her hand.

"Leave your care to me." She considered the cook's size, and the difficulty in moving her. "Can you get to your feet with my help?"

Instead of answering, Mabel began to struggle upward.

"Careful." Together they managed it, though Susanna's leg had begun to throb well before she had the cook on her feet. Mabel swayed, then gave a start and stared. "Where be we, madam?"

"In the cellar, Mabel. Among the supplies and seeds. Do you remember why you came in here?"

A frown creased her countenance as she struggled to recall. It was possible she'd be unable to, Susanna knew. She had a few blank spots in her own memory from hitting her head in the vault.

"I got up to start the baking," Mabel said after a moment longer. " 'Tis a thing I do often, in the wee hours. I do not sleep as well as I once did and it does give me an early start on the day." She frowned and lightly fingered the sore spot on her head. "I were scarce dressed when I heard a noise. I went to look. Meant to give any intruder a piece of my mind, I did, ghost or no, but there weren't no ghost. No one at all that I saw."

"Someone saw you first," Susanna reasoned. Fully dressed, she added to herself, relieved to have at least one small question answered.

Mabel managed a faint smile. "Good thing I've a hard head."

In spite of the mysteries which remained unsolved, Susanna grinned back at her. "Aye. A good thing indeed."

CHAPTER 35

"I mean to leave here," Jennet said. She'd made her decision the moment Lady Appleton announced that she wanted a guard posted from sunset to dawn. Jennet hadn't slept a wink all night and now, in the early morning, when she was obliged to take up Mabel's duties in the kitchen until the cook recovered, she was not in any mood to hold back her feelings.

Mark heaved an exasperated sigh. "You cannot go now, no matter how much you may wish to. 'Tis the middle of winter." He helped himself to a heel of black bread. " 'Twould be sheer folly to try to travel all the way back to Kent on your own."

"I'd not be on my own if you went with me."

"And leave Lady Appleton here with none but Fulke and Lionel to guard her?"

"We could all go."

"She will not leave. You know that, Jennet."

Yes, she did know how stubborn her mistress was, but she also knew Lady Appleton would not insist that any of her retainers stay on if they really wanted to leave. And if they all wanted to go, then she would have no choice but to go with them, or at the least move into Manchester. She would be out of danger then, wouldn't she? Why, it was a service Jennet was performing, to insist upon leaving Appleton Manor.

"If you do not care what happens to me, Mark, then think of your own safety. It might as easily have been you injured in that attack as Mabel."

"Do you care so much, then, Jennet?"

"Do not mock me." She cared too much, which was just the trouble. Since he'd been visiting that wench in Manchester, he had not so much as tried to kiss her.

As if he'd read her mind, Mark sent a smugly superior, very masculine smile in her direction. Jennet had seen the like on Sir Robert's face when he thought he was winning an argument with Lady Appleton. "I think you want to go so that I'll be removed from the . . . temptations of Manchester."

"You do manage to visit there often enough. Even in bad weather."

"I'll not venture out as often when winter truly sets in. I have been told it is impossible to find even the path from Appleton to Denholm when there is wind and blowing snow."

"What a cheerful thought! And ample reason in itself to head south while we yet may." Jennet clenched her hands into fists at her sides. She hated to feel so helpless. Frustration ate at her, pushing her into words she'd never meant to say. "I will make it worth your while to take me safely away."

Mark froze in the act of slicing bread. "Are you that desperate?" he muttered, more to himself than to her.

After months of tormenting him, allowing kisses and caresses but never permitting him to possess her completely, though she'd often wanted to let their lovemaking go further, Jennet had in one moment lost her advantage. She'd been letting him think she saved herself for marriage and that she did not want to marry so soon, but he could not mistake her offer. It did not involve even the most informal of marriage vows. Blushing furiously, she waited for Mark's decision.

It would not be so bad, she told herself. If he would take her back to Leigh Abbey, it would be worth the price. And Mark was an honorable man. He'd marry her if there were any unwanted consequences from their coupling.

Prepared for victory, Jennet could not at first believe that what she saw in his eyes was regret. He meant to refuse her, to reject her.

Before he could do so aloud, she turned away, hiding the tears that sprang into her eyes. It was the girl in Manchester. She was sure of it. Mark had given his heart to another.

"I will manage on my own," she whispered brokenly.

"Jennet—"

He caught her arm, but she jerked away from him. Angry now, as well as hurt, she struck out the only way she knew how. "I am sure my offer will interest some other man. I have but to get to Manchester to find one."

Suddenly his anger matched hers. "You'll be hard-pressed to get that far in this weather."

She went to the door. Two inches of snow already lay on the ground and it was still falling fast and furious. Dismayed, she returned to the kitchen.

"A small sample of what the next months will bring," Mark said with insufferable smugness. "Accept it, Jennet. We'll neither of us be going to Manchester, nor even as far as Gorebury."

"It will stop snowing. Then will I go."

But Mark shook his head. "Even if this snow does not continue long, another storm will follow. 'Tis certain we'll be kept close in each other's company for days, even weeks, perhaps for months to come. Why do you think Lady Appleton laid in so many provisions?"

Jennet wanted to run, but if she did there would be no one to prepare Lady Appleton's breakfast. Scowling fiercely, she brushed past Mark and went toward the hearth. She might have to remain in his company, but she did not have to be civil to him. Indeed, she did not even have to acknowledge his existence.

Determined that he should never know how much he had hurt her by his callous rejection, she reached for a heavy iron pot.

"If I had as much knowledge as some do," she muttered loudly enough for him to hear, "I'm thinking I'd be making a marrow-bone pie."

CHAPTER 36

Catherine Denholm stared out at the fury of the snowstorm, the second of the winter so far. She was torn between gratitude and dismay. She was glad no one from Denholm could travel on such a day, but sorry indeed that she had to be stuck here, with only her parents and the servants for company.

She did not like being confined. She'd have enjoyed paying more visits to the invalid mistress of Appleton Manor after the first. She'd grown very fond of Lady Appleton in the short time she'd spent with her. Knowing her had also increased Catherine's awareness that those at Denholm Hall were ... different.

She longed to escape, to live a normal life, but for the nonce her parents had complete control of her—of her person and her dowry and her disposition in marriage. If she ran away from home, she would have nothing.

A shadow caught Catherine's attention and she narrowed her eyes, trying to make out the shape. Slowly it resolved itself into a man on horseback, head bent as he struggled forward against the wind. Catherine quickly uncurled from her perch on the window seat and called for her cloak. The poor man would be frozen, and hospitality was one thing country folk did without stinting, even here at Denholm Hall.

She reached the stables just as he was dismounting. A groom had already taken charge of his mount and the man himself was brushing off an encrustation of snow. He turned at the small sound she made at the door and the light from the stable's lantern shone full on his face.

Catherine bit back a gasp. She knew who he was, though he'd already left Lancashire by the time she was born. She knew his features as well as she knew her own, the narrow face and high forehead, the dark brown hair and the bottomless brown eyes. At a glance, she took in the broad shoulders and well-formed legs that qualified him as one of the most handsome of the queen's courtiers, but it was his bearing that provided the final proof.

With startling abruptness, the one piece that had been missing from the puzzle of her life fell into place.

She took a deep breath to steady herself. He was waiting for her to speak and she knew she must greet him properly. This was no time to shirk her duty.

"Good day to you, Sir Robert," Catherine said. "Welcome to Denholm Hall."

CHAPTER 37

Sir Robert arrived at Appleton a day late, forced to shelter at Denholm overnight because of the intensity of the storm. He found his wife in the kitchen, tasting the contents of an iron pot.

"Have you no cook to do that?" he demanded irritably.

"She is at present nursing a broken head. 'Tis delightful to see you, too, my dear. Did you have a good journey?"

"I had a wretched trip, as you well can imagine. I was told you were nigh unto death."

"My accident was weeks ago and I am fully recovered now. I hope it does not disappoint you to find me so well." She gave whatever was in the pot another stir with a long wooden spoon, replaced the lid, and turned at last to face him.

New lines had been inscribed in her face by the pain she had borne, but Robert hardened his heart. She did not deserve sympathy. She had disobeyed him.

"What prompted Grimshaw's last letter?" he demanded.

"What, indeed? 'Tis plain Grimshaw wants your presence here. Have you any idea why?"

"He wanted me here months ago to settle the matter of hiring a new steward."

Susanna frowned. She began adding herbs to a second huge cook pot, from which a tantalizing odor emerged, drifting toward him and making his mouth water. "I have taken care of that. Mark shall have the post. With your approval, of course."

"Do whatever you like." His temper fraying rapidly, he glared at his wife.

"Robert, come and sit down." When she left the hearth he noticed that she used a stout stick to steady her steps.

"How bad is it?" He sat as she'd directed, pulling a stool up to the kitchen worktable.

"Tolerable. I was never in mortal danger, no matter what Grimshaw may have told you, but this cold weather increases the stiffness. I presume you got my letter, as well as the lawyer's?"

"Aye. I did. And that came no closer to presenting me with the true situation here than did his."

With a rather grim smile, Susanna eased onto one end of a long bench. Robert reached for the pitcher at the center of the table and poured himself a cup of what he hoped would be ale. He grimaced at the taste of pears and set the drink aside as Susanna told him all that had happened since her arrival at Appleton Manor.

"At first I did think someone wanted me gone and the house empty," she concluded, "but I have begun to believe now that I have been used to lure you here."

"Why? And why would anyone pretend to be a ghost?"

"I know not why. I may know who. Catherine is the most likely possibility."

"Catherine Denholm? A girl of fourteen? Why would she haunt us?"

"If I knew, I'd not be asking you." The stubborn look in Susanna's eyes was one he knew well. " 'Tis obvious that if someone means you harm, then it must be someone you know. And it is equally obvious that you know more than you're telling me, else you'd not have objected so strenuously when I first proposed coming here. Go back over your past, Robert, I beg of you. Consider everything. Review in particular your relationship with your father.''

"You ask too much of me."

"Why did you leave here fifteen years ago? Why was there no marriage between you and Jane Denholm?"

Because I told my father I preferred to become a priest.

For a moment Robert feared he'd spoken aloud, but Susanna's expression did not change. He'd confined the memory to his own mind and there it would have to stay. He could not trust anyone, not even his sworn helpmate, to keep such a dangerous secret.

"Well?" Susanna's impatience jerked him back to the present.

"I left home to enter service in a noble household," he answered.

"No other reason?"

"What other reason could there have been?"

"Jane—"

"Jane had naught to do with anything! I was destined for a career at court, a career which is in greater jeopardy with every day I linger here. I must return as soon as possible."

"Was there a precontract?"

"Trying to get rid of me?" If he'd been legally betrothed to Jane, a commitment that was in fact a form of marriage, both his union with Susanna and Jane's with his father would be invalid.

"Was there?"

"No. Matters never progressed that far. And to be truthful, I did not care for Jane nor she for me."

"What has liking to do with marriage?" Susanna reached for his neglected cup and took a sip of the perry, then pushed it back across the table toward him. "It would be easier to discover the identity of our murderer with your cooperation, Robert."

"You have no proof of any murder. Only speculation."

"Let me speculate, then, upon the murder of your father by pushing him down the stairs and the murder of John Bexwith by poison and the rumored haunting devised to drive everyone away."

"I thought you said the haunting was to lure me here?"

"Would that not be the result with any landholder who cared about his profits? When I arrived in your stead, a newly embodied ghost was used to entice me into a trap. The fall that injured me might as easily have killed me, but I do not believe that was the intent."

"And did your ghost also strike Mabel down?"

" 'Twas the person behind the ghost, I do think."

"Why?"

"I do not know. Possibly our villain was here to do more mischief, but was discovered before he could accomplish his purpose."

Robert had learned never to discount anything his clever wife said, no matter how outrageous, but he had his doubts about her logic in this case. "You say you think it is Catherine who plays at being a ghost, but another who did murder?"

Her expression earnest, Susanna leaned closer to him. "Aye, it does seem reasonable to me that Catherine is obeying her father's orders. There is no doubt that Randall Denholm knows his herbs and so has easy access to poison. And I told you about the strange expression I saw in his eyes upon our first meeting."

Robert considered the account she'd just given him, her usual thorough, efficient analysis of the situation. "You said you thought, at the time, that his animosity was directed at his wife."

"That was my impression. But what sense does that make? What if it was resentment toward me for arriving in your place?"

Robert hesitated. "You have heard of my father's . . . amorous nature?"

Frowning, Susanna nodded.

"I came upon him once when I was a young boy, with Mistress Denholm. Something in their manner made it seem they were . . . more than just neighbors."

Shock made her eyes widen. "Euphemia Denholm was your father's mistress?"

"She was not always as she is now."

"But he married her daughter."

"Years later. And I cannot be sure he had the mother first." Amusement tinged his words. "If he did, he'd have claimed he was just aping his betters. He was wont to repeat that old rumor that King Henry married Anne Boleyn after first having known both her mother and her sister."

"Papist lies."

"Mayhap, but my father believed it. And if you are looking for a motive for Randall Denholm, why there it is. No man can abide being cuckolded."

"Why wait so long for revenge?"

Just like Susanna to take the other side the moment he began to see the logic of her original argument. "I do but try to prove your case, my dear. Randall Denholm may have been carrying a grudge for years, though I cannot say I sensed any animosity toward me last night."

"Last night?"

"Did I not tell you? I availed myself of our neighbors' hospitality because of the storm. They were most gracious."

She turned pale at his words, proof she believed her own theory. Her obvious concern for his safety was pleasing to him, but he also sensed that they were venturing onto dangerous ground. So far, Susanna did not seem to have gotten any hint of his early papist leanings. Accuse Randall Denholm of murder, however, and they would quickly become common knowledge.

"Leave it be, Susanna," he said quietly.

"And if he lured you here to kill you, too, Robert? You ignore this matter at your own peril."

"Think, Susanna. Even if Randall Denholm did kill my

father and John Bexwith, would he force his own daughter to be part of this? 'Twas plain to me last night that he dotes upon the girl.'' And it had been plain, too, that the man did not have all his wits about him. His mind seemed to wander off without warning.

"He is mad. That is the only answer. Mad but devious. For some reason, he does not believe his revenge will be complete until he murders you, ending the Appleton line forever."

Susanna would drive *him* mad if she persisted in this. Impatiently, Robert left the table and prowled the kitchen. "From what you told me earlier, you had many suspects, Susanna. Too many to prove any one of them is the killer. No, Susanna," he said sharply when she looked as if she meant to speak, "you must heed me in this. Let the matter go. We will leave for Kent as soon as the roads are passable."

She came to her feet in as much of a rush as she could manage with her game leg. "Two men have died under unusual circumstances. Both Mabel and I have been injured. You—"

"I mean to leave Lancashire as soon as the weather clears. And you will go with me."

"Concern for my well-being, Robert?" She hobbled up to him, thrusting out that stubborn jaw she'd inherited from her father, challenging him with her glare as well as her words.

He sensed she was barely hanging on to her temper, but did not care. He'd brook no disobedience in this matter. He dared not. "Sarcasm does not become you, my dear."

"Robert, I—"

"No more!" With every appearance of being as angry as she was, he glowered down at his wife. "There is no need for further discussion. You will never prove that murder was done. Therefore you will cease your meddling at once. Devote your energies to packing and making arrangements to move back to Leigh Abbey."

"What if I am right about Randall? What if he did lure you here with intent to harm you?"

"Since I am the intended victim, then it behooves you to

allow me to decide what is best to do. I say we deal with this threat, real or imagined, by leaving here as soon as it is possible to travel south.'' He'd rather seem a coward than let this investigation continue. And he did not greatly care if Denholm had killed his father and Bexwith. Neither man's passing was cause for regret.

Rebellion lurked in Susanna's eyes but something in his manner must have convinced her he would not change his mind. Though it plainly pained her, she paid lip service to his position as head of the household.

''It is your decision,'' she agreed, ''but, Robert, I do beg you to be very careful as long as we remain here.''

''Concern for my well-being?'' he mocked her.

He left the kitchen without giving her an opportunity to reply.

CHAPTER 38

Jennet stayed hidden in the pantry until Sir Robert had stormed past on his way toward the great hall. What she had overheard had been illuminating. Elated by the prospect of leaving Appleton Manor soon, her first thought was to find Mark and tell him the good news. Then she remembered that Sir Robert had also given tacit approval to Mark's appointment as steward. Good news indeed, but for whom? Mark would stay behind. Doubtless he'd marry that girl from Manchester. And then where would Jennet be?

Back home in Kent, she told herself. Where she'd wanted to stay all along. But for the first time she realized that if she left, she might never see Mark again. He would marry, if not Temperance Strelley, then some other woman. And she'd have only herself to blame.

Chewing industriously on her lower lip, Jennet considered her choices. She remembered how arrogant Mark had been the last time he'd gotten her alone. He'd caught her in his arms and pulled her close, covering her mouth with his. The kiss had made her forget, if only for a moment, both her fears about Appleton Manor and her reservations about marriage.

"Your choice, Jennet," he'd whispered bluntly. "Marry me or I will find someone who will. I have lived long enough without a wife."

"Get away with you," she'd cried, suddenly angry. "I am not of a mind to marry."

"You kiss as if you were."

Jennet had retreated a few more steps, confused by her own response to him. He deserved a clout on the head, but what she'd wanted most was to go on kissing him and see where that led.

"I may kiss whatever man I like," she'd said, annoyed to discover that her voice sounded breathless.

He'd had the gall to laugh at her. Advancing slowly, a determined gleam in his eyes, he'd stalked her. "You do not know what you want, woman. That is doubtless why men have been given dominion over all those of your sex."

"Dominion, is it?" Truly incensed, she'd shouted at him, saying things she'd later wished she could take back. "You could be the last man left on the face of the earth," she'd vowed, "and I would not marry you. Nay, nor kiss you again, neither."

A shutter flew open, caught by the wind, bringing Jennet's reverie to an abrupt end. Glad of something to do, she ordered Lionel to fix it. Only then did she realize that she'd not seen Mark since Sir Robert arrived. Fulke had been busy elsewhere, so Mark had taken charge of Vanguard, the master's horse.

Odd he'd not yet returned to the house from the stable, she thought. 'Twas passing cold outside. More worried than she'd admit, even to herself, Jennet put on a warm wool cloak and stepped out into the kitchen garden.

The storm that had delayed Sir Robert's arrival at Appleton Manor had passed, but in its aftermath a frigid, howling wind gusted, creating of the newly fallen snow such deep drifts that Jennet knew she must abandon all hope of an immediate departure for Kent. They would be obliged to wait until at least some of that snow melted.

She hesitated, but the outbuildings were not far from the house and she felt an overwhelming need to find Mark. She had news to convey, she told herself. It was not that she was concerned about him.

There was no light burning in the stable, a circumstance odd in itself on a day so dark. And as soon as Jennet entered the building she heard the sounds of a restless animal. She fumbled in the dimness until she found the lantern she knew was always kept by the door. Once she'd lit it, she advanced cautiously deeper into the shadowy interior.

"Mark?"

A low moan fixed his location. Jennet turned, holding the light high, then almost dropped it when she caught sight of her beloved lying on the ground in front of one of the stalls. His head was bloodied and his clothing torn.

Jennet had no memory of crossing the stable, but when she knelt beside Mark everything was suddenly vivid. She felt the straw prickling her knees through cloak and skirt and petticoat. She smelled horse and sweat and blood and another scent she knew but could not identify. Sir Robert's stallion had backed off, seemingly content with the amount of damage he had already done. He snorted, but did not attack.

Beneath her trembling fingers, Jennet tried to discern the flutter of Mark's pulse, but it was not until she pressed her ear to his chest and listened hard that she could make out the faint beating of his heart. A moment later she saw the shallow rise and fall of his chest and her own breath, which she hadn't realized she was holding, came out in a great sob. For one horrible moment, she had feared that moan had been his last, that he was dead.

Tears streamed down Jennet's face as she shifted position so that she could cradle Mark's head in her lap and cling to his limp hand. She could not control them, not even when she saw him open his eyes. He smiled weakly as he recognized her.

"Oh, Mark" was all she could manage to say.

In a voice that was scarcely more than a whisper, he asked, "Does this mean you love me after all?"

CHAPTER 39

The Appletons hurried into the stable together, summoned by a distraught Fulke, who'd heard Jennet's cries for help. Robert rushed straight to Vanguard. Susanna knelt by her man-servant's side.

None of Mark's injuries looked serious, though they might well have been. He'd been kicked at least once, but most of the damage had been done when he fell.

"Another accident?" She sent Robert a pointed look.

"What happened?" he demanded. "What did you do to my horse?"

"Naught." Mark defended himself. "Fair maddened he was from the start. I had scarce begun to remove his saddle when he reared up, eyes rolling."

"He seems calm enough now," Susanna noted. The saddle and saddle pad had been bucked off. One side of the stall had been kicked in. Mark was fortunate indeed to have sustained no worse injuries.

With Jennet's help, Susanna got to her feet and left Mark's side to peer more closely at both horse and tack. She inhaled the normal scents of hay and dung. Another aroma, out of place in the stable, teased her nostrils.

"Bodykins!" Careful to stay clear of Vanguard's hooves, she flipped the fallen saddle pad over and sniffed delicately. "Here's your answer. Someone has rubbed lye into this cloth. As soon as Vanguard worked up a sweat, it began to burn him."

If the saddle had not already been loosened, the horse would have done far more damage to both Mark and the stable. If he'd felt the pain sooner, he'd likely have tossed his rider into a snowbank. If Robert hadn't broken his neck in a fall, he might well have frozen to death before anyone found him.

It was a most inefficient way to kill someone. And yet there was no doubt in Susanna's mind that someone from Denholm Hall had hoped the stallion would bolt and injure his rider during the ride to Appleton. Only the excessively cold weather had prevented the plan from working. Vanguard had not begun to sweat until the journey's end. In fact, had Mark removed the saddle even seconds sooner, the horse might not have suffered at all.

"Put a little bee's leaf ointment on the raw spot when he's had his oats," she told Fulke. As the groom hastened to see to Vanguard's needs, Susanna turned back to the others. "Mark, you need to be put to bed."

"Nay, madam. I'll be right as rain in a minute. Just wait and see."

"No doubt that is why you wince with every movement. Help him, Jennet."

As the maidservant obeyed, Susanna lowered her voice and spoke to her husband. "Who saddled your horse at Denholm?"

"Denholm's groom."

"Did Randall see you on your way?"

"Aye," Robert reluctantly admitted.

Susanna stared at him, wishing she understood why he was loath to pursue this. Even if he did not care to avenge his father, he ought to be looking out for himself. He'd always put his own well-being first in the past. His present attitude made no sense to her.

"The man has lost his reason, Robert. We cannot guess what he will do next."

"We need not. We are leaving here as soon as may be."

"We might call the constable and have Randall questioned about the lye on the saddle pad. It was a deliberate act of violence, and against a valuable beast, too."

"We will call no one. We will leave," Robert repeated. "Here's an end to it, Susanna."

She gave up trying to argue with him. She opened the stable door and limped out into the wind, followed by Mark and Jennet and leaving her exasperating husband to do as he would.

"Did Master Denholm poison the steward?" Jennet hissed.

Susanna sighed. She should have known the wench's sharp ears would miss nothing.

"I do believe so. What simpler than that a man known to grow all manner of herbs would be able to make Bexwith believe a poisonous root was a powerful love potion?"

Jennet nodded, her face serious. "Mayhap he convinced Bexwith that he ate of it himself before he got Mistress Catherine on his wife."

CHAPTER 40

The next day the sun came out and the snow began to melt and Susanna was faced with a dilemma. She believed Randall Denholm was behind all the violence at Appleton Manor and she was determined to bring him to justice. Robert's arbitrary commands made that more difficult, giving her little time in which to act. If the weather remained clear, they'd soon be on their way south. Still, the task was not impossible, not if she sent word to Denholm Manor right away and kept Robert from guessing what she had planned.

Her continuing lameness prevented her from walking over the snow-covered fields herself. Neither Mark nor Mabel was up to making such a journey, either, and if any of them tried to take a horse, Robert was sure to notice. He was quite concerned about the condition of his stallion, paying regular visits to the stable.

That left Jennet.

The first challenge was to get her away from Mark. While Susanna was glad they had resolved their differences, she grew impatient with the change in her maidservant. If Jennet did not have a care, she'd be deferring to her prospective husband in everything.

At the same time Susanna had to decide what message to send. Which would work better, threats or promises? And how, she wondered, did one deal best with the matter of divided loyalties within a family? After several tries, she composed a letter that she hoped would produce the desired result.

There was danger in what she was doing, of course. It was possible her actions would provoke another attempt on Robert's life. But how could she not continue? Was it not worth the risk to end the killing, to bring a murderer to justice?

"We leave tomorrow," Robert announced at midday, only minutes after Susanna had sent Jennet off toward Denholm.

Shortly thereafter, the message she had sent yielded its desired result when Catherine arrived. Careful not to let Robert see the girl, Susanna whisked Catherine into the stillroom, where they could be private.

"You know why I sent for you," she said.

Catherine nodded. "Will you have me locked up?" she asked in a small voice.

"Not if you tell me the truth." Susanna took a deep breath and hoped she could be convincing. It was essential that Catherine believe Susanna knew more than she did. "You have been pretending to be a ghost, have you not?"

Again the girl nodded.

"Was it your own idea?"

"No."

The whisper of sound was almost inaudible and Susanna's heart ached. It was important that she confirm Randall's guilt and attempt to learn what had motivated him. The questions she had to ask Catherine probed delicate areas. They were necessary, to protect Robert, but Susanna vowed to spare her young friend in every way she could.

"I know it is a hard thing for a child to speak ill of a parent," she began. Her hand on Catherine's elbow, she guided her to the low bench that ran beneath the window. They both sat.

Catherine's sniffle was answer enough to that question.

"Would it be easier if we spoke of 'mine enemy' instead? We both know who I mean."

Plainly fighting tears, confused, and not a little frightened to be enduring this inquisition at all, Catherine managed another nod. Her hands had been resting in her lap. Now she clasped them together as she bowed her head, squeezing her eyes tightly shut.

"I must ask you hard questions, Catherine, and for some you may not have answers. Just do the best you can."

Catherine went very still, tensing against the verbal blows to come.

"Let us go back to the beginning," Susanna said gently. "Did your mother know Sir George Appleton well?"

Catherine made a sound halfway between a laugh and a cry of pain. She lifted her head, opening deep brown eyes to meet Susanna's puzzled blue ones. "How else should I look so much like your husband?" she asked.

Startled, Susanna stared hard at the girl before her. Whatever she had expected to learn today, it had not been this. And yet, now that she had been told, the truth was obvious.

"Sir George was my father," Catherine confessed. "I am your husband's half sister." She made another strangled sound. "Look at me. Look at him. How can anyone deny the relationship?"

There was one other way to explain the resemblance, Susanna thought. Catherine might be Robert's child by Jane Denholm. She quickly dismissed that conjecture. Two things argued against it. Given Robert's apparent inability to father any children, he'd have seized on any such proof of his virility. More to the point, had Jane conceived a child, unwed, Robert would have been fetched home from the Dudley household and forced to marry her.

"You are Sir George's daughter," Susanna said aloud. "Did he know?"

"I do not believe so," Catherine said. "I did not realize it myself until Sir Robert stopped at Denholm Hall two nights past."

"But Randall Denholm did know."

"He must have." Silent tears began to fall. Susanna put one hand over Catherine's and squeezed and gave her a moment to collect herself. She could well understand the girl's reluctance to talk about this. She'd grown up thinking Randall was her father and was confused to learn he was not. She loved him, no matter what he had done.

"I am sorry, Catherine, but I must ask more questions. Did . . . mine enemy . . . push Sir George to his death?"

"I do not know."

"Do you know what poison was used to kill John Bexwith?"

Catherine shook her head.

"But it was murder?"

"Both the recipe for the marrow-bone pie and the gift of candied eryngo came from Denholm Hall," Catherine said carefully.

"Was a poisonous root substituted for the eryngo?"

"I am not sure. I was not told anything. I did not even suspect until I was told I must pretend to be a ghost to frighten you away."

"Then that was the first time you appeared as a ghost? *After* I arrived here?"

"Yes. Before that the ghost was but a rumor. I believe all Grizel saw that night was the white tom, come to court your Dame Cat."

"But you played the ghost a second time, to lure me into the chapel. Who opened the vault?"

"My . . . your enemy."

"I know how hard this is for you, my dear, but you must see that the truth is important. No one can be allowed to get away with murder. No one."

Reluctance palpable in the gesture, Catherine nodded once more.

"Good. Now, how did you know I would be the one to investigate? Or would anyone have done?"

"I threw hard-packed snow at your window first, in the hope of waking you. Then I moaned a bit. 'Twas certain no one else would go out in the dead of night. They were too afraid." Catherine managed a fleeting smile. "You are very brave. You chased me the first time, and almost caught me, too."

Brave? Say rather, foolish. Aloud, Susanna asked, "Did you know the vault was open?"

Sobering quickly, Catherine again hung her head in shame. "No. I was horrified when I heard you'd fallen. I never meant you any harm. It was then I realized my playacting was more than a prank. Then I began to think about what I had heard, what I knew about Appleton Manor and the deaths there. I wanted to tell someone, but I was afraid. And I didn't understand so much of it. It was not until I met Sir Robert that I began to see what must have happened and why."

"This was all meant to lure Robert north, into danger."

"That is what I believe. No one tells me anything. They just give me orders."

For a moment she sounded like any other fourteen-year-old girl despairing her lack of freedom. Susanna remembered the feeling very well. At Catherine's age, she'd been informed by her guardian that she was going to marry Robert Appleton, a man she'd never met. They had not actually wed until four years later, but she'd never forgotten how helpless that bald announcement had made her feel.

"Your ordeal is nearly done, Catherine. I have but a few questions more." And a task to ask the girl to perform, but discussion of that could wait awhile. "Who attacked my cook?"

"I know not."

"Was Matthew Grimshaw involved in all this?"

"Yes, but by his manner he was coerced into doing things he did not want to do. The only act of which I know him to be guilty is paying your servant Bess to steal a letter written to you by Sir Robert. I stole it back and burned it to keep it from falling into another's hands."

She'd deal with Grimshaw later, Susanna decided. Catherine was doubtless correct in thinking he was merely a pawn, as she had been herself.

And now it was Susanna's turn to make use of Catherine. She despised the necessity, but with Robert's safety at stake, she did not see that she had any other choice.

"Lady Appleton?"

"Yes, Catherine."

"I cannot go back to Denholm Hall. Will you hide me here? Will you take me away with you when you leave?"

"Oh, my dear. You are already part of this family. But we cannot run from our responsibility to see justice done. I sent for you in part to lure a killer here. By now, you'll have been missed. Your parents will be searching for you and, as I intended, they will come here."

Panic-stricken, Catherine jumped up from the bench and tried to run, but Susanna caught her arm. "Nay! You do not have to face them just yet, child. Listen while I tell you my plan."

CHAPTER 41

It was just dusk when the frantic knocking came. Mark, now recovered enough to resume some of his duties, went to open the door. A moment later, Euphemia Denholm swept into the hall, followed by her husband and the maid Grizel.

"What have you done with Catherine?" she demanded.

"I have given her a sleeping potion," Lady Appleton said. "She was . . . distraught."

Looking most put out, Euphemia Denholm demanded to be taken to her daughter.

Outside, the winter weather was worsening again. The precipitation was not snow this time, but sleet. One look at that had Lady Appleton smiling. "You must stay the night," she insisted.

Jennet did not think Sir Robert looked happy about the invitation, but country landholders were required to offer hospitality even in good weather.

"We will go and take Catherine with us," Randall said. " 'Tis better so."

"If she is exposed to this wind and weather, she'll not survive till dawn," Lady Appleton told him bluntly. "She was near frozen when she arrived here, from walking across the fields with no cloak."

As Lady Appleton described imaginary symptoms in great detail, Mistress Denholm grumbled, but not too loudly. Cloaks came off. Hot possets were sent for.

"Go and help in the kitchen, Grizel," Mistress Denholm ordered.

The maid fled the great hall, arriving ahead of Jennet at the buttery. Together they fetched the cider and carried it to the kitchen.

"Why did Mistress Catherine flee her home?" Jennet asked, all innocence. She knew full well why Catherine had come to Appleton Manor. She'd carried the message to summon her hence herself. In addition, listening at a keyhole had been spectacularly profitable this day. Jennet now knew all manner of secrets . . . except the last. When Lady Appleton had begun to tell Catherine her plan, she'd lowered her voice until her words became too faint for Jennet to hear.

"I think she were told she must marry Master Grimshaw," Grizel announced. She tried to sound self-important, but spoiled the effect by looking over her shoulder, as if she feared she'd be caught gossiping by her mistress.

Jennet gaped at her, wondering where she had gotten that idea. Trust Grizel to find the strangest interpretation possible for things. "Why do you think so?"

Mabel, now recovered enough to be cooking again, refused to relinquish command of her kitchen. She relieved the two maidservants of the cider and banished them to a quiet corner to wait for it. Jennet continued her inquisition in low tones while Mabel heated the cider and added cinnamon.

"I did accompany Mistress Denholm to Manchester a week past," Grizel confided at Jennet's prodding. "When she did come out of Master Grimshaw's house, she were talking to herself. 'There's Catherine's future settled,' she said. What else could that mean?'' Grizel again glanced apprehensively in the direction of the great hall.

"Your mistress is busy with mine,'' Jennet assured her. "And then she'll be taken to see Mistress Catherine in the room above the storage cellar, the one Sir George used to sleep in.'' Grizel knew more than she was saying, Jennet thought. "You know, Grizel, Lady Appleton would protect you if you chose to leave Denholm Hall.''

"Could she?''

"Aye. She is the cleverest woman in all England. And a good mistress, too. Now, Grizel, tell me what it is you fear and I will make sure she helps you.''

What worked for Lady Appleton with Catherine Denholm failed completely for Jennet with Grizel. Jennet couldn't even get her to confess that it might have been a cat she'd seen the night John Bexwith died.

"It were a ghost,'' Grizel insisted. "Mistress Denholm says if I saw what I saw I should not hide it.''

Jennet's conviction wavered. There could have been a real ghost *that* night. Jane Denholm's come after Master Bexwith. There *were* spirits, no matter what Lady Appleton wanted to think.

A delicious shiver passed through Jennet at the thought that Grizel *had* seen a ghost, a *real* ghost . . . the ghost that only appeared when someone at Appleton Manor was about to die.

"Here, girl,'' Mabel interrupted. "Ye must take this mulled cider to thy master and mistress. Then get ye back to me, for if I be obliged to feed extra mouths, then I will have extra hands to do the work. I've work for ye, as well, Jennet,'' she added.

Jennet stuck out her tongue as soon as the cook turned her broad back. When she was acting as mistress here as Mark's wife, Jennet decided, Mabel would have to go.

"I will serve the possets,'' she declared. Let Grizel stay and turn the spit!

Taking the tray, she flounced off in the direction of the great hall.

CHAPTER 42

Robert hauled his wife into the passageway between the great hall and the service rooms and glared at her. "If all you believe is true, how can you be sure it is safe to sup with them?"

A faint smile flashed across Susanna's face at his sarcasm. She suspected it masked a very real fear of poison, but she refrained from pointing that out. Doubtless it made Robert feel more in control to badger her.

"First, Mabel prepared the food and she has promised not to leave the kitchen unguarded. Second, they did not expect to stay. They'll not have come prepared to do murder. Third, the attacks have become progressively more violent and direct. Going back to poison seems unlikely."

"Then you expect Randall to seize up a sword sooner than add something to the meal?"

Susanna gave him an arch smile. "Or stab you while you sleep." She'd have Randall's confession long before they retired for the night. She was sure of it. Then they'd lock him in the storage cellar under guard until he could be taken to the gaol in Manchester.

"Your attitude begins to annoy me, madam."

"If you are worried about poison, eat only what Randall Denholm eats." She pulled free of his grip, impatient to get back to their guests. She did not want either of them slipping back upstairs to visit Catherine and discovering she'd already left her bed, miraculously restored to consciousness.

"This will be an interminable meal," Robert grumbled.

"I am quite looking forward to it." Indeed, had the storm not obliged the Denholms to stay, she'd have contrived some other means to keep them at Appleton Manor. The inclement weather had saved her a good deal of trouble.

As they took their seats at the refectory table on the dais, Robert put on his courtier's mask and became the perfect host, even singing Mabel's praises as Mark, Jennet, and Grizel brought in her plain but hearty fare. She'd prepared roast mutton and baked oatmeal bread. There were also baked chewits, the finely chopped meat delicately spiced.

The smells were tempting, but Susanna found that her appetite had completely disappeared. She picked at the bread, eating almost none of it, and touched nothing else. Robert ate with his usual enthusiasm, helping himself to each dish only after Randall had already tasted it.

It might have been an ordinary meal, shared by longtime neighbors. Soon Robert had launched into a spirited discussion of fish days among the French as opposed to English practices. "They have meatless days every Friday and Sunday and on the eves of all feasts, and during Advent and Lent," he told them, speaking loudly for Randall's benefit, "and the French forbid eggs, milk, butter, and cheese as well as meat."

"Are their fish tolerably prepared?" Randall asked. There was no hint of vagueness about him this evening, making Susanna wonder if he was mad in truth or if his bouts of addlepated behavior were all an act. She almost hoped for the latter explanation. The mad were much too unpredictable.

"There is a fish called brochet that is excellent," Robert answered, "though I must confess most French fish dishes are not so good as one might expect. Still, sole, salmon, and sturgeon are plentiful in the estuaries of the Loire and the Seine."

"The French are papists," Randall murmured.

"Not all of them." Susanna said. She noticed that Robert's grip on his goblet tightened, though he gave no other sign of increased agitation.

"Just like Lancashire, then? Some of the old religion and some of the new and many who waver between the two?" Randall's smile looked a trifle sly. "At least in France a man can still be a priest if he has a mind to."

"It is much more sensible to enter the clergy in England," Robert shot back, "for here he may do so and keep a wife, as well."

Susanna was puzzled by the exchange, but before she could comment she heard the sound she'd been waiting for, a faint rustle on the staircase at the opposite end of the hall. Randall sat facing that way and Susanna watched him closely. His eyes grew wide and his skin turned pale at the sight that met his eyes.

Sending his chair tumbling over backward, Randall sprang to his feet. Robert stood, too, and might have taken some precipitous action had Susanna not caught his arm.

"Wait," she cautioned him in a whisper. "To move too soon will prevent us from learning the truth."

Slowly, backlit by a branched candelabra that had been strategically placed, a ghostly figure began its descent. Halfway down the stairs, it stopped and turned toward the company assembled on the dais.

In the breathless silence, Catherine boldly threw back her veil. Her dark eyes blazed in the eerie light. Then her arm lifted in a flutter of white fabric and she extended her hand, one finger pointed.

"You killed my real father," she said in clear, bell-like tones.

Susanna's mouth dropped open in surprise. It was not Randall Denholm she accused.

She was pointing at her mother.

"No!" Euphemia's face turned a bright, mottled red.

"Yes. You did. And John Bexwith, too. And you have tried to harm these other good folk. No more, Mother. No more."

The hatred had returned to Randall Denholm's eyes, but this time Susanna had no doubt about its object. He reached out with both hands toward his treacherous wife. He'd actually grasped her around the neck before a spasm of pain made him release her and cry out. His hands fell away as he groaned aloud and clutched at his belly. His face reflected excruciating pain.

Euphemia began to laugh. "It is too late. Too late! We are all going to die."

Robert's face paled. "Poison?"

"What poison?" Susanna demanded. She was almost certain she knew which one had killed Bexwith, but even if she was correct she had no assurance that Effie would use the same thing twice.

Susanna was painfully aware she'd already been wrong once tonight. She had been convinced that Randall killed Sir George and Bexwith. Now she realized that Catherine had never once confirmed it during their talk in the stillroom. She'd agreed to no more than that one of her parents had been behind the haunting of Appleton Manor.

Randall collapsed, froth forming on his lips.

"Die, you poor excuse for a man," Effie said. Then she rounded on her daughter, rage vying with anguish in her voice. "How could you betray me when I did it for you? You will inherit everything now. Denholm and Appleton. Matthew will see to it, or I vow I will come back to haunt him!"

"What is she saying?" Robert demanded.

"Catherine is your sister, Robert," Susanna said.

"What?"

Euphemia Denholm's howl of pain nearly drowned out his roar of outrage. She had consumed the poison, too.

Mark caught Effie as she doubled over. With Jennet's reluctant assistance he lowered her to the floor.

Catherine turned tortured eyes to Susanna. "Help them," she begged. "You have your confession now. Use your knowledge of herbs to save them."

"I must know what poison." Susanna knelt beside Bexwith's murderer and seized Effie's fleshy shoulders. She gave her a shake, forcing her to open her eyes. The pupils were already dilated.

Behind her, she heard Robert groan as the first effects of the poison made themselves felt in his bigger, bulkier body. She forced herself to block out her empathy for his pain and shook Effie again. "What poison?"

If it was one that speeded the heart, the antidote Queen Catherine had recommended might help. If it was of another sort, if its effects were different, the queen mother's recipe could hasten death, or make it even more ghastly.

Euphemia's body convulsed. Her features were contorted by her suffering but a triumphant light shone in her eyes. "It is too late. It acts too quickly. Bexwith's death proved that."

"Cowbane," Susanna said with more conviction than she felt. "You sent a root to him and told him it was eryngo."

In spite of the increasingly violent manifestations of the herb's effects, Effie managed a smile.

"Very clever," Susanna told her. While Effie retched, Susanna grasped Jennet's arm. "Quickly. Fetch the two small green glass bottles on my worktable in the stillroom. Mark, I need three goblets." If she administered the queen mother's antidote at once, it might still have a prayer of working.

As soon as Jennet returned, Susanna poured equal portions from the first bottle into each of the cups.

Catherine seized one and took it to Randall Denholm. No matter who her natural father had been, it was Randall who had raised her. She held the potion to his lips and helped him to drink.

Turning to Robert, Susanna did the same. He gulped it down, but she saw the rising panic in his eyes. He knew, as she did, that there was no guarantee the antidote would work. Indeed, the queen mother might have deliberately given him a false recipe. She was known to be a cruel woman, and devious. Even more so than Effie Denholm.

"This potion has emetic and cathartic effects." As did the poison itself. "It must be followed in a few minutes by two ounces of the second mixture."

Jennet attempted to administer the third goblet's contents to Euphemia Denholm but Effie kept knocking it aside. Nearly half the contents had already spilled out into the rushes.

"Do you want to die?" Catherine asked her. She took the cup from Jennet, but her mother still refused it.

Certain she had succeeded, she was laughing even as she moaned and writhed with the terrible effects of the poison. She believed she'd triumphed, that she'd killed all her enemies, that she'd had her revenge on the Appletons and secured her daughter's future. In some twisted way, she thought killing Robert would allow her child to inherit Sir George's estate.

Tears streaming down her cheeks, Catherine turned away from her mother and offered the cup to Susanna instead. "You might have eaten of the poison, as well."

Susanna shook her head. She felt no symptoms. It had been lack of appetite, however, not clear thinking, that had saved her. She had not believed another attempt would be made so soon. At worst, she'd thought Randall might try to kill himself when his crimes were revealed. Guilt plagued her as she prayed the antidote would work.

"She did poison me chewits!" Mabel's bellow was so loud it made Susanna jump. The cook had Grizel in a painful head lock and was dragging her, kicking and crying, into the great hall.

"Release her, Mabel," Susanna ordered. When she'd grudgingly complied, Susanna addressed Effie's maidservant. "What did you add, Grizel? A powder?"

"I did not know it were poison!" Grizel wailed, throwing herself at Susanna's feet. "It weren't my fault."

"Mistress Denholm gave you the powder and told you to put it in the food?"

"Aye." Grizel was sobbing now.

Absently, Susanna patted the girl's shoulder. This was good news. Dried, powdered cowbane was less toxic than the whole root which Bexwith had eaten.

A sound from Robert drew Susanna's attention. Pain creased his features. Like the others, he had been violently sick to his stomach. "God's blood, Susanna," he gasped. "I should never have listened when you said it was safe to eat."

"I did not think she would use poison again either," Catherine told her newly discovered brother. "You must not blame Lady Appleton."

Susanna felt her husband's weak, rapid pulse and reached for the second part of the antidote.

Catherine whispered to Susanna, "She meant to kill you, too."

"Yes," Susanna agreed.

"There was no need. She's often said a widow's lot is better than a wife's. She must have known you'd look after me if you lived."

Susanna's head jerked up and she stared at the young woman who was now her sister-by-marriage. Under English law, a widow *did* have complete freedom over her own life. She was no longer the possession, the chattel, of a husband or a father.

An insidiously tempting idea crept into Susanna's mind. She had not expected that poison would be used again, but now that it had, Robert's life was in her hands. The power she held in this moment in time was both appalling and appealing. Was this how Euphemia had felt? This sense of being in control? It was a heady sensation, one difficult to experience and then give up.

She divided the second potion into two portions and, taking one goblet, turned to Robert. He had heard her entire exchange with Catherine. She saw the doubt in his eyes. And the fear. If she was inclined to reclaim her freedom, it was the work of a moment to ensure his death. She had only to withhold the remainder of the antidote.

Immediately, she felt ashamed of herself. How could she even think it? True, she might be better off without him, but Robert was her husband. She was bound to him till death, and that death must come as God willed, not because of anything she did or did not do. Very gently, Susanna lifted his head to make it easier for him to swallow the antidote.

"They may yet die," she warned Catherine. "All three of them. And neither of us is to blame if they do. We have done all we can for them, but in the end we can only wait and pray."

Several long hours passed. Effie became delirious and endured violent convulsions. And then, just at dawn, she breathed her last. An hour later, Randall Denholm also died, in spite of the antidote, for he had too many years and too many ailments to fight off the effects of the poison.

Susanna left Catherine grieving noisily over the body of the man she still thought of as her father and went up to the solar to which Robert had been carried earlier. In Robert, the poppy mixture had controlled the convulsions while his body voided itself of toxins. He was already on the mend, although he was still feeling a great deal of pain.

"Randall is gone," she told him.

"Good" was all Robert said before he lapsed into brooding silence.

Susanna stared at him. Good that Randall had died? Robert must be confused. Randall was another victim in all this. Wasn't he?

She stayed with her husband, bathing him, watching over him while he drifted in and out of the healing sleep she induced with an herb water of chamomile, dittany, scabious, and pennyroyal. At midmorning, Robert was much stronger. By noontime, he was well enough to sit up and take some broth.

"There must be no scandal," he said.

"And how do we explain two dead bodies?"

That earned her a glare, but a moment later Robert took control again. "Explain how Catherine can be my sister," he demanded, "and then tell me all else you have learned. Then we will send for Master Grimshaw."

"In his capacity as justice of the peace?"

"In his capacity as conspirator."

"I have already dispatched Mark with a message. The storm cleared early this morning."

Robert scowled, but it was too late now to change what she had done. He settled for growling at her to give him a full account of all she knew to date.

The telling took some time, interrupted as it was by Robert's questions. Susanna could not answer them all. She accepted that they might never know why Mabel had been attacked or why Effie seemed so convinced that her illegitimate daughter could inherit once Robert was out of the way. She did not know, either, a precise motive for Sir George's murder.

"Grizel told Jennet that Effie visited Master Grimshaw last week," she added as an afterthought.

By evening, Robert was able to walk about a bit. He was up and dressed when the lawyer was shown into the solar.

"Sir Robert. I am relieved to see you so fit. I did fear . . . that is, I . . ." Suddenly awkward, Grimshaw's eyes sought Susanna, then jerked away when he found no sympathy there.

"What did Mistress Denholm talk to you about when she visited you a week ago?" Robert demanded.

"I cannot betray a client's secrets."

"Not even when that client is dead?"

"Dead?" Grimshaw's face reflected his every reaction. Shock. Confusion. Relief. "She's dead?"

"Aye. And Randall, too." Susanna made her voice soothing.

In spite of all they suspected he'd done, she found herself feeling sorry for the man.

Tugging on his ruff, Grimshaw choked out a question. "How?"

"Poison. The same she used to kill John Bexwith."

"You know, then. Know it all." He sagged visibly. Susanna pushed a stool in his direction. Robert proffered wine.

"Not all," Susanna admitted.

"Enough to send you to the gallows," Robert put in.

Grimshaw sat down abruptly and gulped the wine. "I did not know. Not at first. I had no part in murder."

"Your silence nearly cost Sir Robert his life," Susanna reminded him.

Robert refilled the wineglass. "Here is what will happen, Master Grimshaw. In return for our silence about your part in Effie Denholm's crimes, you will certify, as justice of the peace, that the Denholms died of exposure to the cold after being caught out in the storm while searching for their runaway daughter."

No Appleton servant would contradict that story. They were all too loyal to Susanna. Grizel was too frightened for her own life.

"Anything," Grimshaw promised.

"In addition, you will tell us now, in as much detail as you know, why this madwoman was driven to kill and kill again."

"I can only guess at some of it," Grimshaw warned.

"Guess, then," ordered Sir Robert.

Grimshaw drew in a strengthening breath. "She claimed to have had a secret precontract for marriage to your father, agreed upon soon after your mother's death."

Robert started to object, but for once Grimshaw was not cowed. He rushed on with his astonishing story.

"She told me he cast her aside to marry a wealthier woman. Believing she had no other choice, she then wed with Randall Denholm, the man her father had picked for her. In fact, the precontract between Sir George and Aunt Euphemia, a precontract witnessed by mine own mother, as she did admit only yesterday, was legally binding on both parties. All subsequent marriages were invalid.''

"Then Jane was illegitimate, but not Catherine. And Catherine does have a claim on Appleton Manor." How unexpected, Susanna thought. "Why did Sir George marry Jane?"

"To hurt Aunt Euphemia. They'd had a long and bitter relationship. I cannot begin to understand or explain it, but she kept going back to him. He'd encourage her for a time, then grow tired of her and go off after another woman. During one of their reconciliations, Catherine was conceived."

Susanna had an understanding of the law unusual for a woman. She knew that a precontract followed by consummation became a legal marriage. Effie might not have realized that, but Sir George undoubtedly had. He just hadn't cared.

"Did my father know Catherine was his?" Robert asked.

"My aunt said he did not, not until the last night of his life. After the maidservant fled, Aunt Euphemia was waiting for him. She'd tried to kill Randall once, thinking that with him out of the way she could persuade Sir George to marry her, this time at the church door. She was prepared to make a second attempt on Randall's life and wanted Sir George's help. To that end, she told him Catherine was his. He just laughed, then suggested they make another bastard together. Furious at his callous attitude, she pushed him away from her. I do not think she meant to kill him, but when he tumbled down the stairs he broke his neck. Aunt Euphemia then fled, leaving the body for Bexwith to discover."

"What about Bexwith? Did he know? Was he demanding money for his silence?"

"He did not guess she killed Sir George. He might have been more careful if he had. I wish I didn't know," he added in an undertone.

"But he was extorting money from someone," Susanna reminded him.

"Yes. What Bexwith had only recently realized, since he

rarely saw Catherine, was how much she resembled Sir George. He threatened to tell Randall he'd been cuckolded if Aunt Euphemia did not pay him to keep silent. I fear my aunt was not always coherent when she talked about her feelings toward Bexwith. She sometimes seemed as outraged that he'd been usurping Sir George's place at Appleton Manor as she was by his demands. She was on the verge of madness, I do think. Why else would she later become so obsessed with killing Sir Robert, too?''

Mad? If so, then she'd been made so by her thwarted love for Robert's father. And yet, there was a certain twisted logic to what she'd done. Effie had judged Bexwith unworthy to take Sir George's place. Was it such a leap to decide Robert had forfeited what legitimate claim he had by his absence and neglect?

It was not for Jane, Susanna suddenly realized, that Effie had kept on mourning, but for her true husband, for Sir George, no matter how little he deserved her devotion. She'd have abandoned her black in far less than eight years if she'd worn it for Jane. Widow's weeds lasted a lifetime.

Sure of her reasoning, Susanna went on to other questions. ''How did your aunt kill Bexwith?'' she asked.

''She said she pretended to agree to his terms and then offered him a secret she claimed Randall had discovered through his experiments with herbs. She promised him youth and virility and gave him death.''

''What man could resist,'' Robert muttered in disgust.

''Which is of more value, I do wonder,'' Susanna mused in a voice too low for Grimshaw to hear. ''A man's life, or his ability to impress a mistress?''

Robert regarded her with wary eyes and seemed to read something in her face. ''I have been considering selling a certain house I own in Dover,'' he said in an undertone. ''I do not intend to use it in future.''

''The money would be welcome to continue renovations

here.'' She lowered her eyes to hide a glint of triumph. It was not at all a bad thing to have him owe her his life.

"We'll not often be in the north.'' He hesitated. "Unless there is work for me in Scotland."

"In that event, it would be most useful to maintain a second house here. With Mark and Jennet in charge, every comfort would be available for your visits."

She took his grunt for assent.

'Twas a gift she'd not looked for. She had meant to make only two demands of her husband. Thinking of them, she turned her speculative gaze on Master Grimshaw. Since he was already here, the lawyer might as well be useful.

"Robert, my dear, we must provide for your sister. Indeed, it might be wise to take Catherine south with us when we return to Leigh Abbey."

"Think carefully, Susanna. To claim her as my sister would cost her any inheritance she's due as Denholm's only child."

"That is a consideration. Still, I am certain we can find a way for Catherine to have all she deserves."

"If she calls herself Appleton, she'll be exposed to the worst sort of speculation."

As he would be. Susanna began to understand his reluctance. Robert did not want to become the subject of gossip. Not even indirectly. One never knew what could threaten a promising career at court. "Perhaps we should let Catherine decide what surname to use."

"She seems a sensible girl," Robert mused.

"As is her brother."

He grimaced, but gave in. "Agreed. Grimshaw, arrange to buy her wardship for me. That will give me control of Denholm properties. If she can be persuaded to keep that heritage."

"She's fourteen," Susanna reminded them. "Unless she is already betrothed . . . ?"

Grimshaw shook his head.

"Then she inherits outright. She is not required to have a guardian and may dispose of her property and her person as she sees fit. She has asked to join our household," she added as Robert started to bluster.

He sighed, then addressed Grimshaw again. "Advise your young cousin well, lawyer. She may not be my ward, but she will be under my protection."

"Aye, Sir Robert."

"Before you settle the Denholm estate, Master Grimshaw," Susanna put in, "there is a document I would have you draw up for Sir Robert to sign." She smiled sweetly at her husband, knowing full well that what she was about to say would irritate him. She was also certain he would accept her proposal.

He did owe her his life.

"Now, Master Grimshaw, this document will say that Lady Appleton is no longer obliged to ask her husband's permission before she draws on her own monies. And she may travel when and where she wills. Further, when Sir Robert Appleton is away from home, he will make no attempt to dictate how his wife spends her time."

Grimshaw looked at Robert. Robert made an impatient gesture. "Write whatever she tells you to, Grimshaw. I will sign it."

"But, it is most irregular, Sir Robert. Why, it will be as if your wife has the freedoms of a widow without first incurring the loss of her spouse."

"An appropriate analogy," Robert muttered. "Do as you are told, lawyer, or I will have to reconsider my earlier generosity."

"Of course, Sir Robert." Grimshaw was too weak-willed, too easily intimidated, to do anything but keep his opinions to himself and obey. He took the parchment and quill Susanna handed him, seated himself at a small table, and began to record her wishes.

"Thank you, my dear," Susanna told her scowling husband.

A sense of deep and abiding satisfaction filled her soul. From this day forward, she thought happily, Lady Appleton would do exactly as she pleased.

Please turn the page for an exciting sneak peek of Kathy Lynn Emerson's next Susanna, Lady Appleton mystery FACE DOWN UPON AN HERBAL coming in paperback from Kensington Books in November 2000.

PROLOGUE

Lord Glenelg was once again cleaning his fingernails with his elaborate little bye-knife when the person he'd been waiting for appeared on the balcony just outside Lord Madderly's study.

"You have kept me waiting," Glenelg complained.

"So I have." There was a certain pleasure in thwarting this offensive Scots nobleman, a heady excitement in the danger of it.

"You were warned." Glenelg bristled like an affronted hedgehog, but he still seemed to think he had the situation under control, that he was in command.

He was wrong.

"Warned or not, there is no help for it. I've no intention of letting you enter this room."

"You will regret your rashness."

"What do you think lies inside, that you are so determined to see?"

"More proof of your guilt, mayhap." Glenelg's annoying chuckle was as counterfeit as a passport bought for twopence at a fair. There was no true mirth in his soul. If he even had a soul.

"I think you wish to gain entry for the sheer perverse pleasure you get from knowing and doing what others do not."

Glenelg did not like this insubordination. His small eyes glittered with animosity. "You will do as I say or I will see to it that all your wicked deceptions are revealed to the world."

"By doing so, you would implicate yourself."

"I will be long gone ere my part in this business comes out. You alone will suffer. Do you know what they do to traitors? 'Tis a horrible death." For emphasis, Glenelg gestured with his knife as he described in loving detail the torment of being hung, then cut down alive to be drawn and quartered. "A quick death is far better," he concluded.

"Then you shall have one."

Glenelg looked surprised when his blade was knocked away, plucked up, and thrust back at him, piercing his heart as it plunged through plum-colored velvet and into his chest.

He crashed back against the door to the study and was bounced forward by the impact. The book he'd had tucked into the waist of his doublet fell free, landing with a thump on the wooden floor. A moment later, Glenelg lay sprawled on top of it.

The killer left him there. Face down upon an herbal, the dead man awaited discovery by whatever person next entered Lord Madderly's library.

CHAPTER 1

Leigh Abbey, Kent
November 1561

Upon his arrival at Leigh Abbey, Sir Robert Appleton's country house, Walter Pendennis insisted he be shown directly into Lady Appleton's presence.

"She is in her stillroom, sir," the housekeeper said.

"Then take me there."

He thought he knew what to expect. He had known Robert since they were young men together and although he had never met Lady Appleton, Pendennis had heard a great deal about her.

Some of it had been unflattering. Robert most often complained about her intelligence. She'd been educated like a man by a doting father, which in Robert's opinion had spoiled her for true womanliness.

"She'll not be pleased to be interrupted," the housekeeper warned. A woman of middling height who appeared to be about to give birth, she addressed him with an asperity that was anything but servile.

"I fear I must insist. I bring a message from the queen."

Relenting, though she did still seem annoyed, the woman escorted him to a large stone building separate from the house. "Wait here," she instructed and left him cooling his heels in the herb garden while she went in alone. Before he had time to do more than glance at his surroundings, she was back, her expression sullen. "Go in if you must, but do not interfere with Lady Appleton's work."

Pendennis had been under the impression that activity in the stillroom reached its peak during the summer months, when most herbs were prepared for storage. Then he remembered. Lady Appleton experimented with powders and decoctions. Her preoccupation with poisons kept her busy year-round.

He sniffed cautiously as he ducked to miss the low lintel of the door and was rewarded with a pungent combination of odors. He had an excellent nose, but these aromas were at first too well mingled for him to sort out any single one.

A tall, slender young woman met him just inside the door. This was not Lady Appleton, but from her uncanny likeness to Sir Robert, Pendennis could guess her identity. One night, late, at Queen Elizabeth's court, when Robert had been deep in his cups and brooding, he'd confessed more than was his wont. He'd confided that he had a half sister, a girl whose existence he'd not even suspected until that business in Lancashire two years ago.

"You are Catherine," Pendennis said.

"Aye, sir. Catherine Denholm." As he moved past her, deeper into the stillroom, he caught the scent of violets. The housekeeper came in after him, closing the door behind her and leaning back against it. Fascinated by Catherine, Pendennis dismissed the servant from his thoughts.

"My name is Walter Pendennis."

"Sir Robert's friend." She smiled, charming him.

"Aye."

If Robert did not want to acknowledge the relationship, Pendennis thought, he'd best keep Catherine close in the country. To any who had ever met Robert Appleton, the resemblance would be impossible to miss. Catherine shared with her half brother a narrow face, a high forehead, and distinctively dark brown eyes. The most likely assumption would be that she was his bastard daughter. By Pendennis's reckoning, Catherine was just sixteen.

"I am sorry to interrupt your work," he said, "but I have been sent by Her Majesty the queen."

The woman standing at the long wooden table at the center of the room glanced his way. When their eyes met, he was startled by the intensity of her gaze. Her eyes were blue, most ordinary in color and shape, and yet Pendennis was suddenly certain that this was a woman who missed nothing. Apparently confident that his presence did not signify distressing tidings about her spouse, she gave a curt nod in acknowledgment of his arrival and went back to her work.

"Lady Appleton will be free to speak with you in a moment," Catherine said. There was no note of apology in her voice. She was simply stating a fact.

The hands busy with mortar and pestle, grinding some sort of dried root to powder, were strong and work-hardened and stained with the residue of various herbal preparations. Delicate, lily-white fingers such as those seen at the royal court had no place here.

"No beauty," Robert had said of his wife. 'Twas true. She was tall for a woman, square-jawed and sturdily built. And yet she had an aura of competence about her that was attractive in itself. Pendennis, an avid student of architecture, had learned to appreciate both form and function.

"Master Pendennis." Catherine's lilting voice interrupted his thoughts. "May I have your assistance?"

She handed him a down pillow, the casing open at one end, and as soon as she was sure he had a good grip on the edges she began to stuff in crushed and dried leaves and flowers from each of several containers.

Sniffing cautiously, he identified two. "Violets," he said. "Your favorite, I do think. And chamomile."

The girl's smile was sweet and shy. "Aye. And hops, balm, and mullein. These herbs, replaced every few weeks, encourage peaceful sleep."

Pendennis held more pillows, a task which allowed him to study his surroundings at the same time. Robert's wife was now mixing the powder she had made into a stiff paste. When she was satisfied with its consistency, she rolled it out on a board as if it were bread dough. After considerable kneading and pounding, she began to pinch off small bits and form them into tiny balls with her hands. It was then Pendennis realized she was making pills.

On the table where Lady Appleton worked sat all manner of equipment for distillation—alembic, pelican, matrass—as well as empty jars, pots, and other vessels made of stoneware, ceramic, glass, horn, pewter, and iron. From force of habit, Pendennis began to assess the contents of the stillroom. He counted thirty large containers, labeled and dated, and over a hundred smaller vessels. Some had parchment tied over the mouths while the covers on others were made of thin skin.

Drying herbs hung in bunches from the beams above his head, but what, he wondered, was kept in that black chest in the darkest corner of the room? Phials of poison? He had reason to think that might be so.

Lady Appleton startled him by speaking his name.

Pendennis saw that the pills were all shaped and had been left to dry on the board. Lady Appleton wiped her hands on her apron and tucked an unruly strand of dark brown hair back up under her embroidered cap.

"This is an unexpected pleasure, Master Pendennis," she said. "Your pardon, sir, for my rudeness in ignoring you, but even a short delay in the preparation can spoil the result."

"It is I must beg your pardon, madam, for disturbing you, but I have come with a message from the queen."

"So you said, but if you hope to find my husband here, I fear your journey was in vain. He has been gone since before Michaelmas. By now he should be in Scotland."

Pendennis had to hide a smile. He well knew where Robert was, and something of what his old friend had been obliged to deal with during the last few weeks.

"My message is for you, Lady Appleton. Queen Elizabeth would have a favor of you."

Many a woman would have been flustered by that announcement. Not Lady Appleton. Pendennis supposed he should not be surprised, given what he'd heard of her.

"Damnably self-assured," Robert had once called her. The description fit.

Susanna Appleton's first impression of Walter Pendennis was that he had a typical courtier's face—bland except for the eyes. It amused her to note that he had grown his beard in the style favored by Lord Robin Dudley, the queen's acknowledged favorite. Susanna recognized it because her husband had done the same.

A pity, she thought now, that the effect was so unflattering. The Dudley style consisted of a mustache that drooped down on each side to the corners of the mouth, a tuft of hair beneath the lower lip, and below that a short chin beard.

Pendennis was a bit taller than Susanna, with a figure that suggested he liked beer, ale, and French wines a bit too well, though she thought perhaps 'twas muscle yet, not fat. She could see little of the structure of his arms beneath the heavy sleeves of his buff-colored doublet, but the legs beneath the padded, pleated skirt looked strong and well-shaped. This was amply revealed by the current form-fitting fashion in thigh-high leather riding boots. Her gaze flicked to his padded and decorated codpiece with only cursory interest before her attention was captured by what he was saying.

"The queen wants you to pay a visit to Madderly Castle."

"Why?" She had recently been in correspondence with Lady Madderly, who was engaged in compiling an account of every plant found in England, including their properties, virtues, and descriptions.

"Lady Madderly is writing an herbal, but she progresses slowly," Pendennis said. "It is Her Majesty's desire that the author of *A Cautionary Herbal* go thither to assist her ladyship in the preparation of this great work. The queen believes Eleanor Madderly's book will be definitive, a godsend to wives and apothecaries alike. It could become a fixture in every household, second only to the Bible in importance."

"And how," Susanna asked, "does Lady Madderly feel about having me thrust upon her?"

She studied Pendennis's eyes as she waited for his answer. He had an intelligent look to him and there had been kindness in his gaze when he'd helped Catherine with the pillows, but she could not help being suspicious.

What had Robert told her about this man? That he was lazy. That he collected the most useless bits of information, which on occasion were surprisingly helpful. And that he was a sometime intelligence gatherer for the queen, as well as a courtier and diplomat, as was Robert himself.

"Lady Madderly welcomes your assistance," Pendennis assured her.

Susanna had her doubts, but one did not argue with a royal command. For all Pendennis's pretty phrasing, she understood that she was obliged to accept this assignment. It would reflect ill on Robert if she refused.

A glance at her companions revealed that Catherine seemed intrigued by the conversation. Jennet, once Susanna's tiring maid, long her friend and companion, and now her housekeeper, affected boredom but was in fact hanging on every word.

"When does the queen wish me to arrive at Madderly Castle?" she asked Pendennis. "It is in Gloucestershire, which is some distance from Kent." Lady Madderly had indicated it was near the border with Warwickshire, in the Cotswold Hills. Susanna knew little of the region save that the sheep raised there were popularly known as Cotswold lions.

"The sooner you can begin, the better," Pendennis answered. "The best route to take is by way of London and Oxford. From Oxford the road runs north to Burford, then west and north toward Campden, some thirty miles beyond."

Campden, Susanna recalled, was the nearest market town to Madderly Castle. "How long am I expected to stay?"

"Until the herbal is ready for publication."

She hid a grimace. 'Twas plain he had no inkling of how much work was involved. Lady Madderly even meant to include woodcuts to illustrate the plants. It was an ambitious project, one which might well take years to complete. "You ask me to abandon my household on a moment's notice and for an indefinite period of time."

"You will be amply compensated."

Susanna knew all about the queen's idea of compensation. She expected her courtiers to spend their own money in her service and rarely rewarded them with material goods or property. Even when she lavished a peerage on one of her subjects, it was likely to come without a sufficient source of income to support the title.

Susanna was about to suggest that they go into the house, there to take refreshment while she discussed the matter with Catherine and Jennet, when Catherine spoke.

"You must accept, Susanna," she said. "The queen expects no less."

"To go at once means I'll not be present when Jennet needs me." The younger woman was due to give birth in less than two weeks. A midwife was already in residence.

Jennet herself gave a snort of wry laughter at that. "This child, like the last, cares little who is present at the birth. Go you to Gloucestershire. Never mind about me."

Susanna fought a smile. She knew Jennet well. Even in childbed she'd enjoy being the center of attention. And since her husband was the newly appointed steward here at Leigh Abbey, having successfully filled that post at another Appleton property for nearly two years, she would be treated as well as any gentlewoman of the household when her time came.

"I do not like to leave you," Susanna protested. "Indeed, I do wish I could take you along."

That was clearly impossible, but Susanna had the feeling she'd have need of a friend at Madderly Castle. Something in Pendennis's manner suggested he was not telling her everything about this mission.

That suspicion, however, was not enough to make her refuse the queen's request. It was not every day that a woman's scholarship and expertise on a subject were recognized, let alone sought out. In a way she was flattered. Master John Day of London had printed her book at the end of the previous year, but anonymously. Few people knew she was the S.A. who had painstakingly compiled it.

"If you mean to go, go. You should be glad of something to do in the winter, since it is such a slow season. 'Twill be especially dull with Sir Robert gone."

"Could I come with you, Susanna?" Catherine seemed taken with the idea.

Perhaps it was time for the girl to explore a wider circle of friends, Susanna thought. This seemed a painless way to achieve that end. "Are there any objections to my bringing a companion, Master Pendennis?"

"You may bring an entire retinue if you wish."

She lifted an eyebrow at that. He was much too eager for her to agree, confirming her suspicion that there was more going on at Madderly Castle than he had revealed. No matter, she decided. She would deal with whatever else awaited her there when she arrived. The sooner the better, as Pendennis had said.

"Very well, Master Pendennis," she said. "Catherine and I will be ready to leave in two days' time."

BOOK YOUR PLACE ON OUR WEBSITE AND MAKE THE READING CONNECTION!

We've created a customized website just for our very special readers, where you can get the inside scoop on everything that's going on with Zebra, Pinnacle and Kensington books.

When you come online, you'll have the exciting opportunity to:

- View covers of upcoming books
- Read sample chapters
- Learn about our future publishing schedule (listed by publication month *and author*)
- Find out when your favorite authors will be visiting a city near you
- Search for and order backlist books from our online catalog
- Check out author bios and background information
- Send e-mail to your favorite authors
- Meet the Kensington staff online
- Join us in weekly chats with authors, readers and other guests
- Get writing guidelines
- AND MUCH MORE!

**Visit our website at
http://www.kensingtonbooks.com**

THRILLS AND CHILLS
The Mysteries of Mary Roberts Rinehart

__The After House	0-8217-4242-6	$3.99US/$4.99CAN
__The Album	1-57566-280-9	$5.99US/$7.50CAN
__The Case of Jennie Brice	1-57566-135-7	$5.50US/$7.00CAN
__The Circular Staircase	1-57566-180-2	$5.50US/$7.00CAN
__The Door	1-57566-367-8	$5.99US/$7.50CAN
__The Great Mistake	1-57566-198-5	$5.50US/$7.00CAN
__A Light in the Window	0-8217-4021-0	$3.99US/$4.99CAN
__Lost Ecstasy	1-57566-344-9	$5.99US/$7.50CAN
__Miss Pinkerton	1-57566-255-8	$5.99US/$7.50CAN
__The Red Lamp	1-57566-213-2	$5.99US/$7.50CAN
__The Swimming Pool	1-57566-157-8	$5.50US/$7.00CAN
__The Wall	1-57566-310-4	$5.99US/$7.50CAN
__The Yellow Room	1-57566-119-5	$5.50US/$7.00CAN

Call toll free **1-888-345-BOOK** to order by phone or use this coupon to order by mail.

Name _____

Address _____

City _____ State _____ Zip _____

Please send me the books I have checked above.

I am enclosing	$_____
Plus postage and handling*	$_____
Sales tax (in New York and Tennessee only)	$_____
Total amount enclosed	$_____

*Add $2.50 for the first book and $.50 for each additional book.
Send check or money order (no cash or CODs) to:
Kensington Publishing Corp., 850 Third Avenue, New York, NY 10022
Prices and Numbers subject to change without notice.
All orders subject to availability.
Check out our website at **www.kensingtonbooks.com**